PRAISE FOR
THE SHACK

P9-DWI-606

"When the imagination of a writer and the passion of a theologian cross-fertilize, the result is a novel on the order of THE SHACK. This book has the potential to do for our generation what John Bunyan's *Pilgrim's Progress* did for his. It's that good!"

— Eugene Peterson, professor emeritus of spiritual theology,
Regent College, Vancouver, B.C.

"While reading THE SHACK, I realized the questions unfolding in this captivating novel were questions I was carrying deep within me. The beauty of this book is not that it supplies easy answers to grueling questions, but that it invites you to come in close to a God of mercy and love, in whom we find hope and healing."

— Jim Palmer, author of *Divine Nobodies*

"THE SHACK is a one-of-a-kind invitation to journey to the very heart of God. Through my tears and cheers, I have been indeed transformed by the tender mercy with which William Paul Young opened the veil that too often separated me from God and from myself. With every page, the complicated do's and don'ts that distort a relationship into a religion were washed away as I understood Father, Son, and Spirit for the first time in my life."

— Patrick M. Roddy, Emmy Award–winning producer for ABC News

"Wrapped in creative brilliance, THE SHACK is spiritually profound, theologically enlightening, and life-impacting. It has my highest recommendation. We are joyfully giving copies away by the case."

— Steve Berger, pastor of Grace Chapel, Leipers Fork, TN

"Finally! A guy-meets-God novel that has literary integrity and spiritual daring. THE SHACK cuts through the clichés of both religion and bad writing to reveal something compelling and beautiful about life's integral dance with the divine. This story reads like a prayer—like the best kind of prayer, filled with sweat and wonder and transparency and surprise. When I read it, I felt like I was fellowshipping with God. If you read one work of fiction this year, let this be it."

— Mike Morrell, zoecarnate.com

"An exceptional piece of writing that ushers you directly into the heart and nature of God in the midst of agonizing human suffering. This amazing story will challenge you to consider the person and the plan of God in more expansive terms than you may have ever dreamed."
—David Gregory, author of *Dinner with a Perfect Stranger*

"THE SHACK will change the way you think about God forever."
—Kathie Lee Gifford,
cohost, NBC's *Today Show*

"I really thought that this book was just another book. Trust me, folks—*it's not!* When bandwagons come along I usually let them go right on by. When it comes to THE SHACK, I'm not only on the bandwagon, I keep asking the driver to stop and pick up all of my friends. I can't remember the last time a book, let alone a work of fiction, had this much of a healing impact on my life."
—Drew Marshall, radio host, *The Drew Marshall Show*

"If God is all-powerful and full of love, why doesn't He do something about the pain and evil in our world? This book answers that age-old question with startling creativity and staggering clarity. By far one of the best books I have ever read."
—James Ryle, author of *Hippo in the Garden*

"Riveting, with twists that defy your expectations while teaching powerful theological lessons without patronizing. I was crying by page one hundred. You cannot read it without your heart becoming involved."
—Gayle E. Erwin, author of *The Jesus Style*

"This book goes beyond being the well-written, suspenseful page-turner that it is. Since the death of our son Jason, the Lord has led us to a small number of life-changing books and this one heads the list. When you close the back cover, you will be changed."
—Dale Lang (rockcanada.org), father of student killed in
Columbine copycat shooting

"THE SHACK is a beautiful story of how God comes to find us in the midst of our sorrows, trapped by disappointments, betrayed by our own presumptions. He never leaves us where He finds us, unless we insist."
—Wes Yoder, Ambassador Speakers Bureau

"You will be captivated by the creativity and imagination of THE SHACK, and before you know it you'll be experiencing God as never before. William Young's insights are not just captivating, they are biblically faithful and true. Don't miss this transforming story of grace."
—Greg Albrecht, editor, *Plain Truth Magazine*

"Your work is a masterpiece! There are tears in my eyes and a lump in my throat. All I can think of is the others who need to read your words. I'm just as convinced that each one who reads it has those who also need your words."
—Chyril Walker, PhD

"THE SHACK is the most absorbing work of fiction I've read in many years. My wife and I laughed, cried, and repented of our own lack of faith along the way. THE SHACK will leave you craving the presence of God."
—Michael W. Smith, recording artist

"This book eloquently captures the shift from being highly responsible people in a religious system to walking in intimacy as we respond to the fragrance of Christ in daily life."
—Arthur Burk, Sapphire Leadership Group, Inc.

"Don't miss this! If there's a better book out there capturing God's engaging nature and His ability to crawl into our darkest nightmare with His love, light, and healing, I've not seen it. For the most ardent believer or newest spiritual seeker, THE SHACK is a must read."
—Wayne Jacobsen, author of *So You Don't Want to Go to Church Anymore*

"My biggest disappointment with Christian books is that almost all of them seem to say the same things in the same way. Not so with THE SHACK! It reads like no other book and tells a story I guarantee you have not heard before. Enjoy the adventure!"
—Bart Campolo, Founder of Mission Year

"It is not often that you have an opportunity to read such a spellbinding account from a contemporary author that so captures the true meaning of forgiveness and redemption."
—Rev. Ron Hooker, pastor emeritus, Grace United Church of Christ, Columbus, OH

"Brilliant! One of the most faith-enhancing books I have ever read."
—Bear Grylls, youngest Briton to climb Everest, star of *Man vs. Wild* and *Born Survivor*

THE
SHACK

Where Tragedy Confronts Eternity

A novel by
WM. PAUL YOUNG
*In collaboration with Wayne Jacobsen
and Brad Cummings*

windblown
MEDIA
Los Angeles, California

THE SHACK
by Wm. Paul Young

www.theshackbook.com

This book is a work of fiction. Names, characters, places, and incidents are the product of the author's imagination or are used fictitiously. Any resemblance to actual events, locales, or persons, living or dead, is coincidental.

Copyright © 2007 by William P. Young
Author's note copyright © 2016 by William P. Young
Motion picture artwork © 2016 Summit Entertainment, LLC.
All rights reserved.

Hachette Book Group supports the right to free expression and the value of copyright. The purpose of copyright is to encourage writers and artists to produce the creative works that enrich our culture.

The scanning, uploading, and distribution of this book without permission is a theft of the author's intellectual property. If you would like permission to use material from the book (other than for review purposes), please contact permissions@hbgusa.com. Thank you for your support of the author's rights.

Published by Windblown Media, 4680 Calle Norte,
Newbury Park, CA 91320 • office@windblownmedia.com
Phone: (805) 498- 2484 • Fax: (805) 499- 4260

Published in association with Hachette Book Group, Inc.

First trade paperback edition: July 2008
First trade paperback media tie-in edition: September 2016

Lyrics used in chapter 1: Larry Norman, "One Way."
© 1995 Solid Rock Productions, Inc. All rights reserved.
Lyrics reprinted by permission.

Lyrics used in chapter 10: "New World," by David Wilcox.
© 1994 Irving Music, Inc., and Midnight Ocean Bonfire Music.
All rights administered by Irving Music, Inc.
Used by permission. All rights reserved.

Page layout by Dave Aldrich

The publisher is not responsible for websites (or their content) that are not owned by the publisher.

ISBN: 978-1-4555-6760-7 (trade pbk. media tie-in), 978-0-9647292-9-2 (ebook)

Printed in the United States of America

LSC-C

10 9 8 7

CONTENTS

This story was written for my children:

Chad—the Gentle Deep
Nicholas—the Tender Explorer
Andrew—the Kindhearted Affection
Amy—the Joyful Knower
Alexandra (Lexi)—the Shining Power
Matthew—the Becoming Wonder

And dedicated first, to:

Kim, my Beloved, thank you for saving my life;

and second, to:

". . . All us stumblers who believe Love rules.
Stand up and let it shine."

FOREWORD

Who wouldn't be skeptical when a man claims to have spent an entire weekend with God, in a shack no less? And this was *the* shack.

I have known Mack for a bit more than twenty years, since the day we both showed up at a neighbor's house to help him bale a field of hay to put up for his couple of cows. Since then he and I have been, as the kids say these days, hangin' out, sharing a coffee—or for me a chai tea, extra hot with soy. Our conversations bring a deep sort of pleasure, always sprinkled with lots of laughs and once in a while a tear or two. Frankly, the older we get, the more we hang out, if you know what I mean.

His full name is Mackenzie Allen Phillips, although most people call him Allen. It's a family tradition: the men all have the same first name but are commonly known by their middle names, presumably to avoid the ostentation of I, II, and III or Junior and Senior. It works well for identifying telemarketers too, especially the ones who call as if they were your best friend. So he and his grandfather, father, and now his oldest son all have the given name of Mackenzie but are commonly referred to by their middle names. Only Nan, his wife, and close friends call him Mack (although I have heard a few total strangers yell, "Hey Mack, where'd you learn to drive?").

Mack was born somewhere in the Midwest, a farm boy in an Irish-American family committed to calloused hands and rigorous rules. Although externally religious, his overly strict church-elder father was a closet drinker, especially when the rain didn't come, or came too early, and most of the times in between. Mack never talks much about him, but when he does his face loses emotion like a tide going out, leaving dark and lifeless eyes. From the few stories Mack has told me, I know his daddy was not a fall-asleep-happy kind of alcoholic but a vicious, mean, beat-your-wife-and-then-ask-God-for-forgiveness drunk.

It all came to a head when thirteen-year-old Mackenzie reluctantly bared his soul to a church leader during a youth revival. Overtaken by the conviction of the moment, Mack confessed in tears that he hadn't done anything to help his mama as he witnessed, on more than one occasion, his drunken dad beat her unconscious. What Mack failed to consider was that his confessor worked and churched with his father, and by the time he got home his daddy was waiting for him on the front porch, with his mama and sisters conspicuously absent. He later learned that they had been shuttled off to his aunt May's in order to give his father some freedom to teach his rebellious son a lesson about respect. For almost two days, tied to the big oak at the back of the house, he was beaten with a belt and Bible verses every time his dad woke from a stupor and put down his bottle.

Two weeks later, when Mack was finally able to put one foot in front of the other again, he just up and walked away from home. But before he left, he put varmint poison in every bottle of booze he could find on the farm. He then unearthed from next to the outhouse the small tin box housing all his earthly treasures: one photograph of the family with everybody squinting as they looked into the sun (his daddy standing off to one side), a 1950 Luke Easter rookie baseball card, a little bottle that contained about an ounce of Ma Griffe (the only perfume his mama had ever worn), a spool of thread and a couple needles, a small silver die-cast U.S. Air Force F-86 jet, and his entire life savings—$15.13. He crept back into the house and slipped a note under his mama's pillow while his father lay snoring off another binge. It just said, "Someday I hope you can forgive me." He swore he would never look back, and he didn't—not for a long time.

Thirteen is too young to be all grown up, but Mack had little choice and adapted quickly. He doesn't talk much about the years that followed. Most of it was spent overseas, working his way around the world, sending money to his grandparents, who passed it on to his mama. In one of those distant countries I think he even picked up a gun in some kind of terrible conflict; he's hated war with a dark passion ever since I've known him. Whatever happened, in his early twenties he eventually ended up in a seminary in Australia. When Mack had had his fill of theology and philosophy he came back to the States, made peace with his mama and sisters, and moved out to Oregon where he met and married Nannette A. Samuelson.

In a world of talkers, Mack is a thinker and doer. He doesn't say much unless you ask him directly, which most folks have learned not to do. When he does speak you wonder if he isn't some sort of alien who sees the landscape of human ideas and experiences differently than everybody else.

The thing is, he usually makes uncomfortable sense in a world where most folks would rather just hear what they are used to hearing, which is often not much of anything. Those who know him generally like him well enough, provided he keeps his thoughts mostly to himself. And when he does talk, it isn't that they stop liking him—rather, they are not quite so satisfied with themselves.

Mack once told me that he used to speak his mind more freely in his younger years, but he admitted that most of such talk was a survival mechanism to cover his hurts; he often ended up spewing his pain on everyone around him. He says that he had a way of pointing out people's faults and humiliating them while maintaining his own sense of false power and control. Not too endearing.

As I pen these words, I reflect on the Mack I've always known—quite ordinary, and certainly not anyone particularly special, except to those who truly know him. He is just about to turn fifty-six, and he is a rather unremarkable, slightly overweight, balding, short white guy, which describes a lot of men in these parts. You probably wouldn't notice him in a crowd or feel uncomfortable sitting next to him while he snoozes on the MAX (metro transit) during his once-a-week trip into town for a sales meeting. He does most of his work from a little home office at his place up on Wildcat Road. He sells something high-tech and gadgety that I don't pretend to understand: techno gizmos that somehow make everything go faster, as if life weren't going fast enough already.

You don't realize how smart Mack is unless you happen to eavesdrop on a dialogue he might be having with an expert. I've been there when suddenly the language being spoken hardly resembles English, and I find myself struggling to grasp the concepts spilling out like a tumbling river of gemstones. He can speak intelligently about most anything, and even though you sense he has strong convictions, he has a gentle way about him that lets you keep yours.

His favorite topics are all about God and creation and why people believe what they do. His eyes light up and he gets this smile that curls at the corners of his lips, and suddenly, like a little kid, the tiredness melts away and he becomes ageless and hardly able to contain himself. But at the same time, Mack is not very religious. He seems to have a love/hate relationship with religion, and maybe even with the God he suspects is brooding, distant, and aloof. Little barbs of sarcasm occasionally spill through the cracks in his reserve like piercing darts dipped in poison from a well deep inside. Although we sometimes both show up on Sundays at the same local pew and pulpit Bible church (the Fifty-fifth Independent Assembly of Saint John the Baptist, we like to call it), you can tell that he is not too comfortable there.

Mack has been married to Nan for just more than thirty-three mostly happy years. He says she saved his life and paid a high price to do it. For some reason beyond understanding, she seems to love him now more than ever, even though I get the sense that he hurt her something fierce in the early years.

I suppose that since most of our hurts come through relationships, so will our healing, and I know that grace rarely makes sense for those looking in from the outside.

In any case, Mack married up. Nan is the mortar that holds the tiles of their family together. While Mack has struggled in a world with many shades of gray, hers is mostly black and white. Common sense comes so naturally to Nan that she can't even see it for the gift it is. Raising a family kept her from pursuing dreams of becoming a doctor, but as a nurse she has excelled and gained considerable recognition for her chosen work with oncology patients who are terminal. While Mack's relationship with God is wide, Nan's is deep.

This oddly matched pair are the parents of five unusually beautiful kids. Mack likes to say that they all got their good looks from him, " 'cause Nan still has hers." Two of the three boys are out of the house: Jon, newly married, works in sales for a local company; and Tyler, a recent college grad, is off at school working on a master's degree. Josh and one of the two girls, Katherine (Kate), are still at home and attend the local community college. Then there is the late arrival, Melissa—or Missy, as we were fond of calling her. She . . . Well, you'll get to know some of them better in these pages.

The last few years have been, how might I put this, remarkably peculiar. Mack has changed; he is now even more different and special than he used to be. In all the time I have known him he has been a rather gentle and kind soul, but since his stay in the hospital three years ago, he has been . . . well, even nicer. He's become one of those rare people who are totally at home in their own skin. And I feel at home around him like I do with nobody else. When we go our separate ways it seems that I have just had the best conversation of my life, even though I usually have done most of the talking. And with respect to God, Mack is no longer just wide, he has gone way deep. But the dive cost him dearly.

These days are very different from seven or so years ago,

when *The Great Sadness* entered his life and he almost quit talking altogether. About that time and for almost two years our hanging out stopped, as if by some unspoken mutual agreement. I saw Mack only occasionally at the local grocery store or even more rarely at church, and although a polite hug was usually exchanged, not much of any consequence was spoken. It was even difficult for him to look me in the eyes; maybe he didn't want to enter a conversation that might tear the scab off his wounded heart.

But that all changed after a nasty accident with . . . But there I go again, getting ahead of myself. We'll get to all that in due time. Just to say that these last few years seem to have given Mack his life back and lifted the burden of *The Great Sadness*. What happened three years ago totally changed the melody of his life, and it's a song I can't wait to play for you.

Although he communicates well enough verbally, Mack is not comfortable with his writing skills—something that he knows I am passionate about. So he asked if I would ghost-write this story—his story, "for the kids and for Nan." He wanted a narrative to help him express to them not only the depth of his love, but also to help them understand what had been going on in his inside world. You know that place: where there is just you alone—and maybe God, if you believe in him. Of course, God might be there even if you *don't* believe in him. That would be just like him. He hasn't been called the Grand Interferer for nothing.

What you are about to read is something that Mack and I have struggled with for many months to put into words. It's a little, well . . . no, it is a *lot* on the fantastic side. Whether some parts of it are actually true or not, I won't be the judge. Suffice it to say that while some things may not be scientifically provable, they can still be true nonetheless. I will tell you honestly that being a part of this story has affected me deep inside, in places I had never been before and didn't even know existed; I confess to you that I desperately want everything Mack has told me to be true. Most days I am right there with him, but on others—when the visible world of concrete and computers seems to be the *real* world—I lose touch and have my doubts.

A couple of final disclaimers: Mack would like you to know that if you happen upon this story and hate it, he says, "Sorry . . . but it wasn't primarily written for you." Then again, maybe it was. What you are about to read is the best Mack can remember about what happened. This is *his* story, not mine, so the few times I show up, I'll refer to myself in the third person—from Mack's point of view.

Memory can be a tricky companion at times, especially with the accident, and I would not be too surprised, in spite of our concerted effort toward accuracy, if some factual errors and faulty remembrances are reflected in these pages. They are not intentional. I can promise you that the conversations and events are recorded as truthfully as Mack can remember them, so please try to cut him a little slack. As you'll see, these are not easy things to talk about.

—Willie

1

A CONFLUENCE OF PATHS

Two roads diverged in the middle of my life,
I heard a wise man say
I took the road less traveled by
And that's made the difference every night and every day

—Larry Norman *(with apologies to Robert Frost)*

March unleashed a torrent of rainfall after an abnormally dry winter. A cold front out of Canada then descended and was held in place by a swirling wind that roared down the Gorge from eastern Oregon. Although spring was surely just around the corner, the god of winter was not about to relinquish its hard-won dominion without a tussle. There was a blanket of new snow in the Cascades, and rain was now freezing on impact with the frigid ground outside the house; enough reason for Mack to snuggle up with a book and a hot cider and wrap up in the warmth of a crackling fire.

But instead, he spent the better part of the morning telecommuting into his downtown desktop. Sitting comfortably in his home office wearing pajama pants and a T-shirt, he made his sales calls, mostly to the East Coast. He paused frequently, listening to the sound of crystalline rain tinging off his window and watching the slow but steady accumulation of frozen ice thickening on everything outside. He was becoming inexorably trapped as an ice-prisoner in his own home—much to his delight.

There is something joyful about storms that interrupt routine. Snow or freezing rain suddenly releases you from expectations, performance demands, and the tyranny of appointments and schedules. And unlike illness, it is largely a corporate rather than individual experience. One can almost hear a unified sigh rise from the nearby city and surrounding countryside where Nature has intervened to give respite to the weary humans slogging it out within her purview. All those affected this way are united by a mutual excuse, and the heart is suddenly and unexpectedly a little giddy. There will be no apologies needed for not showing up to some commitment or other. Everyone understands and shares in this singular justification, and the sudden alleviation of the pressure to produce makes the heart merry.

Of course, it is also true that storms interrupt business, and, while a few companies make a bit extra, some companies lose money—meaning there are those who find no joy when everything shuts down temporarily. But they can't blame anyone for their loss of production, or for not being able to make it to the office. Even if it's hardly more than a day or two, somehow each person feels like the master of his or her own world, simply because those little droplets of water freeze as they hit the ground.

Even commonplace activities become extraordinary. Routine choices become adventures and are often experienced with a sense of heightened clarity. Late in the afternoon, Mack bundled up and headed outdoors to struggle the hundred or so yards down the long driveway to the mailbox. The ice had magically turned this simple everyday task into a foray against the elements: the raising of his fist in opposition to the brute power of nature and, in an act of defiance, laughing in its face. The fact that no one would notice or care mattered little to him—just the thought made him smile inside.

The icy rain pellets stung his cheeks and hands as he carefully worked his way up and down the slight undulations of the driveway; he looked, he supposed, like a drunken sailor gingerly heading toward the next watering hole. When you face the force of an ice storm, you don't exactly walk boldly forward in a show of unbridled confidence. Bluster will get you battered. Mack had to get up off his knees twice before he was finally hugging the mailbox like some long-lost friend.

He paused to take in the beauty of a world engulfed in crystal. Everything reflected light and contributed to the heightened brilliance of the late afternoon. The trees in the neighbor's field had all donned translucent mantles, and each now stood unique but unified in its presentation. It was a glorious world and for a brief moment its blazing splendor almost lifted, even if only for a few seconds, *The Great Sadness* from Mack's shoulders.

It took almost a minute to knock off the ice that had already sealed shut the door of the mailbox. The reward for his efforts was a single envelope with only his first name typewritten on the outside; no stamp, no postmark, and no return address. Curious, he tore the end off the envelope, which was no easy task with fingers beginning to stiffen from the cold. Turning his back to the breath-snatching wind, he finally coaxed the single small rectangle of unfolded paper out of its nest. The typewritten message simply said:

```
Mackenzie,

It's been a while. I've missed you.

I'll be at the shack next weekend if you
want to get together.
                              —Papa
```

Mack stiffened as a wave of nausea rolled over him and then just as quickly mutated into anger. He purposely thought about the shack as little as possible, and even when he did, his thoughts were neither kind nor good. If this was someone's idea of a bad joke, he had truly outdone himself. And to sign it "Papa" just made it all the more horrifying.

"Idiot," he grunted, thinking about Tony the mailman, an overly friendly Italian with a big heart but little tact. Why would he even deliver such a ridiculous envelope? It wasn't even stamped. Mack angrily stuffed the envelope and note into his coat pocket and turned to start the slide back in the general direction of the house. Buffeting gusts of wind, which had initially slowed him, now shortened the time it took to traverse the mini glacier that was thickening beneath his feet.

He was doing just fine, thank you, until he reached that place in the driveway that sloped a little downward and to the left. Without any effort or intention he began to build up speed, sliding on shoes with soles that had about as much traction as a duck landing on a frozen pond. Arms flailing wildly in hopes of somehow maintaining the potential for balance, Mack found himself careening directly toward the only tree of any substantial size bordering the driveway—the one whose lower limbs he had hacked off only a few short months before. Now it stood eager to embrace him, half naked and seemingly anxious for a little retribution. In a fraction of a thought he chose the chicken's way out and tried to plop himself down by allowing his feet to slip out from under him—which is what they had naturally wanted to do anyway. Better to have a sore butt than pick slivers out of his face.

But the adrenaline rush caused him to overcompensate, and in slow motion Mack watched his feet rise up in front of him as if jerked up by some jungle trap. He hit hard, back of the head first, and skidded to a heap at the base of the shimmering tree, which seemed to stand over him with a smug look mixed with disgust and not a little disappointment.

The world went momentarily black, or so it seemed. He lay there dazed and staring up into the sky, squinting as the icy precipitation rapidly cooled his flushed face. For a fleeting pause, everything felt oddly warm and peaceful, his ire momentarily knocked out by the impact. "Now who's the idiot?" he muttered to himself, hoping that no one had been watching.

Cold was creeping quickly through his coat and sweater, and Mack knew the icy rain that was both melting and freezing beneath him would soon become a major discomfort. Groaning and feeling like a much older man, he rolled onto his hands and knees. It was then that he saw the bright red skid mark tracing his journey from point of impact to final destination. As if birthed by the sudden awareness of his injury, a dull pounding began crawling up the back of his head. Instinctively, he reached for the source of the drumbeat and brought his hand away bloody.

With rough ice and sharp gravel gouging his hands and knees, Mack half crawled and half slid until he eventually made it to a level part of the driveway. With not a little effort he was finally able to stand and gingerly inch his way toward the house, humbled by the powers of ice and gravity.

Once inside, Mack methodically shed the layers of outerwear as best he could, his half-frozen fingers responding with about as much dexterity as oversized clubs at the ends of his arms. He decided to leave the drizzly bloodstained mess right where he doffed it in the entryway and retreated painfully to the bathroom to examine his wounds. There was no question that the icy driveway had won. The gash on the back of his head was oozing around a few small pebbles still embedded in his scalp. As he had feared, a significant lump had already formed, emerging like a humpback whale breaching the wild waves of his thinning hair.

Mack found it a difficult chore to patch himself up by trying to see the back of his head using a small handheld mirror that reflected a reverse image off the bathroom mirror. A short frustration later he gave up, unable to get his hands to go in the right directions and unsure which of the two mirrors was lying to him. By gingerly probing around the soggy gash he succeeded in picking out the biggest pieces of debris, until it hurt too much to continue. Grabbing some first-aid ointment and plugging the wound as best he could, he then tied a washcloth to the back of his head with some gauze he found in a bathroom drawer. Glancing at himself in the mirror, he thought he looked a little like some rough sailor out of *Moby Dick*. It made him laugh, then wince.

He would have to wait until Nan made it home before he would get any real medical attention—that attention being one of the many benefits of being married to a registered nurse. Anyway, he knew that the worse it looked, the more sympathy he would get. There was often some compensation in every trial, if one looked hard enough. He swallowed a couple over-the-counter painkillers to dull the throbbing and limped toward the front entry.

Not for an instant had Mack forgotten about the note. Rummaging through the pile of wet and bloody clothing he finally found it in his coat pocket, glanced at it, and then headed back into his office. He located the post office number and dialed it. As expected, Annie, the matronly postmaster and keeper of everyone's secrets, answered the phone. "Hi, is Tony in by chance?"

"Hey, Mack, is that you? Recognized your voice." Of course she did. "Sorry, but Tony ain't back yet. In fact I just talked to him on the radio and he's only made it halfway up Wildcat, not even to your place yet. Do ya need me to have him call ya, or would ya just like to leave a message?"

"Oh, hi. Is that you, Annie?" He couldn't resist, even though her Midwestern accent left no doubt. "Sorry, I was busy for a second there. Didn't hear a word you said."

She laughed. "Now, Mack, I know you heard every word. Don't you be goin' and tryin' to kid a kidder. I wasn't born yesterday, ya know. Whaddya want me to tell him if he makes it back alive?"

"Actually, you already answered my question."

There was a pause at the other end. "Actually, I don't remember you askin' a question. What's wrong with you, Mack? Still smoking too much dope or do you just do that on Sunday mornings to make it through the church service?" At this she started to laugh, as if caught off guard by the brilliance of her own sense of humor.

"Now, Annie, you know I don't smoke dope—never did, and don't ever want to." Of course Annie knew no such thing, but Mack was taking no chances on how she might remember the conversation in a day or two. Wouldn't be the first time that her sense of humor morphed into a good story that soon became "fact." He could see his name being added to the church prayer chain. "It's okay, I'll just catch Tony some other time, no big deal."

"Okay, then, just stay indoors where it's safe. Don't ya know, an old guy like you coulda lost his sense of balance over the years. Wouldn't wanna see ya slip and hurt your pride. Way things are shapin' up, Tony might not make it up to your place at all. We can do snow, sleet, and darkness of night pretty well, but this frozen rain stuff, it's a challenge to be sure."

"Thanks, Annie. I'll try and remember your advice. Talk to you later. Bye now." His head was pounding more than ever—little trip-hammers beating to the rhythm of his heart. *That's odd*, he thought. *Who would dare put something like that in* our *mailbox?* The painkillers had not yet fully kicked in but were present enough to dull the edge of worry that he was starting to feel, and he was suddenly very tired. Laying his head down on the desk, he thought he had just dropped off to sleep when the phone startled him awake.

"Uh . . . hello?"

"Hi, love. You sound like you've been asleep." It was Nan, sounding unusually cheery, even though he felt he could hear the underlying sadness that lurked just beneath the surface of every conversation. She loved this kind of weather as much as he usually did. He switched on the desk lamp and glanced at the clock, surprised that he had been out for a couple of hours.

"Uh, sorry. I guess I dozed off for a bit."

"Well, you sound a little groggy. Is everything all right?"

"Yup." Even though it was almost dark outside, Mack could see that the storm had not let up. It had even deposited a couple more inches of ice. Tree branches were hanging low, and he knew some would eventually break from the weight, especially if the wind kicked up. "I had a little tussle with the driveway when I got the mail, but other than that, everything is fine. Where are you?"

"I'm still at Arlene's, and I think me and the kids'll spend the night here. It's always good for Kate to be around the family . . . seems to restore a little balance." Arlene was Nan's sister who lived across the river in Washington. "Anyway, it's really too slick to go out. Hopefully it'll break up by morning. I wish I had made it home before it got so bad, but oh well." She paused. "How's it up at the house?"

"Well, it's absolutely stunningly beautiful, and a whole lot safer to look at than walk in, trust me. I for sure don't want you to try and get up here in this mess. Nothing's moving. I don't even think Tony was able to bring us the mail."

"I thought you already got the mail?" she queried.

"Nope, I didn't actually get the mail. I thought Tony had already come and I went out to get it. There"—he hesitated, looking down at the note that lay on the desk where he had placed it—"wasn't any mail yet. I called Annie and she said Tony probably wouldn't be able to make it up the hill, and I'm not going out there again to see if he did.

"Anyway—" He quickly changed the subject to avoid more questions. "How is Kate doing over there?"

There was a pause and then a long sigh. When Nan spoke her voice was hushed to a whisper and he could tell she was covering her mouth on the other end. "Mack, I wish I knew. She is just like talking to a rock, and no matter what I do I can't get through. When we're around family she seems to come out of her shell some, but then she disappears again. I just don't know what to do. I've been praying and praying that Papa would help us find a way to reach her, but"—she paused again—"it feels like he isn't listening."

There it was. Papa was Nan's favorite name for God, and it expressed her delight in the intimate friendship she had with him.

"Honey, I'm sure God knows what he's doing. It will all work out." The words brought him no comfort, but he hoped they might ease the worry he could hear in her voice.

"I know," she sighed. "I just wish he'd hurry up."

"Me too" was all Mack could think to say. "Well, you and the kids stay put and stay safe, and tell Arlene and Jimmy hi, and thank them for me. Hopefully I will see you tomorrow."

"Okay, love. I should go and help the others. Everyone's busy looking for candles in case the power goes out. You should probably do the same. There's some above the sink in the basement, and there's leftover stuffed bread dough in the fridge that you can heat up. Are you sure you're okay?"

"Yeah, my pride is hurt more than anything."

"Well, take it easy, and hopefully we'll see you in the morning."

"All right, honey. Be safe and call me if you need anything. Bye."

That was kind of a dumb thing to say, he thought as he hung up the phone. Kind of a manly dumb thing, as if he could help if they needed anything.

Mack sat and stared at the note. It was confusing and painful trying to sort out the swirling cacophony of disturbing emotions and dark images clouding his mind—a million thoughts traveling a million miles an hour. Finally, he gave up, folded the note, slid it into a small tin box he kept on the desk, and switched off the light.

Mack managed to find something to heat up in the microwave, then he grabbed a couple of blankets and pillows and headed for the living room. A quick glance at the clock told him that Bill Moyer's show had just started, a favorite program that he tried never to miss. Moyer was one of a handful of people whom Mack would love to meet—a brilliant and outspoken man, able to express intense compassion for both people and truth with unusual clarity. One of the stories tonight had something to do with oilman Boone Pickens, who was now starting to drill for water, of all things.

Almost without thinking, and without taking his eyes off the television, Mack reached over to the end table, picked up a photo frame holding a picture of a little girl, and clutched it to his chest. With the other hand he pulled the blankets up under his chin and hunkered deeper into the sofa.

Soon the sounds of gentle snoring filled the air as the media tube turned its attention to a piece on a high school senior in Zimbabwe who had been beaten for speaking out against his government. But Mack had already left the room to wrestle with his dreams; maybe tonight there would be no nightmares, only visions, perhaps, of ice and trees and gravity.

2

THE GATHERING DARK

Nothing makes us so lonely as our secrets.
—Paul Tournier

Sometime during the night an unexpected chinook blew through the Willamette Valley, freeing the landscape from the storm's icy grip, except for those things that lay hidden in the deepest shadows. Within twenty-four hours it was early summer warm. Mack slept late into the morning, one of those dreamless sleeps that seem to pass in an instant.

When he finally crawled off the sofa, he was somewhat chagrined to see that the ice follies had fizzled out so quickly but delighted to see Nan and the kids when they showed up less than an hour later. First came the anticipated and considerable scolding for not putting his bloodied mess in the laundry room, followed by an appropriate and satisfying amount of oohing and ahhing that accompanied her examination of his head wound. The attention pleased Mack immensely, and Nan soon had him cleaned up, patched up, and fed up. The note, though never far from his mind, was not mentioned. He still didn't know what to think of it, and he didn't want Nan included if it turned out to be some kind of cruel joke.

Little distractions like the ice storm were a welcome although brief respite from the haunting presence of his constant companion: *The Great Sadness*, as he referred to it. Shortly after the summer that Missy vanished, *The Great*

Sadness had draped itself around Mack's shoulders like some invisible but almost tangibly heavy quilt. The weight of its presence dulled his eyes and stooped his shoulders. Even his efforts to shake it off were exhausting, as if his arms were sewn into its bleak folds of despair and he had somehow become part of it. He ate, worked, loved, dreamed, and played in this garment of heaviness, weighed down as if he were wearing a leaden bathrobe—trudging daily through the murky despondency that sucked the color out of everything.

At times he could feel *The Great Sadness* slowly tightening around his chest and heart like the crushing coils of a constrictor, squeezing liquid from his eyes until he thought there no longer remained a reservoir. Other times he would dream that his feet were stuck in cloying mud as he caught brief glimpses of Missy running down the wooded path ahead of him, her red cotton summer dress gilded with wildflowers flashing among the trees. She was completely oblivious to the dark shadow tracking her from behind. Although he frantically tried to scream warnings to her, no sound emerged and he was always too late and too impotent to save her. He would bolt upright in bed, sweat dripping from his tortured body, while waves of nausea and guilt and regret rolled over him like some surreal tidal flood.

The story of Missy's disappearance is, unfortunately, not unlike others too often told. It all happened during Labor Day weekend, the summer's last hurrah before another year of school and autumn routines. Mack boldly decided to take the three younger children on a final camping trip to Wallowa Lake in northeastern Oregon. Nan was already booked at a continuing education class in Seattle, and the two older boys were back at college or counseling at a summer camp. But Mack was confident that he possessed the right combination of outdoorsmanship and mothering skills. After all, Nan had taught him well.

The sense of adventure and camping fever gripped everyone, and the place became a whirlwind of activity. If they had done it Mack's way, they would have simply backed a moving van up to the house and shifted most of its contents for the long weekend. At one point in all the confusion, Mack decided he needed a break and settled himself in his daddy chair after shooing off Judas, the family cat. He was about to turn on the tube when Missy came running in, holding her little Plexiglas box.

"Can I take my insect collection camping with us?" asked Missy.

"You want to take your bugs along?" grunted Mack, not paying her much mind.

"Daddy, they're not bugs. They're insects. Look, I've got lots of them in here."

Mack reluctantly turned his attention to his daughter, who, seeing him focus, started explaining the contents of her treasure box.

"See, there are two grasshoppers. And see on that leaf, there is my caterpillar and somewhere . . . There she is! Do you see my ladybug? And I have a fly in here somewhere too and some ants."

As she inventoried her collection, Mack tried his best to show attention, nodding along.

"So," Missy finished, "can I take them along?"

"Sure you can, honey. Maybe we can let them loose in the wild when we're out there."

"No she can't!" came a voice from the kitchen. "Missy, you need to keep your collection at home, honey. Trust me, they're safer here." Nan stuck her head around the corner and lovingly frowned at Mack as he shrugged his shoulders.

"I tried, honey," he whispered to Missy.

"Grrr," growled Missy. But knowing the battle was lost, she picked up her box and left.

By Thursday night the van was overloaded and the pull-behind tent-trailer hitched up with lights and brakes tested. Early Friday, after one last lecture from Nan to her kids about safety, obedience, brushing teeth in the mornings, not picking up cats with white stripes down their backs, and all manner of other things, they headed out: Nan north up Interstate 205 to Washington, and Mack and the three amigos east on Interstate 84. The plan was to return the following Tuesday night, just before the first day of school.

The Columbia River Gorge is worth the trip by itself, with breathtaking panoramas overseen by river-carved mesas standing sleepy guard in the late-summer warmth. September and October can offer some of Oregon's best weather: Indian summer often sets in around Labor Day and hangs on until Halloween, when it quickly turns cold, wet, and nasty. This year was no exception. Traffic and weather cooperated wonderfully, and the crew hardly noticed the time and miles passing by.

The foursome stopped at Multnomah Falls to buy a coloring book and crayons for Missy and two inexpensive, waterproof disposable cameras for Kate and Josh. They then decided to climb the short distance up the trail to the bridge facing the falls. There had once been a path that led around the main pool and into a shallow cave behind the tumbling water, but, unfortunately, it had been blocked off by the park authorities because of erosion. Missy loved it here, and she begged her daddy to tell the legend of the beautiful Indian maid, the daughter of a chief of the Multnomah tribe. It took some coaxing, but Mack finally relented and retold the story as they all stared up into the mists shrouding the falling cascade.

The tale centered on a princess, the only child left to her aging father. The chief loved his daughter dearly and carefully picked out a husband for her, a young warrior chief of the Clatsop tribe, whom he knew she loved. The two tribes came together to celebrate the days of the wedding feast, but before it could begin, a terrible sickness began to spread among the men, killing many.

The elders and the chiefs met to discuss what they could do about the wasting disease that was quickly decimating their warriors. The oldest medicine man among them spoke of how his own father, when aged and near death, had foretold of a terrible sickness that would kill their men, an illness that could be stopped only if a pure and innocent daughter of a chief would willingly give up her life for her people. In order to fulfill the prophecy, she must voluntarily climb to a cliff above the Big River and from there jump to her death onto the rocks below.

A dozen young women, all daughters of the various chiefs, were brought before the council. After considerable debate the elders decided that they could not ask for such a precious sacrifice, especially for a legend they weren't sure was true.

But the disease continued to spread unabated among the men, and eventually the young warrior chief, the husband-to-be, fell ill with the sickness. The princess who loved him knew in her heart that something had to be done, and after cooling his fever and kissing him softly on the forehead, she slipped away.

It took her all night and the next day to reach the place spoken of in the legend, a towering cliff overlooking the Big River and the lands beyond. After praying and giving herself to the Great Spirit, she fulfilled the prophecy by jumping without hesitation to her death on the rocks below.

Back at the villages the next morning, those who had been sick arose well and strong. There was great joy and celebration until the young warrior discovered that his beloved bride was missing. As the awareness of what had happened spread rapidly among the people, many began the journey to the place where they knew they would find her. As they silently gathered around her broken body at the base of the cliff, her grief-stricken father cried out to the Great Spirit, asking that her sacrifice would always be remembered. At that moment, water began to fall from the place where she had jumped, turning into a fine mist that fell at their feet, slowly forming a beautiful pool.

Missy usually loved the telling, almost as much as Mack did. It had all the elements of a true redemption story, not unlike the story of Jesus that she knew so well. It centered on a father who loved his only child and a sacrifice foretold by a prophet. Because of love, the child willingly gave up her life to save her betrothed and their tribes from certain death.

But on this occasion, Missy didn't say a word when the story was finished. Instead, she immediately turned and headed for the van as if to say, "Okay, I am done here. Let's get going."

They made a quick stop for some brunch and a potty break at Hood River and then got right back on the road, reaching La Grande by early afternoon. Here they left I-84 and took the Wallowa Lake Highway, which would take them the final seventy-two miles to the town of Joseph. The lake and campground they were headed for were only a few miles beyond Joseph, and after finding their site they all pitched in and had everything set up in short order—perhaps not exactly the way Nan would have preferred, but functional nonetheless.

The first meal was a Phillips family tradition: flank steak, marinated in Uncle Joe's secret sauce. For dessert they ate the brownies Nan had made the night before, topped with the vanilla ice cream they had packed away in dry ice.

That evening, as he sat among three laughing children watching one of nature's greatest shows, Mack's heart was suddenly penetrated by unexpected joy. A sunset of brilliant colors and patterns played off the few clouds that had waited in the wings to become central actors in this unique presentation. He was a rich man, he thought to himself, in all the ways that mattered.

By the time supper was cleaned up, night had fallen. The deer—routine day visitors and sometimes a serious nuisance—had gone wherever deer go to bed down. Their shift was picked up by the night troublemakers: raccoons, squirrels, and chipmunks that traveled in roving bands looking for any container left slightly open. The Phillips campers knew this from past experience. The first night they had ever spent in these campgrounds had cost them four dozen Rice Krispies Treats, a box of chocolates, and all their peanut butter cookies.

Before it got too late, the four went on a short hike away from the campfires and lanterns, to a dark and quiet spot where they could lie down and gaze in wonder at the Milky Way, stunning and intense when undiminished by the pollution of city lights. Mack could lie and gaze up into that vastness for hours. He felt so incredibly small yet comfortable with himself. Of all the places he sensed the presence of God, out here, surrounded by nature and under the stars, was one of the most tangible. He could almost hear the song of worship they sang to their Creator, and in his reluctant heart he joined in as best he could.

Then it was back to the campsite, and after several trips to the facilities, Mack tucked the three in turn into the safety and security of their sleeping bags. He prayed briefly with Josh before moving across to where Kate and Missy lay waiting, but when it came Missy's turn to pray she wanted to talk instead.

"Daddy, how come she had to die?" It took Mack a moment to figure out whom Missy was talking about, suddenly realizing that the Multnomah princess must have been on her mind since they had stopped earlier.

"Honey, she didn't *have* to die. She *chose* to die to save her people. They were very sick and she wanted them to be healed."

There was silence and Mack knew that another question was forming in the darkness.

"Did it really happen?" This time the question was from Kate, obviously interested in the conversation.

"Did what really happen?"

"Did the Indian princess really die? Is the story true?"

Mack thought before he spoke. "I don't know, Kate. It's

a legend, and sometimes legends are stories that teach a lesson."

"So, it didn't really happen?" asked Missy.

"It might have, sweetie. Sometimes legends are built from real stories, things that really happen."

Again silence, then, "So is Jesus' dying a legend?"

Mack could hear the wheels turning in Kate's mind. "No, honey, that's a true story. And do you know what? I think the Indian princess story is probably true too."

Mack waited while his girls processed their thoughts.

Missy was next to ask, "Is the Great Spirit another name for God—you know, Jesus' Papa?"

Mack smiled in the dark. Obviously, Nan's nightly prayers were having an effect. "I would suppose so. It's a good name for God because he is a spirit and he is great."

"Then how come he's so *mean*?"

Ah, here was the question that had been brewing. "What do you mean, Missy?"

"Well, the Great Spirit makes the princess jump off the cliff and makes Jesus die on a cross. That seems pretty mean to me."

Mack was stuck. He wasn't sure how to answer. At six and a half years old, Missy was asking questions that wise people had wrestled with for centuries.

"Sweetheart, Jesus didn't think his Daddy was mean. He thought his Daddy was full of love and loved him very much. His Daddy didn't *make* him die. Jesus chose to die because he and his Daddy love you and me and everyone in the world. He saved us from our sickness, just like the princess."

Now came the longest silence, and Mack was beginning to wonder if the girls had fallen asleep. Just as he was about to lean over and kiss them good night, a little voice with a noticeable quiver broke into the quiet.

"Daddy?"

"Yes, honey?"

"Will I ever have to jump off a cliff?"

Mack's heart broke as he understood what this conversation had really been about. He gathered his little girl into his arms and pulled her close. With his own voice a little huskier than usual, he gently replied, "No, honey. I will never ask you to jump off a cliff, never, ever, ever."

"Then will God ever ask me to jump off a cliff?"

"No, Missy. He would never ask you to do anything like that."

She snuggled deeper into his arms. "Okay! Hold me close. G'night, Daddy. I love you." And she was out, drifting deep into a sound sleep with only good and sweet dreams.

After a few minutes, Mack placed her gently back in her sleeping bag.

"You okay, Kate?" he whispered as he kissed her good night.

"Yup," she whispered. "Daddy?"

"What, sweetheart?"

"She asks good questions, doesn't she?"

"She sure does. She's a special little girl. You both are, except you're not so little anymore. Now get some sleep—we have a big day ahead of us. Sweet dreams, darlin'."

"You too, Daddy. I love you tons!"

"I love you too, with all my heart. Good night."

Mack zipped up the trailer on his way out, blew his nose, and wiped away the tears that still remained on his cheeks. He prayed a silent thanks to God and then went to brew some coffee.

3

THE TIPPING POINT

The soul is healed by being with children.

—Fyodor Dostoyevsky

Wallowa Lake State Park in Oregon and its surrounding area has been well referred to as the Little Switzerland of America. Wild, rugged mountains rise to almost ten thousand feet, and in between them are hidden innumerable valleys full of streams, hiking trails, and high-elevation meadows overflowing with sprays of wildflowers. Wallowa Lake is the gateway into the Eagle Cap Wilderness Area and Hells Canyon National Recreation Area, which sports the deepest gorge in North America. Carved out over centuries by the Snake River, it reaches a depth of nearly two miles top to bottom in places, and ten miles at times from rim to rim.

Seventy-five percent of the recreation area is roadless, with more than nine hundred miles of hiking trails. Once the domain of the prevailing Nez Percé tribe, the remnants of their presence are scattered throughout this wilderness, as well as those of white settlers traveling through on their way to the West. The nearby town of Joseph was named for a powerful tribal chief whose Indian name meant "Thunder Rolling Down the Mountain." This area is home to an abundance of flora and wildlife including elk, bear, deer, and mountain goat. The presence of rattlers, especially as you get closer to the Snake River, is reason enough to hike cautiously, should you decide to venture off-trail.

Wallowa Lake itself is five miles long and one mile wide, formed, some say, by glaciers nine million years ago. It now sits about a mile from the town of Joseph at an elevation of forty-four hundred feet. The water, though catch-your-breath cold most of the year, is comfortable enough by the end of summer for a leisurely swim, at least close in to shore. Sacagawea, at almost ten thousand feet, looks down on this blue jewel from her snowcapped and timbered heights.

Mack and the kids filled the next three days with fun and leisure. Missy, seemingly satisfied with her daddy's answers, never again raised the issue of the princess, even when one of their day hikes took them by some precipitous cliffs. They spent a few hours traveling the lake shore in paddle boats, tried their best to win a prize at miniature golf, and even went horseback trail-riding. After a morning trip to the historic Wade Ranch that sits about halfway between Joseph and Enterprise, they spent the afternoon visiting the little shops in the town of Joseph itself.

Back at the lake, Josh and Kate raced each other around the go-kart track. Josh came away the winner, but Kate was able to regain bragging rights later that afternoon when she landed three good-sized lake trout. Missy caught one with hook and worm, but neither Josh nor Mack could claim a single tug on their fancier lures.

Sometime during the weekend two other families seemed to magically weave themselves into the Phillipses' world. As often happens, friendships had been struck up initially among the children and then between the adults. Josh had been especially keen on getting to know the Ducettes, whose eldest, Amber, just happened to be a cute young lady about his age. Kate seriously enjoyed tormenting her older brother about the entire matter, and he would reward her taunting by stomping off to the tent-trailer, all bluster and gripe. Amber had a sister, Emmy, who was only a year younger than Kate, and the two spent a lot of time together. Vicki and Emil Ducette had traveled from their home in Colorado, where Emil worked as an agent for the U.S. Fish and Wildlife Service Office of Law Enforcement, and Vicki stayed home to manage the household, which included their surprise son J.J., now almost a year old.

The Ducettes introduced Mack and his children to a Canadian couple they had met earlier, Jesse and Sarah Madison. These two had an easy, unpretentious manner, and Mack took an instant liking to them. Both careered as independent consultants, Jesse in human resources and Sarah in change management. Missy gravitated immediately to Sarah, and both were often together down at the Ducette campsite helping Vicki with J.J.

Monday broke gloriously, and the entire entourage was excited about its plans to take the Wallowa Lake Tramway to the top of Mount Howard—8,150 feet above sea level. When it was constructed in 1970, the tramway had the steepest vertical lift in North America, with a cable length of almost four miles. The trip to the summit takes about fifteen minutes in a tramcar that dangles anywhere from three feet to 120 feet off the ground.

Instead of packing a lunch, Jesse and Sarah insisted on treating everyone to a meal at the Summit Grill. The plan was to eat as soon as they reached the top and then spend the rest of the day hiking to the five viewpoints and overlooks. Armed with cameras, sunglasses, water bottles, and sunscreen, they headed off by mid-morning. As intended, they consumed a veritable feast of hamburgers, fries, and shakes at the Grill. The elevation must have spurred their appetites—even Missy was able to down an entire burger and most of the trimmings.

After lunch they hiked to each of the nearby lookouts, the longest trail being from the Valley Overlook to the Snake River Country and Seven Devils Lookout (a little more than three-quarters of a mile). From the Wallowa Valley Overlook they could see as far as the towns of Joseph, Enterprise, Lostine, and even Wallowa. From the Royal Purple Overlook and the Summit Overlook they enjoyed the crystal clear view, looking into the states of Washington and Idaho. Some even thought they could see across the Idaho panhandle into Montana.

By late afternoon, everyone was tired and happy. Missy, whom Jesse had carried on his shoulders to the last couple of lookouts, was now falling asleep in her father's arms as they bumped and whirred down from the summit. The four young people, along with Sarah, had their faces plastered against the windows, oohing and ahhing at the wonders to be seen along the descent. The Ducettes sat holding hands in quiet conversation, while J.J. slept in his father's arms.

This is one of those rare and precious moments, thought Mack, *that catches you by surprise and almost takes your breath away. If only Nan could be here, it truly would be perfect.* He shifted Missy's weight to a more comfortable position for her, now that she was totally out, and pulled back the hair from her face to look at her. The grime and sweat of the day had done nothing but strangely enhance her innocence and beauty. *Why do they have to grow up?* he mused and kissed her on the forehead.

That evening the three families combined their food for a last supper together. Taco salad was the entrée, with lots of fresh vegetables and dip. And somehow, Sarah had been able to whip up a chocolate dessert with layers of whipped cream, mousse, brownies, and other delights that had everyone feeling decadent and satisfied.

With the remains of supper stashed back in the coolers and the dishes cleaned and put away, the adults sat sipping coffee around a blazing campfire while Emil shared his adventures of breaking up endangered-animal smuggling rings and explaining how they caught poachers and others who hunted illegally. He was a skilled storyteller, and his vocation offered a deep resource for some hilarious tales. It was all fascinating, and Mack realized again that there was much in the world about which he was naive.

As the evening wound down, Emil and Vicki headed for bed first with their sleepy-eyed baby. Jesse and Sarah volunteered to stay awhile before walking the Ducette girls back to their campsite. The three Phillips kids and two Ducettes immediately disappeared into the safety of the tent-trailer to share stories and secrets.

As often happens when a campfire burns long, the conversation turned from the humorous to the more personal. Sarah seemed eager to ask Mack about the rest of his family, especially Nan.

"So what is she like, Mackenzie?"

Mack loved any opportunity to brag about his Nan. "Well, besides being beautiful—and I'm not just saying that—she really is beautiful, inside and out." He looked up sheepishly to see them both smiling at him. He was really missing her and was glad the night shadows hid his embarrassment. "Her full name is Nannette, but almost no one calls her anything but Nan. She has quite a reputation in the medical community, at least in the Northwest. She's a nurse and works with oncology patients—uh, cancer patients—who are terminal. It's tough work, but she really loves it. Anyway, she's written some papers and has been a speaker at a couple of conferences."

"Really?" Sarah prompted. "What does she speak on?"

"She helps people think through their relationship with God in the face of their own death," Mack answered.

"I'd love to hear more about that," encouraged Jesse as he stirred up the fire with a stick, causing it to bloom with renewed vigor.

Mack hesitated. As much as he felt unusually at ease with these two, he didn't really know them, and the conversation had gotten a little deeper than he was comfortable with. He searched quickly for a short answer to Jesse's interest.

"Nan's a lot better at that than I am. I guess she thinks about God differently than most folks. She even calls him Papa because of the closeness of their relationship, if that makes sense."

"Of course it does!" exclaimed Sarah as Jesse nodded. "Is that a family thing, referring to God as Papa?"

"No," said Mack, laughing. "The kids have picked it up some, but I'm not comfortable with it. It just seems a little too familiar for me. Anyway, Nan has a wonderful father, so I think it's just easier for her."

It had slipped out, and Mack inwardly shuddered, hoping no one had noticed, but Jesse was looking right at him. "Your dad wasn't too wonderful?" he asked gently.

"Yeah." Mack paused. "I guess you could say he was not too wonderful. He died when I was just a kid, of natural causes." Mack laughed, but the sound was empty. He looked at the two. "He drank himself to death."

"We're so sorry," Sarah said for both of them, and Mack could sense that she meant it.

"Well," he said, forcing another laugh, "life is hard sometimes, but I have a lot to be thankful for."

An awkward silence followed as Mack wondered what it was about these two that seemed to penetrate his defenses so easily. He was rescued seconds later by a flurry of children pouring out of the trailer and into their midst. Much to Kate's glee, she and Emmy had caught Josh and Amber holding hands in the dark, and now she wanted the whole world to know. By this time, Josh was so smitten that he was willing to put up with any harassment and took what she dished out in stride. He couldn't have wiped the silly grin off his face even if he had tried.

Both Madisons hugged Mack and his children good night, with Sarah giving him an especially tender squeeze before she left. Then, hand in hand with Amber and Emmy, they headed off into the darkness toward the Ducette site. Mack watched them until he could no longer hear their night whispers and the swaying of their flashlight disappeared from sight. He smiled to himself and turned to herd his own brood in the direction of their sleeping bags.

Prayers were said all around, followed by good-night kisses and giggles from Kate in low conversation with her older brother, who would occasionally burst out in a harsh whisper so everyone could hear, "Cut it out, Kate. Grrr . . . I mean it, you are such a brat!" and eventually, silence.

Mack packed up what he could by the light of the lanterns and soon decided to leave the rest till daylight. They weren't planning to leave until early afternoon anyway. He brewed his final nightly cup of coffee and sat sipping it in front of the fire that had burned itself down to a flickering mass of red-hot coals. It was so easy to get lost inside such a bed of glowing undulating embers. He was alone, yet not alone. Wasn't that a line from the Bruce Cockburn song "Rumors of Glory"? He wasn't sure, but if he remembered he would look it up when he got home.

As he sat mesmerized by the fire and wrapped in its warmth, he prayed, mostly prayers of thanksgiving. He had been given so much. *Blessed* was probably the right word. He was content, at rest, and full of peace. Mack did not know it then, but within twenty-four hours his prayers would change drastically.

ᚠᚱᚾᛞᚾᚱ

The next morning, though sunny and warm, didn't start off so well. Mack rose early to surprise the kids with a wonderful breakfast, but he burned two fingers while trying to free flapjacks that had stuck to the griddle. In response to the searing pain, he knocked over the stove and griddle and dropped the bowl of pancake batter onto the sandy ground. The kids, startled awake by the clatter and under-the-breath expletives, had stuck their heads out of the tent-trailer to see what all the commotion was about. They began to giggle as soon as they grasped the situation, but one "Hey, it's not funny!" from Mack and they ducked back into the safety of the tent, still tittering from their hideout while they watched through the mesh windows.

So breakfast, instead of the feast Mack had intended, was cold cereal with half-and-half—since the last of the milk had gone into the pancake batter. Mack spent the next hour trying to organize the site with two fingers stuck in a glass of ice water, which had to be refreshed frequently with chips that Josh broke off the ice block with the back side of a spoon. Word must have gotten out because Sarah Madison showed up with burn first aid, and within minutes of having his fingers slathered in the whitish liquid, he felt the sting recede.

About that time Josh and Kate, having completed their ordered chores, showed up to ask if they could go out in the Ducettes' canoe one last time; they promised to wear life jackets. After the initial mandatory no and the required amount of begging from the kids, especially Kate, Mack finally gave in, reminding them once again of the rules of canoe safety and conduct. He wasn't too concerned. Their campsite was only a stone's throw from the lake, and they promised to stay close to shore. Mack would be able to keep an eye on them while he continued packing up the camp.

Missy was busy at the table, coloring in the book from Multnomah Falls. *She's just too cute*, Mack thought, glancing in her direction as he worked to clean up the mess he had made earlier. She was dressed in the only clean thing she had left, a little red sundress with embroidered wildflowers, a purchase from their first day's trip into the town of Joseph.

About fifteen minutes later, Mack looked up when he heard a familiar voice calling "Daddy!" from the direction of the lake. It was Kate, and she and her brother were paddling like pros out on the water. Both were obediently wearing their life jackets and he waved at them.

It is remarkable how a seemingly insignificant action or event can change entire lives. Kate, lifting her paddle to wave back in response, lost her balance and tipped the canoe. There was a frozen look of terror on her face as almost in silence and slow motion it rolled over. Josh frantically leaned to try to balance, but it was too late and he disappeared from sight in the midst of the splash. Mack was already headed for the water's edge, not intending to go in but to be near when they bobbed up. Kate was up first, sputtering and crying, but there was no sign of Josh. Then suddenly, an eruption of water and legs, and Mack knew instantly that something was terribly wrong.

To his amazement, all the instincts he had honed as a teenage lifeguard came roaring back. In a matter of seconds he hit the water, shoes and shirt off. He didn't even notice the icy shock as he began racing the fifty feet out toward the overturned canoe, ignoring for the moment the terrified sobbing of his daughter. She was safe. His primary focus was Josh.

Taking a deep breath, he dove under. The water, in spite of all the churning, was still fairly clear, with visibility about three feet. He found Josh quickly and also discovered why he was in trouble. One of the straps on his life vest had gotten tangled in the canoe webbing. Try as he might, he couldn't yank it free either, so he tried to signal Josh to push himself deeper inside the canoe, where breathable air was trapped. But the poor boy was panicking, straining against the strap that was keeping him caught under the canoe rim and underwater.

Mack surfaced, yelled at Kate to swim to shore, gulped what air he could, and went under a second time. By his third dive and knowing time was running out, Mack realized that he could either keep trying to free Josh from the vest or flip the canoe. Since Josh in his panic was not letting anyone near him, Mack chose the latter. Whether it was God and angels or God and adrenaline, he would never know for sure, but on only his second attempt he succeeded in rolling the canoe over, freeing Josh from his tether.

The jacket, finally able to do what it was designed for, now kept the boy's face up above water. Mack surfaced behind Josh, who was limp and unconscious, blood oozing from a gash on his head where the canoe had banged him as Mack had righted it. He immediately began mouth-to-mouth on his son as best he could, while others, who had heard the commotion, arrived to pull him and the canoe with the attached vest toward the shallows.

Oblivious to the shouts around him as people barked instructions and questions, Mack focused on his task, his own panic building inside his chest. Just as his feet touched solid ground, Josh began to cough and throw up water and breakfast. A huge cheer erupted from everyone gathered, but Mack couldn't have cared less. Overwhelmed with relief and the adrenaline rush of a narrow escape, he began to cry, and then suddenly Kate was sobbing with her arms around his neck, and everyone was laughing and crying and hugging.

Somehow they all made it to shore. Among those who had been drawn to the scene by the panic and noise were Jesse Madison and Emil Ducette. Through the mayhem of cheers and relief, Mack could hear Emil's voice, like the repetitious chant of a rosary, whispering again and again, "I am so sorry . . . I am so sorry . . . I am so sorry." It was his canoe. It could have been his children. Mack found him, wrapped his arms around the younger man, and emphasized strongly in his ear, "Stop it! This wasn't your fault and everyone's okay." Emil began to sob, emotions suddenly freed from behind a dam of pent-up guilt and fear.

A potential crisis had been averted. Or so Mack thought.

4

THE GREAT SADNESS

Sadness is a wall between two gardens.

—Kahlil Gibran

Mack stood on the shore, doubled over and still trying to catch his breath. It took a few minutes before he even thought about Missy. Remembering that she had been coloring in her book at the table, he walked up the bank to where he could see the campsite, but there was no sign of her. His pace quickened as he hurried to the tent-trailer, calling her name as calmly as he could manage. No response. She was not there. Even though his heart skipped a beat, he rationalized that in the confusion someone had seen to her, probably Sarah Madison or Vicki Ducette, or one of the older kids.

Not wanting to appear overanxious or panicky, he found and soberly informed his two new friends that he couldn't find Missy and asked if they would check with their families. Both quickly headed off to their respective campsites. Jesse returned first to announce that Sarah had not seen Missy at all that morning. He and Mack then headed for the Ducette site, but before they reached it Emil came hurrying toward them, a look of apprehension written clearly on his face.

"No one has seen Missy today, and we don't know where Amber is either. Maybe they're together?" There was a hint of dread in Emil's question.

"I'm sure that's it," said Mack, trying to reassure himself and Emil at the same time. "Where do you think they might be?"

"Why don't we check the bathrooms and showers?" suggested Jesse.

"Good idea," said Mack. "I'll check the one nearest our site, the one my kids use. Why don't you and Emil check the one between your sites?"

They nodded and Mack headed at a slow trot toward the closest showers, noticing for the first time that he was barefoot and shirtless. *What a sight I must be*, he thought. He probably would have chuckled if his mind wasn't so focused on Missy.

Arriving at the restrooms, he asked a teenager emerging from the women's section if she had seen a little girl in a red dress inside, or maybe two girls. She told him that she hadn't noticed but would look again. In less than a minute she was back, shaking her head.

"Thank you anyway," said Mack, and he headed around the back of the building where the showers were located. As he rounded the corner he began calling loudly for Missy. Mack could hear water running, but no one responded. Wondering if Missy might be in one of the showers, he began pounding on each until he got a response. He succeeded only in severely scaring a poor elderly lady when his door banging accidentally opened her shower stall. She shrieked, and Mack, with profuse apologies, quickly shut the door and hurried on to the next one.

Six shower stalls and no Missy. He checked the men's toilet stalls and showers, trying not to think about why he would even bother looking there. She was nowhere and he jogged back toward Emil's, unable to pray anything except "Oh, God, help me find her . . . Oh, God, please help me find her."

When she saw him, Vicki rushed to meet him. She had been trying not to cry but couldn't help it as they embraced. Suddenly Mack desperately wanted Nan to be there. She would know what to do, at least what the right thing was. He felt so lost.

"Sarah has Josh and Kate back at your campsite, so don't worry about them," Vicki told him between sobs.

Oh, God, Mack thought, having totally forgotten about his other two. *What kind of a father am I?* Although he was relieved that Sarah had them, he now wished even more that Nan were here.

Just then, Emil and Jesse burst into camp, Emil appearing relieved and Jesse looking as tense as a wound-up spring.

"We found her!" exclaimed Emil, his face lighting up, then turning somber as he realized what he had implied. "I mean, we found Amber. She just came back from taking a shower at this other place that still had hot water. She said she told her mom, but Vicki probably didn't hear her . . ." His voice trailed off.

"But we didn't find Missy," Jesse added quickly, answering the most important question. "Amber hasn't seen her today either."

Emil, all business now, took charge. "Mack, we need to contact the campground authorities immediately and get the word out to find Missy. Maybe in the ruckus and excitement she got scared and confused and just wandered away and got lost, or maybe she was trying to find us and took a wrong turn. Do you have a picture of her? Maybe there's a copy machine at the office and we could make a few copies and save some time."

"Yeah, I have a snapshot of her in my wallet." He reached for his back pocket and for a second panicked as he found nothing there. The thought flashed through his mind of his wallet sitting at the bottom of Wallowa Lake, and then he remembered that it was still in his van after yesterday's trip up the tram.

The three headed back to Mack's site. Jesse ran ahead to let Sarah know that Amber was safe, but that Missy's whereabouts were still unknown. Arriving at camp, Mack hugged and encouraged Josh and Kate as best he could, trying to appear calm for their sakes. Changing out of his wet clothes, he threw on a T-shirt and jeans, some clean dry socks, and a pair of running shoes. Sarah promised that she and Vicki would keep his older two with them and whispered that she was praying for him and Missy. Mack gave her a quick hug and thanked her, and after kissing his children he joined the other two men as they jogged toward the campground office.

Word of the water rescue had reached the little two-room camp headquarters ahead of them, and everyone there was in high spirits. This changed quickly as the three took turns explaining Missy's disappearance. Fortunately the office had a photocopier, and Mack enlarged half a dozen pictures of Missy, handing them around.

The Wallowa Lake campground has 215 sites divided into five loops and three group areas. The young assistant manager, Jeremy Bellamy, volunteered to help canvass, so they divided the camp into four areas and each headed out armed with a map, Missy's picture, and an office walkie-talkie. One assistant with a walkie-talkie also went back to Mack's site to report in if Missy turned up there.

It was slow, methodical work, much too slow for Mack, but he knew that this was the most logical way to find her if . . . if she was still on the campgrounds. As he walked between tents and trailers, he was praying and promising. He knew in his heart that promising things to God was rather dumb and irrational, but he couldn't help it. He was desperate to get Missy back, and surely God knew where she was.

Many campers were either not at their sites or in the final stages of packing up to head home. No one he asked had seen Missy or anyone looking like her. Periodically the search parties checked in with the office to get an update on the progress, if any, that each was making. Nothing at all, until almost two in the afternoon.

Mack was finishing his section when the call came in on the walkie-talkies. Jeremy, who had taken the area nearest the entrance, thought he had something. Emil instructed them to put a mark on their maps showing where each had left off, and then he gave them the site number where Jeremy had called from. Mack was the last to arrive, and he walked in on an intense conversation involving Emil, Jeremy, and a third young man Mack did not recognize.

Emil quickly brought Mack up to speed, introducing him to Virgil Thomas, a city boy from California who had been camping all summer in the area with some buddies. Virgil and his friends had crashed after partying late into the night, and he had been the only one up who saw an old military-green truck heading out the entrance and down the road toward Joseph.

"About what time was that?" Mack asked.

"Like I told him," Virgil said, pointing his thumb at Jeremy, "it was before noon. I'm not sure how much before noon, though. I was kinda hung over, and we really haven't been paying much attention to clocks since we got here."

Pushing the picture of Missy in front of the young man, Mack asked sharply, "Do you think you saw *her*?"

"When the other fellow first showed me that picture, she didn't look familiar," Virgil answered, looking again at the photo. "But then, when he said that she was wearing a bright red dress, I remembered that the little girl in the green truck was wearin' red and she was either laughing or bellerin', I couldn't really tell. And then it looked like the guy slapped her or pushed her down, but I suppose he coulda been just playin' too."

Mack felt paralyzed. The information was overwhelming to him, but unfortunately it was the only thing they had heard that made any sense. It explained why they had found no trace of Missy. But everything in him didn't want it to be true. He turned and started to run toward the office, but he was halted by Emil's voice.

"Mack, stop! We've already radioed the office and contacted the sheriff in Joseph. They're sending someone here right away and putting out an APB on the truck."

As he finished speaking, as if on cue, two patrol cars pulled into the campgrounds. The first headed directly for the office, while the other turned into the section where they all stood waiting. Mack waved the officer down and hurried to meet him as he emerged from his vehicle. A young man who looked to be in his late twenties introduced himself as Officer Dalton and began taking their statements.

The next hours saw a massive escalation in response to Missy's disappearance. An all-points bulletin was sent out as far west as Portland; east to Boise, Idaho; and north to Spokane, Washington. Police officers in Joseph set up a roadblock on the Imnaha Highway, which led out of Joseph and deeper into the Hells Canyon National Recreation Area. If the child abductor had taken Missy up the Imnaha—only one of many directions he could have gone—the police figured they could get pertinent information by questioning those coming out. Their resources were limited, and rangers in the area were also contacted to be on the lookout.

The Phillipses' campsite was cordoned off as a crime scene and everyone in the vicinity was questioned. Virgil offered as much detail as he could about the truck and its occupants, and the resulting description was flashed out to all relevant agencies.

The FBI field offices in Portland, Seattle, and Denver were put on notice. Nan had been called and was on her way, being driven by her best friend, Maryanne. Even tracking dogs were brought in, but Missy's trail ended in the nearby parking lot, increasing the likelihood that Virgil's story was accurate.

After forensic specialists had combed through his campsite, Officer Dalton asked Mack to reenter the area and carefully look to see if anything was out of place or different from what he remembered. Although already exhausted by the emotions of the day, Mack was desperate to do anything to help and deliberately focused his mind to try to remember whatever he could about the morning. Cautiously, so as not to disturb anything, he retraced his steps. What he would give for a do-over: a chance to have this day start again from the beginning. He would be glad to burn his fingers and drop the pancake batter all over again if only he could take back the events that followed.

He turned back to his assigned task, but nothing seemed to be different from what he remembered. Nothing had changed. He came to the table where Missy had been busy. The book was open to the page she had been coloring, a half-finished picture of the Multnomah Indian princess. The crayons were also there, although Missy's favorite color, red, was missing. He began to look around on the ground to see where it might have fallen.

"If you're looking for the red crayon, we found it over there, by the tree," said Dalton, pointing toward the parking lot. "She probably dropped it when she was struggling with . . ." His voice trailed off.

"How can you tell she was struggling?" Mack demanded.

The officer hesitated but then spoke, almost reluctantly. "We found one of her shoes near there, in the bushes where it was probably kicked off. You weren't here at the time, so we asked your son to identify it."

The image of his daughter fighting off some perverted monster was like a fist to the stomach. Almost succumbing to the sudden blackness that threatened to smother him, Mack leaned on the table to keep from passing out or throwing up. It was then that he noticed a ladybug pin sticking in the coloring book. He snapped to awareness as if someone had opened smelling salts under his nose.

"Whose is that?" he asked Dalton, pointing to the pin.

"Whose is what?"

"This ladybug pin! Who put *that* there?"

"We just assumed it was Missy's. Are you telling me that pin was not there this morning?"

"I'm positive," asserted Mack adamantly. "She doesn't own anything like that. I am absolutely positive that it was not here this morning!"

Officer Dalton was already on his radio, and within minutes forensics was back and had taken the pin into custody.

Dalton took Mack aside and explained. "If what you say is correct, then we have to assume that Missy's assailant left it here on purpose." He paused before adding, "Mr. Phillips, this could be good news or bad."

"I don't understand," responded Mack.

The officer again hesitated, trying to decide whether he should tell Mack what he was thinking. He searched for the right words. "Well, the good news is that we might get some evidence off of it. It's the only thing we have so far linking him to the scene."

"And the bad news?" Mack held his breath.

"Well, the bad news—and I am not saying that this is the case here—but guys who leave something like this usually have a purpose in leaving it, and it usually means that they have done this before."

"What are you saying?" Mack snapped. "That this guy is some kind of serial killer? Is this some sort of mark he leaves behind to identify himself, like he is marking his territory or something?"

Mack was getting angry, and it was evident by the look on Dalton's face that he was sorry for even mentioning it. But before Mack could blow, Dalton received an incoming call on his belt radio patching him through to the FBI field office in Portland, Oregon. Mack refused to leave and listened as a woman identified herself as a special agent. She asked Dalton to describe the pin in detail. Mack followed the officer to where the forensic team had set up a work area. Holding the ziplock bag in which the pin had been secured, Dalton concentrated on describing it as best he could, while Mack eavesdropped from a position slightly behind the group.

"It's a ladybug stickpin that was stuck through some pages of a coloring book, like one of those pins a woman would wear on her lapel, I think."

"Please describe the colors and the number of dots on the ladybug," directed the voice over the radio.

"Let's see," said Dalton, with his eyes almost up to the pouch. "The head is black with a . . . uhh . . . ladybug head. And the body is red, with black edges and divisions. There are two black dots on the left side of the body as you look down from above . . . with the head at the top. Does that make sense?"

"Perfectly. Please go on," the voice said patiently.

"And on the right side of the ladybug there are three dots, so five in all."

There was a pause. "Are you sure there are five dots?"

"Yes, ma'am, there are five dots." He looked up and saw Mack, who had moved to the other side to see better, made eye contact, and shrugged his shoulders as if to ask, *Who cares how many dots?*

"Okay, now, Officer Dabney—"

"Dalton, ma'am, Tommy Dalton." He looked up at Mack again and rolled his eyes.

"Sorry, Officer Dalton. Would you please turn over the pin and tell me what is on the bottom or underside of the ladybug?"

Dalton turned the pouch over and looked carefully. "There is something here engraved on the bottom, Special Agent . . . uh, I didn't get your name exactly."

"Wikowsky, spelled just like it sounds. Is it some letters or numbers?"

"Well, let me see. Yeah, I think you're right. It looks like some kinda model number. Umm . . . C . . . K . . . 1-4-6, I believe; yeah, Charlie, Kilo, 1, 4, 6. It's tough to make out through the Baggie."

There was silence on the other end. Mack whispered to Dalton, "Ask her why or what that means."

Dalton hesitated and then complied. Again there was an extended silence on the other end.

"Wikowsky? Are you there?"

"Yeah, I'm here." Suddenly the voice sounded tired and hollow. "Hey, Dalton, are you someplace private where you can talk?"

Mack nodded with exaggeration and Dalton got the message. "Hold on a sec." He put down the pouch with the pin and moved outside the area, allowing Mack to follow. Dalton was already way beyond protocol with him anyway.

"Yup, I am now. So tell me, what's the scoop on this ladybug?" he inquired.

"We've been trying to catch this guy for almost four years, tracking him across more than nine states now; he's been continually moving west. He's been nicknamed the Little Ladykiller, but we have never released the ladybug detail to the press or anyone else, so please keep that on the downlow. We believe he's responsible for abducting and killing at least four children so far, all girls, all under the age of ten. Each time he adds a dot to the ladybug, so this would be number five. He always leaves the same pin somewhere at the kidnap scene, all with the same model number like he bought a box of them, but we've had no luck tracking down where they originally came from. We haven't found one of the bodies of any of those four little girls, and although forensics has come up with *nothing*, we have good reason to believe that none of the girls have survived. Every crime has taken place at or near a camping area, with a state park or reserve close by. The perpetrator seems to be an expert woodsman and mountaineer. In every case he has left us absolutely nothing—except the pin."

"What about the car? We have a pretty good description of the green truck he left in."

"Oh, you'll probably find it, all right. If this is our guy, it will have been stolen a day or two ago, repainted, full of outdoor gear, and it will be wiped clean."

As he listened to Dalton's conversation with Special Agent Wikowsky, Mack felt the last of his hope draining away. He slumped to the ground and buried his face in his hands. Was there ever a man as tired as he was at this moment? For the first time since Missy's disappearance, he allowed himself to consider the range of horrendous possibilities, and once it started he couldn't stop; the imaginations of good and evil all mixed up together in a soundless but terrifying parade. Even when he tried to shake free of the images, he couldn't. Some were horrible ghastly snapshots of torture and pain: of monsters and demons of the deepest dark with barbwire fingers and razor touches; of Missy screaming for her daddy and no one answering. And mixed throughout these horrors were flashes of other memories: the toddler with her Missy-sippy cup as they had called it, the two-year-old drunk from eating too much chocolate cake, and the one image so recently made as she fell asleep safely in her daddy's arms. Unyielding images. What would he say at her funeral? What could he possibly say to Nan? How could this have happened? God, how could this happen?

ᛈᛉᛟᛞᛉᛈ

A few hours later, Mack and his two children drove to the hotel in Joseph that had become the staging grounds for the growing search. The proprietors had kindly offered them a complimentary room and as he moved a few of his things into it his exhaustion began to get the better of him. He had gratefully accepted Officer Dalton's offer to take his children down to a local diner for some food, and now, sitting down on the edge of the bed, he was swept helplessly away in the unrelenting and merciless grip of growing despair, slowly rocking back and forth. Soul-shredding sobs and groans clawed to the surface from the core of his being. And that is how Nan found him. Two broken lovers, they held each other and wept as Mack poured out his sorrow and Nan tried to hold him in one piece.

That night Mack slept in fits and starts as the images continued to pound him, like relentless waves on a rocky shore. Finally he gave up, just before the sun began to issue hints of its arrival. He hardly noticed. In one day he had spent a year's worth of emotions, and now he felt numb, adrift in a suddenly meaningless world that felt as if it would be forever gray.

After considerable protest from Nan, they agreed it would be best for her to head home with Josh and Kate. Mack would remain to help in any way he could, and to be close, just in case. He simply couldn't leave, not when she might still be out there, needing him. Word had quickly spread, and friends arrived to help him pack up the site and cart everything back to Portland. His boss called, offering any support he could and encouraging Mack to stay as long as he needed. Everyone they knew was praying.

Reporters, with their photographers in tow, began showing up during the morning. Mack didn't want to face them or their cameras, but after some coaching he spent time answering their questions in the parking lot, knowing the exposure could go a long way in aiding the search for Missy.

He had kept quiet about Officer Dalton's overstepping his protocol, and Dalton returned the favor by keeping him inside the information loop. Jesse and Sarah, willing to do anything, made themselves constantly available to the family and friends who came to help. They lifted the huge burden of communication with the public from both Nan and Mack and seemed to be everywhere as they skillfully wove some threads of peace into the turbulence of emotions.

Emil Ducette's parents arrived after driving all the way from Denver to help Vicki and the kids get home safely. Emil, with the blessing of his superiors, had decided to stay behind to do what he could with the Park Service, to help Mack stay informed on that side of things. Nan, who had bonded quickly with both Sarah and Vicki, had distracted herself by helping with little J.J. and then getting her own children ready for their trip back to Portland. And when she broke down, as she frequently did, Vicki or Sarah was always there to weep and pray with her.

When it became clear that the need for their assistance was winding down, the Madisons packed up their own site and then came by for a teary farewell before heading north. As Jesse gave Mack a long hug, he whispered that they would see each other again, and that he would be in prayer for all of them. Sarah, tears rolling down her cheeks, simply kissed Mack on the forehead and then held on to Nan, who again broke into sobs and moans. Sarah sang something, words Mack couldn't quite hear, but it calmed his wife until she was steady enough to let Sarah go. Mack couldn't even bear to watch as the couple finally walked away.

As the Ducettes readied to go, Mack took a minute to thank Amber and Emmy for comforting and reaching out to his own, especially when he couldn't. Josh cried his good-byes; he wasn't brave anymore, at least not today. Kate, on the other hand, had become a rock, busying herself making sure that everyone had everyone else's home and e-mail addresses. Vicki's world had been shaken by the events, and now she had to be almost pried from Nan as her own grief threatened to sweep her away. Nan held her, stroking her hair and whispering prayers into her ear, until she was settled enough to walk to the waiting car.

By noon all of the families were on the road. Maryanne drove Nan and the kids home where family would be waiting to care for and comfort them. Mack and Emil joined Officer Dalton, who was now just Tommy, and headed into Joseph in

Tommy's patrol car. There they grabbed sandwiches, which were barely touched, and then drove to the police station. Tommy Dalton was the father of two daughters himself, his oldest being only five, so it was easy to see that this case struck a particular nerve with him. He extended every kindness and courtesy he could to his new friends, especially Mack.

Now came the hardest part, waiting. Mack felt as if he was moving in slow motion inside the eye of a hurricane of activity happening all around him. Reports filtered in from everywhere. Even Emil was busy networking with the people and professionals he knew.

The FBI entourage arrived mid-afternoon from field offices in three cities. It was clear from the start that the person in charge was Special Agent Wikowsky, a small, slim woman who was all fire and motion, and to whom Mack took an instant liking. She publicly returned the favor, and from that moment on no one questioned his presence at even the most intimate of conversations or debriefings.

After setting up her command center at the hotel, the FBI agent asked Mack to come in for a formal interview, something she insisted was routine in these kinds of circumstances. Agent Wikowsky rose from behind the desk she was working at and held out her hand. As he reached for the handshake, she clasped both her hands around his and smiled grimly.

"Mr. Phillips, I apologize that I haven't been able to spend much time with you so far. We've been frantically setting up communications with all the law enforcement and other agencies involved in trying to get Missy back safely. I'm so sorry that we have to meet under such conditions."

Mack believed her. "Mack," he said.

"I beg your pardon?"

"Mack. Please, call me Mack."

"Well, Mack, then please call me Sam. Short for Samantha, but I grew up kind of a tomboy and beat up the kids who would dare call me Samantha to my face."

Mack couldn't help but smile, relaxing a little into the

chair as he watched her quickly sort through a couple of folders full of papers.

"Mack, are you up for a few questions?" she asked without looking up.

"I'll do my best," he answered, grateful for the opportunity to do anything.

"Good! I won't make you walk through all the details again. I have the reports on everything that you told the others, but I have a couple of important things to go over with you." She looked up, making eye contact.

"Anything I can do to help," confessed Mack. "I'm feeling very useless at the moment."

"Mack, I understand how you feel, but your presence here is important. And believe me, there is not a person here who doesn't care about your Missy. We will do everything in our power to get her back safely."

"Thank you" was all Mack could say, and he looked down at the floor. Emotions seemed so near the surface, and even the least bit of kindness seemed to poke holes in his reserve.

"Okay, now . . . I've had a good off-the-record talk with your friend Officer Tommy, and he filled me in on everything that you and he have talked about, so don't feel like you have to protect his butt. He's all right in my book."

Mack looked up and nodded, then smiled again at her.

"So," she continued, "have you noticed anyone strange around your family these past few days?"

Mack was surprised and sat back in his chair. "You mean he's been stalking us?"

"No, he seems to choose his victims at random, though they were all about the age of your daughter with similar hair color. We think he spots them a day or two before and waits and watches from nearby for an opportune moment. Have you seen anyone unusual or out of place near the lake? Perhaps near the bathrooms?"

Mack recoiled at the thought of his children being watched, being targets. He tried to think past his own imagination but came up blank. "I'm sorry, not that I can remember."

"Did you stop anywhere on your way to the campgrounds or notice anyone strange when you were hiking or sightseeing in the area?"

"We stopped at Multnomah Falls on the way here, and we've been all over the area the past three days, but I don't recall seeing anyone who looked out of the ordinary. Who would have thought . . . ?"

"Exactly, Mack, so don't beat yourself up. Something may come to mind later. No matter how small or irrelevant it might seem, please let us know." She paused to look at another paper on her desk. "What about a green military truck? Have you noticed anything like that around while you were here?"

Mack racked his memory. "I really can't remember seeing anything like it."

Special Agent Wikowsky continued to question Mack for the next fifteen minutes but could not jar his memory enough to provide anything helpful. She finally closed her notebook and stood, extending her hand. "Mack, again, I am so sorry about Missy. If anything breaks, I will personally let you know the minute it happens."

ℬℛℴℴℛ

At 5 p.m. the first promising report finally came in, from the Imnaha roadblock. As she had promised, Agent Wikowsky immediately sought out Mack and filled him in on the details. Two couples had encountered a green military-looking truck matching the description of the vehicle everyone was searching for. They had been exploring some old Nez Percé sites off National Forest 4260 in one of the more-remote areas of the National Reserve, and on their way out they had come face-to-face with the vehicle, just south of the junction where NF 4260 and NF 250 split. Because that section of road was basically one lane, they had to back up to a safe place to allow the truck to pass. They noted that the pickup had a number of gas cans in the back, plus a fair amount of camping gear. The odd part was that the man had bent over toward his passenger side as if looking for something on the floor, pulled his hat down low, and wore a big coat in the heat of the day, almost as if he was afraid of them. They had just laughed him off as probably being one of those militia freaks.

The instant the report was announced to the group, tensions in the station increased. Tommy came over to let Mack know that unfortunately everything he had learned so far fit the Little Ladykiller's MO—to head for remote areas out of which he could eventually hike. It was obvious that he knew where he was going, as the locale where he had been spotted was well off the beaten path. Unlucky for him that someone else had been so far out there as well.

With evening quickly approaching, an intense discussion began regarding the efficacy of immediate pursuit or holding off until daybreak. It seemed that all who spoke, regardless of their point of view, were deeply affected by the situation. Something in the hearts of most human beings simply cannot abide pain inflicted on the innocent, especially children. Even broken men serving in the worst correctional facilities will often first take out their own rage on those who have caused suffering to children. Even in such a world of relative morality, causing harm to a child is still considered absolutely wrong. Period!

Standing near the back of the room, Mack listened impatiently to what seemed like time-wasting bickering. He was almost ready to kidnap Tommy if he had to and go after the guy himself. It felt as if every second counted.

Although it certainly felt longer to Mack, the various departments and personalities agreed quickly, and unanimously, to set out in pursuit just as soon as a few arrangements could be made. Although there weren't many ways to drive out of the area—and roadblocks were being set up immediately to prevent this—there was a very real concern that a skilled hiker could pass undetected into the Idaho wilderness to the east or Washington State to the north. While officials in the towns of Lewiston, Idaho, and Clarkston, Washington, were being contacted and notified of the situation, Mack quickly called Nan to give her an update and then left with Tommy.

By now he had only one prayer left: "Dear God, please, please, please take care of my Missy. I just can't right now." Tears traced their way down his cheeks and then spilled off onto his shirt.

ᏍᎦᏙᏍᏆ

By 7:30 p.m. the convoy of patrol cars, FBI SUVs, pickups carrying dogs in kennels, and some Ranger vehicles headed up the Imnaha Highway. Instead of turning east onto the Wallowa Mountain Road, which would have taken them directly into the National Reserve, they stayed on the Imnaha and headed north. Eventually they took the Lower Imnaha Road and finally Dug Bar Road into the Reserve.

Mack was glad he was traveling with someone who knew the area. It seemed at times that Dug Bar Road went in all directions simultaneously. It was almost as if whoever had named these roads had run out of ideas or simply got tired or drunk and began naming everything Dug Bar just so he could go home.

The roads, with frequent narrow switchbacks edging steep drop-offs, became even more treacherous in the pitch dark of night. Progress slowed to a crawl. Finally, they passed the point where the green pickup had last been seen, and a mile later they came to the junction where NF 4260 went farther north-northeast and NF 250 headed southeast. There, as planned, the caravan split into two, with a small group heading north up the 4260 with Special Agent Wikowsky, while the rest, including Mack, Emil, and Tommy, went southeast on the 250. A few difficult miles later, this larger group split again, Tommy and a dog truck continuing down the 250 where, according to the maps, the road would end, and the rest taking the more easterly route through the park on NF 4240 down toward the Temperance Creek area.

At this point all search efforts slowed even more. The trackers were now on foot and backed up by powerful flood-lights while they looked for signs of recent activity on the roads—anything that might suggest the particular area they were examining was something other than a dead end.

Almost two hours later, as they were moving at a snail's pace toward the end of 250, a call came in to Dalton from Wikowsky. Her team had caught a break. About ten miles from the junction where they had separated, an old unnamed road left the 4260 and headed straight north for almost two miles. It was barely visible and deeply potted. They would either have missed it entirely or ignored it, except that one of the trackers had flashed his floodlight off a hubcap less than fifty feet from the main road. Out of curiosity he retrieved it, and under the covering of road dust found it splattered with specks of green paint. The hubcap had probably been lost when the truck had tussled with one of the many deep potholes strewn in that direction.

Tommy's group immediately turned back the way it had come. Mack didn't want to let himself begin to hope that perhaps, by some miracle, Missy might still be alive, espe-cially when everything he knew told him otherwise. Twenty minutes later, another call from Wikowsky, this time to tell them they had found the truck. Choppers and search planes would never have seen it from the sky, hidden as it was under a carefully built lean-to of limbs and brush.

It took Mack's crew almost three hours to reach the first team and by then it was all over. The dogs had done the rest, uncovering a descending game trail that led more than a mile into a small hidden valley. There they found a run-down little shack near the edge of a pristine lake barely half a mile across, fed by a cascading creek a hundred yards away. A century or so earlier this had probably been a settler's home. It had two good-sized rooms, enough to house a small family. Since that time, it had most likely served as an occasional hunter's or poacher's cabin.

By the time Mack and his friends arrived, the sky was beginning to show the grays of predawn. A base camp had been set up well away from the battered little cabin in order to preserve the crime scene. The moment Wikowsky's group had found the place, dog trackers had been sent out in different directions to try to locate a scent. Occasionally, the baying indicated that they had found something, only to have it disappear again. Now they were all returning to regroup and plan the day's strategy.

Special Agent Samantha Wikowsky was sitting at a card table doing some map-work and drinking a large dripping bottle of water when Mack walked up. She offered him a grim smile, which he didn't return, and an extra bottle, which he accepted. Her eyes were sad and tender but her words were all business.

"Hey, Mack." She hesitated. "Why don't you pull up a chair?"

Mack didn't want to sit down. He needed to do something to stop his stomach from churning. Sensing trouble, he stood and waited for her to continue.

"Mack, we found something, but it's not good news."

He fumbled for the right words. "Did you find Missy?" It was the question that he didn't want to hear the answer to, but he desperately needed to know.

"No, we didn't find her." Sam paused and started to stand up. "But I do need you to come and identify something we found down in that old shack. I need to know if it was—" She caught herself, but it was too late. "I mean, if it *is* hers."

His gaze went to the ground. He again felt a million years old, almost wishing he could somehow turn himself into a big unfeeling rock.

"Oh, Mack, I'm so sorry," Sam apologized, standing up. "Look, we can do this later if you like. I just thought . . ."

He couldn't look at her and even found it difficult to come up with words he could speak without falling apart. He could feel the dam about to burst again. "Let's do it now," he mumbled softly. "I want to know everything there is to know."

Wikowsky must have signaled the others because, although Mack didn't hear anything, he suddenly felt Emil and Tommy each take one of his arms as they turned and followed the special agent down the short path to the shack. Three grown men, arms locked in some special grace of solidarity, walking together, each one toward his own worst nightmare.

A member of the forensic team opened the door of the shack to let them in. Generator-powered lighting illuminated every part of the main room. Shelving lined the walls surrounding an old table, a few chairs, and an old sofa that someone had hauled in with no little effort. Mack immediately saw what he had come to identify and, turning, crumpled into the arms of his two friends and began to weep uncontrollably. On the floor by the fireplace lay Missy's torn and blood-soaked red dress.

ᚠᚱᚫᚫᚱ

For Mack, the next few days and weeks became a numbing blur of interviews with law enforcement and the press, followed by a memorial service for Missy with a small empty coffin and an endless sea of faces, all sad as they paraded by, no one knowing what to say. Sometime during the weeks that followed, Mack began the slow and painful trek back into everyday life.

The Little Ladykiller, it seemed, was credited with taking his fifth victim, Melissa Anne Phillips. As was true in the other four cases, authorities didn't recover Missy's body, even though search teams had scoured the forest around the shack for days after its discovery. As in every other instance, the killer had left no fingerprints and no DNA. He'd left no useful evidence anywhere, only the pin. It was as if the man were a ghost.

At some point in the process, Mack attempted to emerge from his own pain and grief, at least with his family. They had lost a sister and daughter, but it would be wrong for them to lose a father and husband as well. Although no one involved was left unmarked by the tragedy, Kate seemed to have been affected the most, disappearing into a shell, like a turtle protecting its soft underbelly from anything potentially dangerous. It seemed that she would poke her head out only when she felt fully safe, which was becoming less and less often. Mack and Nan both worried increasingly about her but couldn't seem to find the right words to penetrate the fortress she was building around her heart. Attempts at conversation would turn into one-way monologues, with sounds bouncing off her stone visage. It was as if something had died inside her and now was slowly infecting her from the inside, spilling out occasionally in bitter words or emotionless silence.

Josh fared much better, due in part to the long-distance relationship he had kept up with Amber. E-mail and the telephone gave him an outlet for his pain, and she had given him the time and space to grieve. He was also preparing to graduate from high school with all the distractions that his senior year provided.

The Great Sadness had descended and in differing degrees cloaked everyone whose life had touched Missy's. Mack and Nan weathered the storm of loss together with reasonable success, and in some ways they were closer for it. Nan had made it clear from the start, and repeatedly, that she did not blame Mack in any way for what happened. Understandably, it took Mack much longer to let himself off the hook, even a little bit.

It is so easy to get sucked into the if-only game, and play-

ing it is a short and slippery slide into despair. *If only* he had
decided not to take the kids on that trip; *if only* he had said
no when they asked to use the canoe; *if only* he had left the
day before; *if only, if only, if only.* And then to have it all end
with nothing. The fact that he was unable to bury Missy's
body magnified his failure as her daddy. That she was still out
there somewhere alone in the forest haunted him every day.
Now, three and a half years later, Missy was officially presumed to have been murdered. Life would never be normal
again, not that any time is really ever normal. It would be so
empty without his Missy.

The tragedy had also increased the rift in Mack's own
relationship with God, but he ignored this growing sense of
separation. Instead, he tried to embrace a stoic, unfeeling
faith, and even though Mack found some comfort and peace
in that, it didn't stop the nightmares where his feet were stuck
in the mud and his soundless screams could not save his precious Missy. The bad dreams were becoming less frequent,
and laughter and moments of joy were slowly returning, but
he felt guilty about these.

So when Mack received the note from "Papa" telling him
to meet him back at the shack, it was no small event. Did
God even write notes? And why *the shack*—the icon of his
deepest pain? Certainly God would have had better places to
meet with him. A dark thought even crossed his mind that
the killer could be taunting him or luring him away to leave
the rest of his family unprotected. Maybe it was all just a
cruel hoax. But then why was it signed "Papa"?

Try as he might, Mack could not escape the desperate
possibility that the note just might be from God after all,
even if the thought of God's passing notes did not fit well
with his theological training. In seminary he had been taught
that God had completely stopped any overt communication
with moderns, preferring to have them only listen to and follow sacred Scripture, properly interpreted, of course. God's
voice had been reduced to paper, and even that paper had to

be moderated and deciphered by the proper authorities and intellects. It seemed that direct communication with God was something exclusively for the ancients and uncivilized, while educated Westerners' access to God was mediated and controlled by the intelligentsia. Nobody wanted God in a box, just in a book. Especially an expensive one bound in leather with gilt edges, or was that guilt edges?

The more Mack thought about it, the more confused and irritated he became. Who sent the damn note? Whether it was God or the killer or some prankster, what did it matter? Whichever way he looked at it, he felt as if he were being toyed with. And anyway, what good was following God at all? Look where it got *him*.

But in spite of his anger and depression, Mack knew that he needed some answers. He realized he was stuck, and Sunday prayers and hymns weren't cutting it anymore, if they ever really had. Cloistered spirituality seemed to change nothing in the lives of the people he knew, except maybe Nan. But she was special. God might really love her. She wasn't a screwup like him. He was sick of God and God's religion, sick of all the little religious social clubs that didn't seem to make any real difference or effect any real changes. Yes, Mack wanted more, and he was about to get much more than he bargained for.

5

GUESS WHO'S COMING
TO DINNER

*We routinely disqualify testimony that would plead for extenuation. That
is, we are so persuaded of the rightness of our judgment as to invalidate
evidence that does not confirm us in it. Nothing that deserves to be called
truth could ever be arrived at by such means.*

—Marilynne Robinson, *The Death of Adam*

There are times when you choose to believe something that would normally be considered absolutely irrational. It doesn't mean that it is *actually* irrational, but it
surely is not rational. Perhaps there is suprarationality: reason beyond the normal definitions of fact or data-based
logic; something that makes sense only if you can see a
bigger picture of reality. Maybe that is where faith fits in.

Mack wasn't sure about a lot of things, but at some time
in his heart and mind during the days following his tiff with
the icy driveway, he became convinced that there were three
plausible explanations for the note. It was either from God,
as absurd as that sounded; a cruel joke; or something more
sinister from Missy's killer. Regardless, the note dominated
his thoughts every waking minute and his dreams at night.

Secretly, he began to make plans to travel to the shack
the following weekend. At first he told no one, not even Nan.
He had no reasonable defense in any exchange that would
result after such a disclosure, and he was afraid that he might

get locked up and the key thrown away. Anyway, he rationalized such a conversation would only bring more pain with no resolution. "I am keeping it to myself for *Nan's* sake," he told himself. Besides, acknowledging the note would mean admitting that he had kept secrets from her, secrets he still justified in his own mind. Sometimes honesty can be incredibly messy.

Convinced of the rightness of his impending journey, Mack began to consider ways to get the family away from home for the weekend without rousing any suspicions. There was the slim possibility that the killer was trying to lure him out of town, leaving the family unprotected, and that was not acceptable. But he was stumped. Nan was too perceptive for him to show his hand in any way, and doing so would just lead to questions that he was not ready to answer.

Fortunately for Mack, it was Nan herself who proffered a solution. She had been toying with the idea of visiting her sister and family up in the San Juan Islands, off the coast of Washington. Her brother-in-law was a child psychologist, and Nan thought that getting his insights on Kate's increasingly antisocial behavior might be very helpful, especially since neither she nor Mack was having any success getting through to her. When she brought up the possibility of the trip, Mack was almost too eager in his response.

"Of course you are going" was his reaction when Nan told him.

That was not the reply she had anticipated, and she gave him a quizzical look.

"I mean," he floundered, "I think that's a great idea. I will miss you all, of course, but I think I can survive alone for a couple days, and I have lots to do anyway."

She shrugged it off, perhaps grateful that the path for her to leave had opened so easily.

"I just think it would be good for Kate, especially, to get away for a few days," she added, and he nodded in agreement.

A quick call to Nan's sister and their trip was set. The house soon became a whirlwind of activity. Josh and Kate were both delighted; this would extend their spring break for a week. They loved visiting their cousins and were an easy sell on the whole idea, not that they really had any choice in the matter.

On the sly, Mack called up Willie and, while trying rather unsuccessfully to not divulge too much information, asked if he could borrow his friend's four-wheel-drive Jeep. Since Nan was taking the van, he needed something better than his own little car to negotiate the pitted roads in the Reserve, which would most likely still be buried in winter's grip. Mack's odd request predictably started a barrage of questions from Willie, questions Mack tried to answer as evasively as he could. When Willie bluntly asked if Mack's intention was a trip to the shack, Mack told him that while he could not answer his questions at that moment, he would explain fully when Willie came over in the morning to exchange vehicles.

Late Thursday afternoon, Mack saw Nan, Kate, and Josh off with hugs and kisses all around, and then he slowly began his own preparations for the long drive to northeastern Oregon—to the place of his nightmares. He reasoned that he wouldn't need much if *God* had sent the invitation, but just in case, he loaded up a cooler with much more than enough for the miles he would be traveling and then added a sleeping bag, some candles, matches, and a number of other survival items. There was, no doubt, the possibility that he had turned into a complete idiot or was the butt of some ugly prank, but he would then be free to just drive away.

A knock at the door startled Mack from his concentration, and he could see that it was Willie. Their conversation must have been sufficiently perplexing to warrant an early visit. Mack was just relieved that Nan had already left.

"I'm in here, Willie. In the kitchen," Mack called out.

A moment later, Willie poked his head around the hall corner and shook his head looking at the mess Mack had made. He leaned against the doorjamb and crossed his arms. "Well, I brought the Jeep and it's full of gas, but I am not handing over the keys until you tell me what exactly is going on."

Mack continued piling things into a couple of bags for the trip. He knew it was no use lying to his friend, and he needed the Jeep. "I'm going back to the shack, Willie."

"Well, I figured that much out already. What I want to know is why you even want to go back there, especially at this time of year. I don't know if my old Jeep'll even keep us on the roads up there. But just in case, I put some chains in the back if we need them."

Without looking at him, Mack walked to the office, pried the lid off the small tin box, and took out the note. Reentering the kitchen, he handed it to Willie.

His friend unfolded the paper and read silently. "Geez, what kind of loony kook would write you something like this? And who is this Papa?"

"Well, you know, Papa—Nan's favorite name for God." Mack shrugged, not sure what else to say. He took back the note and slid it into his shirt pocket.

"Wait—you aren't thinking this is really from God, are you?"

Mack stopped and turned to face him. He had just about finished packing anyway. "Willie, I'm not sure what to think about this. I mean, at first I thought it was just a hoax, and it made me angry and sick to my stomach. Maybe I'm just losing it. I know it sounds crazy, but somehow I feel strangely drawn to find out for sure. I gotta go, Willie, or it'll drive me nuts forever."

"Have you thought of the possibility that this might be the killer? What if he's luring you back for some reason?"

"Of course I've thought of that. Part of me won't be disappointed if it is. I have a score to settle with him," he said grimly and paused. "But that doesn't make a lot of sense either. I'm not thinking the killer would sign this note 'Papa.' You'd have to *really* know our family to come up with that."

Willie was perplexed.

Mack continued, "And no one who knows us *that* well would ever send a note like this. I'm thinking only God would . . . maybe."

"But God doesn't do stuff like that. At least I've never heard of him sending someone a note. Not that he couldn't, but, you know what I mean. And why would he want you to return to the shack, anyway? I can't think of a worse place . . ."

The silence that hung between them grew awkward.

Mack leaned back against the counter and stared a hole through the floor before speaking. "I'm not sure, Willie. I guess part of me would like to believe that God would care enough about me to send a note. I'm so confused, even after all this time. I just don't know what to think and it isn't getting better. I feel like we're losing Kate, and that's killing me. Maybe what happened to Missy is God's judgment for what I did to my own dad. I just don't know." He looked up into the face of a man who cared more about him than anyone he knew, except Nan. "All I know is that I need to go back."

There was silence between them before Willie spoke again. "So, when do we leave?"

Mack was touched by his friend's willingness to jump into his insanity. "Thanks, buddy, but I really need to do this alone."

"I thought you'd say that," Willie responded as he turned and walked out of the room. He returned a few moments later with a pistol and a box of shells in his hands. He gently laid them on the counter. "I figured I wouldn't be able to talk you out of going, so I thought you might need this. I believe you know how to use it."

Mack looked at the gun. He knew Willie meant well and was trying to help. "Willie, I can't. It's been thirty years since I last touched a gun, and I don't intend to now. If I learned anything back then, it was that using violence to solve a problem always landed me in a worse problem."

"But what if it is Missy's killer? What if he's waiting for you up there? What are you going to do then?"

He shrugged. "I honestly don't know, Willie. I'll take my chances, I guess."

"But you'll be defenseless. There's no telling what he has in mind, or in hand. Just take it, Mack." Willie slid the pistol and shells across the counter toward him. "You don't have to use it."

Mack looked down at the gun and after some deliberation reached slowly for it and the shells, putting them carefully in his pocket. "Okay, just in case." He then turned to pick up some of his equipment and, arms loaded, headed out toward the Jeep. Willie grabbed the large duffel bag remaining, finding it heavier than he had anticipated, and grunted as he hoisted it.

"Geez, Mack, if you think God is going to be up there, why all the supplies?"

Mack smiled rather sadly. "I just thought I'd cover my bases. You know, be prepared for whatever happens . . . or doesn't."

They made their way out of the house to the driveway where the Jeep sat. Willie pulled the keys out of his pocket and handed them to Mack.

"So," Willie said, breaking the silence, "where is everybody, and what did Nan think of you heading out for the shack? I can't imagine *she* was real pleased."

"Nan and the kids are visiting her sister up in the Islands, and . . . I didn't tell her," Mack confessed.

Willie was obviously surprised. "What? You never keep secrets from her. I can't believe you lied to her!"

"I didn't lie to her," Mack objected.

"Well, excuse me for splitting hairs," Willie snapped back. "Okay, you didn't *lie* to her because you didn't tell her the whole truth. Oh, yeah, she's going to understand that, all right." He rolled his eyes.

Mack ignored the outburst and walked back to the house and into his office. There he found the spare set of keys for his car and home and, hesitating for just a moment, picked up the small tin box. He then headed back out toward Willie.

"So, what do you think he looks like?" Willie chuckled as he approached.

"Who?" asked Mack.

"God, of course. What do you think he'll look like, if he even bothers to show up, I mean? Boy, I can just see you scaring the living daylights out of some poor hiker—asking him if he's God and then demanding answers an' all."

Mack grinned at the thought. "I don't know. Maybe he's a really bright light, or a burning bush. I've always sort of pictured him as a really big grandpa with a long white flowing beard, sort of like Gandalf in Tolkien's *Lord of the Rings*."

He shrugged and handed Willie his keys and they exchanged a brief hug. Willie climbed into Mack's car and rolled down the driver's window.

"Well, if he does show, say hi for me," Willie said with a smile. "Tell him I have a few questions of my own. And Mack, try not to piss him off." They both laughed. "Seriously," Willie continued, "I am concerned for you, buddy. I wish I was going with you, or Nan or someone else was. I hope you find everything you need up there. I will be saying a prayer or two for you."

"Thanks, Willie. I love you too." He waved as Willie backed out of the driveway. Mack knew that his friend would keep his word. He probably could use all the prayers he could get.

He watched until Willie was around the corner and out of sight, then slipped the note from his shirt pocket, read it one more time, and placed it in the little tin box, which he deposited on the passenger seat among some of the other gear stacked there. Locking the doors, he headed back into the house and a sleepless night.

Well before dawn on Friday, Mack was already out of town and traveling down I-84. Nan had called the night before from her sister's to let him know that they had made it safe and sound, and he didn't expect to get another call until at least Sunday. By that time he would probably be on his way back, if he wasn't home already. He forwarded the house phone to his cell, just in case, not that he would have any reception once he was into the Reserve.

He retraced the same path they had taken three and a half years before, with a few minor changes: not as many potty breaks, and he sailed by Multnomah Falls without looking. He had pushed away any thoughts of the place since Missy's disappearance, sequestering his emotions securely in the padlocked basement of his own heart.

On the long stretch up the Gorge, Mack felt a creeping panic begin to penetrate his consciousness. He had tried to avoid thinking about what he was doing and just keep putting one foot in front of the other, but like grass pushing through concrete, the repressed feelings and fears somehow began to poke through. His eyes darkened and his hands tightened on the steering wheel as he fought the temptation at every off-ramp to turn around and go home. He knew he was driving straight into the center of his pain, the vortex of *The Great Sadness* that had so diminished his sense of being alive. Flashes of visual memory and stabbing instants of blistering fury now came in waves, attended by the taste of bile and blood in his mouth.

He finally reached La Grande, where he gassed up and then took Highway 82 out to Joseph. He was half tempted to stop and look in on Tommy but decided against it. The fewer people who thought he was a raving lunatic, the better. Instead, he topped off his tank and headed out.

Traffic was light, and the Imnaha and smaller roads were remarkably clear and dry for this time of year, much warmer than he had expected. But it seemed that the farther he drove, the slower he traveled, as if the shack were somehow repelling his approach. The Jeep crossed the snow line as he climbed the last couple of miles to the trail that would take him down to the shack. Above the whine of the engine he could hear the tires crunch doggedly through the deepening snow and ice. Even after a couple of wrong turns and some backtracking, it was only early afternoon when Mack finally pulled over and parked at the barely visible trailhead.

He sat there for almost five minutes reprimanding himself for being such a fool. With every mile that he had traveled from Joseph, the memories had come back with adrenaline-enforced clarity, and now he was mentally certain that he wanted to go no farther. But the inner compulsion to press on was irresistible. Even as he argued with himself, he buttoned up his coat and reached for his leather gloves.

He stood and stared down the path, deciding to leave everything in the car and hike the mile or so down to the lake; at least that way he wouldn't have to lug anything back up the hill when he returned to leave, which he now expected would be in very short order.

It was cold enough that his breath hung in the air around him, and it even felt as if it might snow. The pain that had been building in his stomach finally pushed him into panic. After only five steps, he stopped and retched so strongly that it brought him to his knees.

"Please help me!" he groaned. He stood up on shaky legs and took another step away from the car. Then he stopped and turned back. He opened the passenger door and reached in, rummaging around until he felt the small tin box. He pried the lid off and found what he was looking for, his favorite picture of Missy, which he removed along with the note. Replacing the lid, he left the box on the seat. He paused for a moment, looking at the glove box. Finally he opened it and grabbed Willie's gun, checking to make sure it was loaded and the safety was on. Standing up, he closed the door, reached under his coat, and stuck the gun in his belt in the small of his back. He turned and faced the path once more, taking one last look at Missy's picture before sliding it into his shirt pocket alongside the note. If they found him dead, at least they would know who had been on his mind.

The trail was treacherous, the rocks icy and slippery. Every step took concentration as he descended into the thickening forest. It was eerily quiet. The only sounds he could hear were the crunch of his steps on the snow and the heaviness of his breathing. Mack started feeling as if he was being watched, and once he even spun around quickly to see if anyone was there. As much as he wanted to turn and run back to the Jeep, his feet seemed to have a will of their own, determined to continue down the path and deeper into the dimly lit and increasingly dense woods.

Suddenly, something moved close by. Startled, he froze, silent and alert. With his heart pounding in his ears and his mouth suddenly dry, he slowly reached behind his back, sliding the pistol from his belt. Snapping off the safety, he peered intensely into the dark underbrush, trying to see or hear anything that might explain the noise and slow the rush of adrenaline. But whatever had moved had now stopped. Was it waiting for him? Just in case, he stood motionless for a few minutes before he again began inching his way farther down the trail, trying to be as quiet as possible.

The forest seemed to close in around him, and he began to seriously wonder if he had taken the wrong path. Out of the corner of his eye, he again saw movement and instantly crouched down, peering between the low branches of a nearby tree. Something ghostly, like a shadow, slipped into the brush. Or had he only imagined it? Again he waited, not shifting a muscle. Was that God? He doubted it. Maybe an animal? He couldn't remember if there were wolves up here, and deer or elk would make more noise. And then the thought he had been avoiding: *What if it is something worse? What if I have been lured up here? But for what?*

Slowly rising from his hiding place, gun still drawn, he took a step forward when suddenly the bush behind him seemed to explode. Mack whipped around, scared and ready to fight for his life, but before he could squeeze the trigger he recognized the rear end of a badger scampering back up the trail. He slowly exhaled the breath he hadn't realized he had been holding, lowered his gun, and shook his head. Mack the Courageous had been reduced to just another scared boy in the woods. Snapping the safety back on, he tucked the gun away. *Someone could get hurt*, he thought with a sigh of relief.

Taking another deep breath and exhaling slowly, he calmed himself. Determined that he was done being afraid, he continued down the path, trying to look more confident than he felt. He hoped he hadn't come all this way for nothing. If God was really meeting him here, he was more than ready to get a few things off his chest, respectfully, of course.

A few turns later he stumbled out of the woods and into a clearing. At the far side and down the slope he saw it—the shack. He stood staring, his stomach a ball of motion and turmoil. On the surface it seemed that nothing had changed other than the winter's stripping of the deciduous trees and the white shroud of snow that blanketed the surroundings. The shack itself looked dead and empty, but as he stared it seemed for a moment to transform into an evil face, twisted in some demonic grimace, looking straight back at him and daring him to approach. Ignoring the rising panic he was feeling, Mack walked with resolve down the last hundred yards and up onto the porch.

The memories and horror of the last time he'd stood at this door came flooding back, and he hesitated before pushing it open. "Hello?" he called, not too loudly. Clearing his throat he called again, this time louder. "Hello? Anybody here?" His voice echoed off the emptiness inside. Feeling bolder, he stepped completely across the threshold and stopped.

As his eyes adjusted in the dimness, he began to make out the details of the room by the afternoon light filtering in through the broken windows. Stepping into the main room, he recognized the old chairs and table. Mack couldn't help himself as his eyes were drawn to the one place he could not bear to look. Even after a few years, the faded bloodstain was still clearly visible in the wood near the fireplace where they had found Missy's dress. *I'm so sorry, honey.* Tears began to well up in his eyes.

And finally his heart exploded like a flash flood, releasing his pent-up anger and letting it rush down the rocky canyons of his emotions. Turning his eyes heavenward, he began screaming his anguished questions. "Why? Why did you let this happen? Why did you bring me here? Of all the places to meet you—why *here*? Wasn't it enough to kill my baby? Do you have to toy with me too?"

In a blind rage, Mack grabbed the nearest chair and flung it at the window. It smashed into pieces. He picked up one of the legs and began destroying everything he could. Groans and moans of despair and fury burst through his lips as he beat his wrath into the terrible place. "I hate you!" In a frenzy he pounded out his rage until he was exhausted and spent.

Despairing and defeated, Mack slumped to the floor next to the bloodstain. He touched it carefully. This was all that was left of his Missy. As he lay next to the stain, his fingers tenderly traced the discolored edges and he softly whispered, "Missy, I'm so sorry. I'm sorry I couldn't protect you. I'm sorry I couldn't find you."

Even in his exhaustion the anger seethed, and he once again took aim at the indifferent God he imagined somewhere beyond the roof of the shack. "God, you couldn't even let us find her and bury her properly. Was that just too much to ask?"

As the mix of emotions ebbed and flowed, his anger giving way to pain, a fresh wave of sorrow began to mix with his confusion. "So where are you? I thought you wanted to meet me here. Well, I'm here, God. And you? You're nowhere to be found! You've never been around when I've needed you—not when I was a little boy, not when I lost Missy. Not now! Some 'Papa' you are!" He spat out the words.

Mack sat there in silence, the *emptiness* of the place invading his soul. His jumble of unanswered questions and far-flung accusations settled to the floor with him and then slowly drained into a pit of desolation. *The Great Sadness* tightened around him, and he almost welcomed the smothering sensation. *This* pain he knew. He was familiar with it, almost like a friend.

Mack could feel the gun in the small of his back, an inviting cold pressed against his skin. He pulled it out, not sure what he was going to do. Oh, to stop caring, to stop feeling the pain, to never feel anything again. Suicide? At the moment that option was almost attractive. *It would be so easy*, he thought. *No more tears, no more pain . . .* He could almost see a black chasm opening up in the floor behind the gun he was staring at, a darkness sucking any last vestiges of hope from his heart. Killing himself would be one way to strike back at God, if God even existed.

Clouds parted outside, and a sunbeam suddenly spilled into the room, piercing the center of his despair. But . . . what about Nan? And what about Josh and Kate and Tyler and Jon? As much as he longed to stop the ache in his heart, he knew he could not add to their hurt.

Mack sat in his emotionally spent stupor, weighing the options in the feel of the gun. A cold breeze brushed past his face and part of him wanted to just lie down and freeze to death, he was so exhausted. He slumped back against the wall and rubbed his weary eyes. He let them fall closed as he mumbled, "I love you, Missy. I miss you so much." Soon he drifted without effort into a dead sleep.

It was probably only minutes later that Mack woke with a jerk. Surprised that he'd nodded off, he stood up quickly. Stuffing the gun back into his waistband and his anger back into the deepest part of his soul, he started for the door. "This is ridiculous! I'm such an idiot! To think that I hoped God might actually care enough to send me a note!"

He looked up into the open rafters. "I'm done, God," he whispered. "I can't do this anymore. I'm tired of trying to find you in all of this." And with that, he walked out the door. Mack determined that this was the last time he would go looking for God. If God wanted him, God would have to come find him.

He reached into his pocket and took out the note he had found in his mailbox and tore it up, letting the pieces slowly sift through his fingers, to be carried off by the cold wind that had kicked up. A weary old man, he stepped off the porch and, with heavy footsteps and a heavier heart, started the hike back to the car.

CRGGR

He had barely walked fifty feet up the trail when he felt a sudden rush of warm air overtake him from behind. The chirping of a songbird broke the icy silence. The path in front of him rapidly lost its veneer of snow and ice, as if someone were blow-drying it. Mack stopped and watched as all around him the white covering dissolved and was replaced by emerging and radiant growth. Three weeks of spring unfurled before him in thirty seconds. He rubbed his eyes and steadied himself in the swirl of activity. Even the light snow that had begun to fall had changed to tiny blossoms lazily drifting to the ground.

What he was seeing, of course, was not possible. The snowbanks had vanished, and summer wildflowers began to color the borders of the trail and the forest as far as he could see. Robins and finches darted after one another among the trees. Squirrels and chipmunks occasionally crossed the path ahead, some stopping to sit up and watch him for a moment before plunging back into the undergrowth. He even thought that he glimpsed a young buck emerging from a dark glade in the forest, but on second look it was gone. As if that weren't enough, the scent of blooms began to fill the air, not just the drifting aroma of wild mountain flowers, but the richness of roses and orchids and other exotic fragrances found in more tropical climes.

Mack was no longer thinking about home. A terror gripped him, as if he had opened Pandora's box and was being swept away into the center of madness, to be lost forever. Unsteady, he carefully turned around, trying to hold on to some sense of sanity.

He was stunned. Little, if anything, was the same. The dilapidated shack had been replaced by a sturdy and beautifully constructed log cabin, now standing directly between him and the lake, which he could see just above the rooftop. It was built out of hand-peeled full-length logs, every one scribed for a perfect fit.

Instead of the dark and forbidding overgrowth of brush, briars, and devil's club, everything Mack could see was now postcard perfect. Smoke was lazily wending its way from the chimney into the late-afternoon sky, a sign of activity inside. A walkway had been built to and around the front porch, bordered by a small white picket fence. The sound of laughter was coming from nearby—maybe inside, but he wasn't sure.

Perhaps this was what it was like to experience a complete psychotic breakdown. "I'm losing it," Mack whispered to himself. "This can't be happening. This isn't real."

It was a place that Mack could have imagined only in his best dreams, and this made it all the more suspect. The sights were wondrous, the scents intoxicating, and his feet, as if they had a mind of their own, took him back down the walkway and up onto the front porch. Flowers bloomed everywhere, and the mix of floral fragrances and pungent herbs aroused hints of memories long forgotten. He had always heard that the nose was the best link to the past, that the olfactory sense was the strongest for tapping into forgotten history, and now some long-stored remembrances of his own childhood flitted through his mind.

Once on the porch he stopped again. Voices were clearly coming from inside. Mack rejected the sudden impulse to run away, as if he were some kid who had thrown his ball into a neighbor's flower garden. *But if God is inside, it wouldn't do much good anyway, would it?* He closed his eyes and shook his head to see if he could erase the hallucination and restore reality. But when he opened them, it was all still there. He tentatively reached out and touched the wooden railing. It certainly seemed real.

He now faced another dilemma. What should you do when you come to the door of a house, or cabin in this case, where God might be? Should you knock? Presumably God already knew that Mack was there. Maybe he ought to simply walk in and introduce himself, but that seemed equally absurd. And how should he address him? Should he call him "Father," or "Almighty One," or perhaps "Mr. God," and would it be best if he fell down and worshiped? Not that he was really in the mood.

As he tried to establish some inner mental balance, the anger that he thought had so recently died inside him began to emerge. No longer concerned or caring about what to call God and energized by his ire, he walked up to the door. Mack decided to bang loudly and see what happened, but just as he raised his fist to do so, the door flew open, and he was looking directly into the face of a large, beaming African-American woman.

Instinctively he jumped back, but he was too slow. With speed that belied her size, she crossed the distance between them and engulfed him in her arms, lifting him clear off his feet and spinning him around like a little child. And all the while she was shouting his name—"Mackenzie Allen Phillips"—with the ardor of someone seeing a long-lost and deeply loved relative. She finally set him back on Earth and, with her hands on his shoulders, pushed him back as if to get a good look at him.

"Mack, look at you!" she fairly exploded. "Here you are, and so grown up. I have really been looking forward to seeing you face-to-face. It is so wonderful to have you here with us. My, my, my, how I do love you!" And with that she wrapped herself around him again.

Mack was speechless. In a few seconds this woman had breached pretty much every social propriety behind which he had so safely entrenched himself. But something in the way she looked at him and yelled his name made him equally delighted to see her too, even though he didn't have a clue who she was.

Suddenly, he was overwhelmed by the scent emanating from her, and it shook him. It was the smell of flowers with overtones of gardenia and jasmine, unmistakably his mother's perfume that he kept hidden away in his little tin box. He had already been perched precariously on the precipice of emotion, and now the flooding scent and attendant memories staggered him. He could feel the warmth of tears beginning to gather behind his eyes, as if they were knocking on the door of his heart. It seemed that she saw them too.

"It's okay, honey, you can let it all out . . . I know you've been hurt, and I know you're angry and confused. So, go ahead and let it out. It does a soul good to let the waters run once in a while—the healing waters."

But while Mack could not stop the tears from filling his eyes, he was not ready to let go—not yet, not with this woman. With every effort he could muster, he kept himself from falling back into the black hole of his emotions. Meanwhile, this woman stood with her arms outstretched as if they were the very arms of his mother. He felt the presence of love. It was warm, inviting, melting.

"Not ready?" she responded. "That's okay, we'll do things on your terms and time. Well, come on in. Can I take your coat? And that gun? You don't really need that, do you? We wouldn't want anyone to get hurt, would we?"

Mack wasn't sure what to do or what to say. Who was she? And how did she know? He was rooted to the spot where he stood but slowly and mechanically took off his coat.

The large black woman gathered his coat and he handed her the gun, which she took from him with two fingers as if it was contaminated. Just as she turned to enter the cabin, a small, distinctively Asian woman emerged from behind her.

"Here, let me take those," her voice sang. Obviously she had not meant the coat or gun but something else, and she was in front of him in a blink of an eye.

He stiffened as he felt something sweep gently across his cheek. Without moving, he looked down and could see that she was busy with a fragile crystal bottle and a small brush, like those he had seen Nan and Kate use for makeup, gently removing something from his face.

Before he could ask, she smiled and whispered, "Mackenzie, we all have things we value enough to collect, don't we?"

His little tin box flashed through his mind.

"I collect tears."

As she stepped back, Mack found himself involuntarily squinting in her direction, as if doing so would allow his eyes to see her better. But strangely, he still had a difficult time focusing on her; she seemed almost to shimmer in the light, and her hair blew in all directions even though there was hardly a breeze. It was almost easier to see her out of the corner of his eye than it was to look at her directly.

He then glanced past her and noticed that a third person had emerged from the cabin, this one a man. He appeared Middle Eastern and was dressed like a laborer, complete with tool belt and gloves. He stood easily, leaning against the doorjamb with arms crossed in front of him, wearing jeans covered in wood dust and a plaid shirt with sleeves rolled just above the elbows, revealing well-muscled forearms. His features were pleasant enough, but he was not particularly handsome—not a man who would stick out in a crowd. But his eyes and smile lit up his face, and Mack found it difficult to look away.

Mack stepped back again, feeling a bit overwhelmed. "Are there more of you?" he asked a little hoarsely.

The three looked at one another and laughed.

Mack couldn't help but smile.

"No, Mackenzie." The black woman chuckled. "We is all that you get, and believe me, we're more than enough."

Mack tried again to look at the Asian woman. This wiry-looking person appeared to be of northern Chinese or Nepalese or even Mongolian ethnicity. It was hard to tell, though, because his eyes had to work to see her at all. From her clothing, Mack assumed she was a groundskeeper or gardener. She had gloves folded into her belt, not the heavy leathers of the man, but the lightweight cloth-and-rubber ones that Mack himself used for yard work at home. She was dressed in plain jeans with ornamental designs at the fringes—knees covered in dirt from where she had been kneeling—and a brightly colored blouse with splashes of yellow and red and blue. But he knew all this as more of an impression of her than from actually seeing her, as she seemed to phase in and out of his vision.

The man then stepped in, touched Mack on the shoulder, gave him a kiss on both cheeks, and embraced him strongly. Mack knew instantly that he liked him. As they separated, the man stepped back, and the Asian lady moved toward him again, this time taking his face in both her hands. Gradually and intentionally, she moved her face closer to his and just when he imagined she was going to kiss him, she stopped and looked deep into his eyes. Mack thought he could almost see through her. Then she smiled and her scents seemed to wrap themselves around him and lift a huge weight off his shoulders, as if he had been carting his gear in a backpack.

Mack suddenly felt lighter than air, almost as if he were no longer touching the ground. She was hugging him without hugging him, or really without even touching him. Only when she pulled back, which was probably just seconds later, did he realize that he was still standing on his feet and that his feet were still touching the deck.

"Oh, don't mind her." The big black woman laughed. "She has that effect on everyone."

"I like it," he muttered, and all three burst into more laughter, and now Mack found himself laughing along with them, not knowing exactly why and not really caring either.

When they finally stopped giggling, the large woman put her arm around Mack's shoulders, drew him to her, and said, "Okay, we know who you are, but we should probably introduce ourselves to you. I"—she waved her hands with a flourish—"am the housekeeper and cook. You may call me Elousia."

"Elousia?" asked Mack, not comprehending at all.

"Okay, you don't have to call me Elousia; it's just a name I am rather fond of and has particular meaning to me. So"—she crossed her arms and put one hand under her chin as if thinking especially hard—"you could call me what Nan does."

"What? You don't mean . . ." Now Mack was surprised and even more confused. Surely this was not the Papa who sent the note? "I mean, are you saying, 'Papa'?"

"Yes," she responded and smiled, waiting for him to speak as if he were about to say something, which he was not at all.

"And I," interrupted the man, who looked to be in his thirties and stood a little shorter than Mack himself, "I try to keep things fixed up around here. I enjoy working with my hands, although, as these two will tell you, I take pleasure in cooking and gardening as much as they do."

"You look as if you're from the Middle East, maybe Arab?" Mack guessed.

"Actually, I'm a stepbrother of that great family. I am Hebrew, to be exact, from the house of Judah."

"Then . . ." Mack was suddenly staggered by his own realization. "Then, you are . . ."

"Jesus? Yes. And you may call me that if you like. After all, it has become my common name. My mother called me Yeshua, but I have also been known to respond to Joshua or even Jesse."

Mack stood dumbfounded and mute. What he was looking at and listening to simply would not compute. It was all so impossible . . . but here he was, or was he really here at all? Suddenly, he felt faint. Emotion swept over him as his mind attempted desperately to catch up with all the information. Just as he was about to crumple to his knees, the Asian woman stepped closer and deflected his attention.

"And I am Sarayu," she said as she tilted her head in a slight bow and smiled. "Keeper of the gardens, among other things."

Thoughts tumbled over themselves as Mack struggled to figure out what to do. Was one of these people God? What if they were hallucinations or angels, or God was coming later? That could be embarrassing. Since there were three of them, maybe this was a Trinity sort of thing. But two women and a man and none of them white? Then again, why had he naturally assumed that God would be white? He knew his mind was rambling, so he focused on the one question he most wanted answered.

"Then," Mack struggled to ask, "which one of you is God?"

"I am," said all three in unison. Mack looked from one to the next, and even though he couldn't begin to grasp what he was seeing and hearing, he somehow believed them.

6

A Piece of π

*No matter what God's power may be, the first aspect of God
is never that of the absolute Master, the Almighty. It is that of the God
who puts himself on our human level and limits himself.*

—Jacques Ellul, *Anarchy and Christianity*

Well, Mackenzie, don't just stand there gawkin' with your mouth open like your pants are full," said the big black woman as she turned and headed across the deck, talking the whole time. "Come and talk to me while I get supper on. Or if you don't want to do that, you can do whatever you want. Behind the cabin," she said, gesturing over the roof without looking or slowing down, "you will find a fishing pole by the boat shed that you can use to catch some lake trout."

She stopped at the door to give Jesus a kiss. "Just remember," she said, turning to look back at Mack, "you gotta clean what you catch." Then with a quick smile, she disappeared into the cabin, armed with Mack's winter coat and still carrying the gun by two fingers, a full arm's length away from her.

Mack was standing there with his mouth indeed open and an expression of bewilderment plastered to his face. He hardly noticed when Jesus walked over and put an arm around his shoulder. Sarayu seemed to have just evaporated.

"Isn't she great?" exclaimed Jesus, grinning at Mack.

Mack turned and faced him, shaking his head. "Am I

going crazy? Am I supposed to believe that God is a big black woman with a questionable sense of humor?"

Jesus laughed. "She's a riot! You can always count on her to throw you a curve or two. She loves surprises, and even though you might not think it, her timing is always perfect."

"Really?" said Mack, still shaking his head and not sure if he really believed that. "So now what am I supposed to do?"

"You're not *supposed* to do anything. You're free to do whatever you like." Jesus paused and then continued, trying to help by giving Mack a few suggestions. "I am working on a wood project in the shed. Sarayu is in the garden. Or you could go fishing, canoeing, or go in and talk to Papa."

"Well, I sort of feel obligated to go in and talk to him, uh, her."

"Oh"—now Jesus was serious—"don't go because you feel obligated. That won't get you any points around here. Go because it's what you *want* to do."

Mack thought for a moment and decided that going into the cabin actually was what he wanted to do. He thanked Jesus, who smiled, turned, and headed off to his workshop, and Mack stepped across the deck and up to the door. Again he was alone, but after a quick look around, he carefully opened it. He stuck his head in, hesitated, and then decided to take the plunge.

"God?" he called, rather timidly and feeling more than a little foolish.

"I'm in the kitchen, Mackenzie. Just follow my voice."

He walked in and scanned the room. Could this even be the same place? He shuddered at the whisper of lurking dark thoughts and again locked them out. Across the room a hallway disappeared at an angle. Glancing around the corner into the living room, his eyes searched out the spot near the fireplace, but there was no stain marring the wood surface. He noticed that the room was decorated tastefully, with art that looked as if it had been either drawn or handcrafted by children. He wondered if this woman treasured each of these pieces, as any parent who loves her children would. Maybe that was how she valued anything that was given to her from the heart, the way children seemed to give so easily.

Mack followed her soft humming down a short hallway and into an open kitchen-dining area, complete with a small four-seat table and wicker-backed chairs. The inside of the cabin was roomier than he had expected. Papa was working on something with her back to him, flour flying as she swayed to the music of whatever she was listening to. The song obviously came to an end, marked by a couple of last shoulder and hip shakes. Turning to face him, she took off the earphones.

Suddenly Mack wanted to ask a thousand questions, or say a thousand things, some of them unspeakable and terrible. He was sure that his face betrayed the emotions he was battling to control, and then in a flash of a second he shoved everything back into his battered heart's closet, locking the door on the way out. If she knew his inner conflict, she showed nothing by her expression—still open, full of life, and inviting.

He inquired, "May I ask what you're listening to?"

"You really wanna know?"

"Sure." Now Mack was curious.

"West Coast Juice. Group called Diatribe and an album that isn't even out yet called *Heart Trips*. Actually," she said, winking at Mack, "these kids haven't even been born yet."

"Right," Mack responded, more than a little incredulous. "West Coast Juice, huh? It doesn't sound very religious."

"Oh, trust me, it's not. More like Eurasian funk and blues with a message, and a great beat." She sidestepped toward Mack as if she were doing a dance move and clapped.

Mack stepped back. "So God listens to funk?" Mack had never heard "funk" talked about in any properly righteous terms. "I thought you would be listening to George Beverly Shea or the Mormon Tabernacle Choir—you know, something churchier."

"Now see here, Mackenzie. You don't have to be lookin'

out for me. I listen to everything—and not just to the music itself, but the hearts behind it. Don't you remember your seminary classes? These kids ain't saying anything I haven't heard before; they're just full of vinegar and fizz. Lots of anger and, I must say, with some good reason too. They're just some of my kids, showin' and spoutin' off. I am especially fond of those boys, you know. Yup, I'll be keeping my eye on 'em."

Mack struggled to keep up with her, to make some sense of what was happening. None of his old seminary training was helping in the least. He was at a sudden loss for words and his million questions had all seemed to abandon him. So he stated the obvious.

"You must know," he offered, "calling you 'Papa' is a bit of a stretch for me."

"Oh, really?" She looked at him in mock surprise. "Of course I know. I always know." She chuckled. "But tell me, why do *you* think it's hard for you? Is it because it's too familiar for you, or maybe because I am showing myself as a woman, a mother, or—"

"No small issue there," Mack interrupted with an awkward chuckle.

"Or maybe it's because of the failures of your *own* papa?"

Mack gasped involuntarily. He wasn't used to having deep secrets surface so quickly and openly. Instantly guilt and anger welled up, and he wanted to lash out with a sarcastic remark in response. Mack felt as if he were dangling over a bottomless chasm and was afraid if he let any of it out, he would lose control of everything. He sought for safe footing but was only partially successful, finally answering through gritted teeth, "Maybe it's because I've never known *anyone* I could really call 'Papa.'"

At that she put down the mixing bowl that had been cradled in her arm, and, leaving the wooden spoon in it, she turned toward Mack with tender eyes. She didn't have to say it; he knew she understood what was going on inside him, and somehow he knew she cared about him more than anyone ever had. "If you let me, Mack, I'll be the papa you never had."

The offer was at once inviting and at the same time repulsive. He had always wanted a papa he could trust, but he wasn't sure he'd find it here, especially if this one couldn't even protect his Missy. A long silence hung between them. Mack was uncertain what to say, and she was in no hurry to let the moment pass easily.

"If you couldn't take care of Missy, how can I trust you to take care of me?" There, he'd said it—the question that had tormented him every day of *The Great Sadness*. Mack felt his face flush angry red as he stared at what he now considered to be some odd characterization of God, and he realized his hands were knotted into fists.

"Mack, I'm so sorry." Tears began to trail down her cheeks. "I know what a great gulf this has put between us. I know you don't understand this yet, but I am especially fond of Missy, and you too."

He loved the way she said Missy's name and yet he hated hearing it coming from her. It rolled off her tongue like the sweetest wine, and even through all the fury still raging in his mind he somehow knew she meant it. He *wanted* to believe her, and slowly some of his rage began to subside.

"That's why you're here, Mack," she continued. "I want to heal the wound that has grown inside you and between us."

To gain some control, he turned his eyes toward the floor. It was a full minute before he had enough to whisper without looking up. "I think I'd like that," he admitted, "but I don't see how . . ."

"Honey, there's no easy answer that will take your pain away. Believe me, if I had one, I'd use it now. I have no magic wand to wave over you and make it all better. Life takes a bit of time and a lot of relationship."

Mack was glad they were stepping back from the edge of

his ugly accusation. How near he had come to being totally overwhelmed by it had scared him. "I think it'd be easier to have this conversation if you weren't wearing a dress," he suggested and attempted a smile, as weak as it was.

"If it were easier, then I wouldn't be," she said with a slight giggle. "I'm not trying to make this harder for either of us. But *this* is a good place to start. I often find that getting head issues out of the way first makes the heart stuff easier to work on later . . . when you're ready."

She again picked up the wooden spoon, which was dripping with some sort of batter. "Mackenzie, I am neither male nor female, even though both genders are derived from my nature. If I choose to *appear* to you as a man or a woman, it's because I love you. For me to appear to you as a woman and suggest that you call me 'Papa' is simply to mix metaphors, to help you keep from falling so easily back into your religious conditioning."

She leaned forward as if to share a secret. "To reveal myself to you as a very large, white grandfather figure with flowing beard, like Gandalf, would simply reinforce your religious stereotypes, and this weekend is *not* about reinforcing your religious stereotypes."

Mack almost laughed out loud and wanted to say, "You think? I'm over here barely believing that I'm not starkraving mad!" Instead, he focused on what she had just said and regained his composure. He believed, in his head at least, that God was Spirit, neither male nor female, but in spite of that, he was embarrassed to admit to himself that all his visuals for God were very white and very male.

She stopped talking, but only long enough to put some seasonings in a spice rack on a ledge by the window before turning to face him again. She looked at Mack intently. "Hasn't it always been a problem for you to embrace me as your Father? And after what you've been through, you couldn't very well handle a father right now, could you?"

He knew she was right, and he realized the kindness

and compassion in what she was doing. Somehow, the way she had approached him had skirted his resistance to her love. It was strange and painful and maybe even a little bit wonderful.

"But then"—he paused, still focused on staying rational—"why is there such an emphasis on you being a Father? I mean, it seems to be the way you most reveal yourself."

"Well," responded Papa, turning away from him and bustling around the kitchen, "there are many reasons for that, and some of them go very deep. Let me say for now that we knew once the creation was broken, true fathering would be much more lacking than mothering. Don't misunderstand me, both are needed—but an emphasis on fathering is necessary because of the enormity of its absence."

Mack turned away, a bit bewildered and feeling he was already in over his head. As he reflected, he looked through the window at a wild-looking garden.

"You knew I would come, didn't you?" Mack finally spoke quietly.

"Of course I did." She was busy again, her back to him.

"Then was I free *not* to come? Did I not have a choice in the matter?"

Papa turned back to face him, now with flour and dough in her hands. "Good question—how deep would you like to go?" She didn't wait for a response, knowing that Mack didn't have one. Instead, she asked, "Do you believe you are free to leave?"

"I suppose I am. Am I?"

"Of course you are! I'm not interested in prisoners. You're free to walk out that door right now and go home to your empty house. Or you could go down to The Grind and hang out with Willie. Just because I know you're too curious to go, does that reduce your freedom to leave?"

She paused only briefly and then turned back to her task, talking to him over her shoulder. "Or, if you want to go just a wee bit deeper, we could talk about the nature of freedom itself. Does freedom mean that you are allowed to do whatever you want to do? Or we could talk about all the limiting influences in your life that actively work against your freedom. Your family genetic heritage, your specific DNA, your metabolic uniqueness, the quantum stuff that is going on at a subatomic level where only I am the always-present observer. Or the intrusion of your soul's sickness that inhibits and binds you, or the social influences around you, or the habits that have created synaptic bonds and pathways in your brain. And then there's advertising, propaganda, and paradigms. Inside that confluence of multifaceted inhibitors," she said, sighing, "what is freedom really?"

Mack just stood there, not knowing what to say.

"Only I can set you free, Mackenzie, but freedom can never be forced."

"I don't understand," replied Mack. "I don't even understand what you just told me."

She turned back and smiled. "I know. I didn't tell you so that you would understand right now. I told you for later. At this point, you don't even comprehend that freedom is an incremental process." Gently reaching out, she took Mack's hands in hers, flour-covered and all, and looking him straight in the eyes, she continued, "Mackenzie, the truth shall set you free and the truth has a name; he's over in the woodshop right now covered in sawdust. Everything is about *him*. And freedom is a process that happens inside a relationship with him. Then all that stuff you feel churnin' around *inside* will start to work its way out."

"How can you really know how I feel?" Mack asked, looking back into her eyes.

Papa didn't answer, only looked down at their hands. His gaze followed hers and for the first time Mack noticed the scars on her wrists, like those he now assumed Jesus also had on his. She allowed him to tenderly touch the scars, outlines of a deep piercing, and he finally looked up again into her eyes. Tears were slowly making their way down her face, little pathways through the flour that dusted her cheeks.

"Don't ever think that what my Son chose to do didn't cost us dearly. Love always leaves a significant mark," she stated softly and gently. "We were there *together*."

Mack was surprised. "At the cross? Now wait, I thought you *left* him—you know—'My God, my God, why hast thou forsaken me?'" It was a Scripture that had often haunted Mack in *The Great Sadness*.

"You misunderstand the mystery there. Regardless of what he *felt* at that moment, I never left him."

"How can you say that? You abandoned him just like you abandoned me!"

"Mackenzie, I never left him, and I have never left you."

"That makes no sense to me," he snapped.

"I know it doesn't, at least not yet. Will you at least consider this: when all you can see is your pain, perhaps then you lose sight of me?"

When Mack did not respond, she turned back to her cooking so as to offer him a little needed space. She seemed to be preparing a number of dishes all at once, adding various spices and ingredients. Humming a haunting little tune, she put the finishing touches on the pie she had been making and slid it into the oven.

"Don't forget, the story didn't end in his sense of forsakenness. He found his way through it to put himself completely into my hands. Oh, what a moment that was!"

Mack leaned against the counter, somewhat bewildered. His emotions and thoughts were all jumbled. Part of him wanted to believe everything Papa was saying. That would be nice! But another part was objecting rather loudly, *This can't possibly be true!*

Papa reached for the kitchen timer, gave it a little twist, and placed it on the table in front of them. "I'm not who you think I am, Mackenzie." Her words weren't angry or defensive.

Mack looked at her, looked at the timer, and sighed. "I feel totally lost."

"Then let's see if we can find you in this mess."

Almost as if on cue, a blue jay landed on the kitchen windowsill and began strutting back and forth. Papa reached into a tin on the counter and, sliding the window open, offered Mr. Jay a mixture of grains that she must have kept just for that purpose. Without any hesitation, and with a seeming air of humility and thankfulness, the bird walked straight to her hand and began feeding.

"Consider our little friend here," she began. "Most birds were created to fly. Being grounded for them is a limitation *within* their ability to fly, not the other way around." She paused to let Mack think about her statement. "You, on the other hand, were created to be loved. So for you to live as if you were unloved is a limitation, not the other way around."

Mack nodded his head, not so much in full agreement, but more as a signal that at least he understood and was tracking. That seemed simple enough.

"Living unloved is like clipping a bird's wings and removing its ability to fly. Not something I want for you."

There's the rub. He didn't *feel* particularly *loved* at the moment.

"Mack, pain has a way of clipping our wings and keeping us from being able to fly." She waited a moment, allowing her words to settle. "And if it's left unresolved for very long, you can almost forget that you were ever created to fly in the first place."

Mack was silent. Strangely, the silence was not that uncomfortable. Mack looked at the little bird. The bird looked back at Mack. He wondered if it was possible for birds to smile. At least Mr. Jay looked as if he was, even if only sympathetically.

"I'm not like you, Mack."

It wasn't a put-down; it was a simple statement of fact. But to Mack it felt like a splash of cold water.

"I am God. I am who I am. And unlike you, my wings can't be clipped."

"Well that's wonderful for you, but where exactly does that leave me?" Mack blurted out, sounding more irritated than he would have liked.

Papa began stroking the little bird, brought him up close to her face, and said, "Smack-dab in the center of my love!" as the two cuddled nose-to-beak.

"I'm thinking that bird probably understands that better than I do" was the best Mack could offer.

"I know, honey. That's why we're here. Why do you think I said, 'I'm not like you'?"

"Well, I really have no idea. I mean, you're God and I'm not." He couldn't keep the sarcasm out of his voice, but she ignored it completely.

"Yes, but not exactly. At least not in the way you're thinking. Mackenzie, I am what some would say 'holy, and wholly other than you.' The problem is that many folks try to grasp some sense of who I am by taking the best version of themselves, projecting that to the nth degree, factoring in all the goodness they can perceive, which often isn't much, and then calling *that* God. And while it may seem like a noble effort, the truth is that it falls pitifully short of who I really am. I'm not merely the best version of you that you can think of. I am far more than that, above and beyond all that you can ask or think."

"I'm sorry, but those are just words to me. They don't make much sense." Mack shrugged.

"Even though you can't finally grasp me, guess what? I still want to be known."

"You're talking about Jesus, right? Is this going to be a let's-try-to-understand-the-Trinity sort of thing?"

She chuckled. "Sort of, but this isn't Sunday school. This is a flying lesson. Mackenzie, as you might imagine, there are some advantages to being God. By nature I am completely unlimited, without bounds. I have always known fullness. I live in a state of perpetual satisfaction as my normal state of existence," she said, quite pleased. "Just one of the perks of me being me."

That made Mack smile. This lady was fully enjoying herself, all by herself, and there wasn't an ounce of arrogance to spoil it.

"We created you to share in that. But then Adam chose to go it on his own, as we knew he would, and everything got messed up. But instead of scrapping the whole creation, we rolled up our sleeves and entered into the middle of the mess—that's what we have done in Jesus."

Mack was hanging in there, trying his best to follow her train of thought.

"When we three spoke ourselves into human existence as the Son of God, we became fully human. We also chose to embrace all the limitations this entailed. Even though we have always been present in this created universe, we now became flesh and blood. It would be like this bird, whose nature it is to fly, choosing only to walk and remain grounded. He doesn't stop being a bird, but it does alter his experience of life significantly."

She paused to make sure Mack was still tracking. While there was a definite cramp forming in his brain, he voiced an "Okay . . . ?" inviting her to continue.

"Although by nature he is fully God, Jesus is fully human and lives as such. While never losing the innate ability to fly, he chooses moment-by-moment to remain grounded. That is why his name is Immanuel, 'God with us,' or 'God with *you*,' to be more precise."

"But what about all the miracles? The healings? Raising people from the dead? Don't those prove that Jesus was God—you know, more than human?"

"No, it proves that Jesus is truly human."

"What?"

"Mackenzie, *I* can fly, but humans can't. Jesus is fully human. Although he is also fully God, he has *never* drawn upon his nature as God to do anything. He has only lived out of his relationship with me, living in the very same manner that I desire to be in relationship with every human being. He is just the first to do it to the uttermost—the first to absolutely trust my life within him, the first to believe in my love and my goodness without regard for appearance or consequence."

"So when he healed the blind?"

"He did so as a dependent, limited human being trusting in my life and power to be at work within him and through him. Jesus, as a human being, had no power within himself to heal anyone."

That came as a shock to Mack's religious system.

"Only as he rested in his relationship with me, and in our communion—our co-union—could he express my heart and will into any given circumstance. So, when you look at Jesus and it appears that he's flying, he really is . . . flying. But what you are actually seeing is me, my life in him. That's how he lives and acts as a true human, how every human is designed to live—out of my life.

"A bird is defined not by being grounded but by his ability to fly. Remember this, humans are defined not by their limitations, but by the intentions I have for them; not by what they seem to be, but by everything it means to be created in my image."

Mack felt the onset of information overload. So he pulled up a chair and just sat down. This would take some time to comprehend. "So does this mean that you were limited when Jesus was on Earth? I mean, did you limit yourself only to Jesus?"

"Not at all! Although I have only been limited in Jesus, I have never been limited in myself."

"There's that whole Trinity thing, which is where I kind of get lost."

Papa laughed a long, rich belly laugh that made Mack want to join in. She set the little bird down on the table next to Mack, turned to open the oven, and gave the pie that was baking a quick little look. Satisfied that everything was fine, Papa then pulled up a chair alongside him.

Mack looked at the little bird, who, amazingly, was content to just sit there with them. The absurdity of it all gave Mack a chuckle.

"To begin with, that you can't grasp the wonder of my nature is rather a good thing. Who wants to worship a God who can be fully comprehended, eh? Not much mystery in that."

"But what difference does it make that there are three of you, and you are all one God? Did I say that right?"

"Right enough." She grinned. "Mackenzie, it makes all the difference in the world!" She seemed to be enjoying this. "We are not three gods, and we are not talking about one god with three attitudes, like a man who is a husband, father, and worker. I am one God and I am three persons, and each of the three is fully and entirely the one."

The "huh?" Mack had been suppressing finally surfaced in all its glory.

"Never mind that," she continued. "What's important is this: if I were simply one God and only one person, then you would find yourself in this creation without something wonderful, without something essential even. And I would be utterly other than I am."

"And we would be without . . . ?" Mack didn't even know how to finish the question.

"Love and relationship. All love and relationship is possible for you *only* because it already exists within me, within God myself. Love is *not* the limitation; love is the flying. I *am* love."

As if in response to her declaration, the timer dinged and the little bird took off and flew out the window. Watching the jay in flight took on a whole new level of delight. Mack turned back to Papa and just stared at her in wonder. She was so beautiful and astonishing, and even though he was feeling a little lost and even though *The Great Sadness* still attended him, he felt himself settling down somewhat into the safety of being close to her.

"You do understand," she continued, "that unless I had an object to love—or, more accurately, a someone to love—if I did not have such a relationship within myself, then I would not be capable of love at all? You would have a god who could not love. Or maybe worse, you would have a god who, when he chose, could love only as a limitation of his nature. That kind of god could possibly act without love, and that would be a disaster. And that is surely *not* me."

With that, Papa stood up, went to the oven door, pulled out the freshly baked pie, set it on the counter, and, turning around as if to present herself, said, "The God who is—the I am who I am—cannot act apart from love!"

Mack knew that what he was hearing, as hard as it was to understand, was something amazing and incredible. It was as if her words were wrapping themselves around him, embracing him and speaking to him in ways beyond just what he could hear. Not that he actually believed any of it. If only it were true. His experience told him otherwise.

"This weekend is about relationship and love. Now, I know you have a lot you want to talk to me about, but right now you'd better go wash up. The other two are on their way in for supper." She began to walk away but paused and turned back.

"Mackenzie, I know that your heart is full of pain and anger and a lot of confusion. Together, you and I, we'll get around to some of that while you're here. But I also want you to know that there is more going on than you could imagine or understand, even if I told you. As much as you are able, rest in what trust you have in me, no matter how small, okay?"

Mack had lowered his head and was looking at the floor. *She knows*, he thought. Small? His "little" must be barely to the right of none. Nodding agreement, he looked up and noticed again the scars on her wrists.

"Papa?" Mack finally said in a way that felt very awkward, but he was trying.

"Yes, honey?"

Mack struggled for the words to tell her what was in his heart. "I'm so sorry that you, that Jesus, had to die."

She walked around the table and gave Mack another big hug. "I know you are, and thank you. But you need to know that we aren't sorry at all. It was worth it. Isn't that right, Son?"

She turned to ask her question of Jesus, who had just entered the cabin.

"Absolutely!" He paused and then looked at Mack. "And I would have done it even if it were *only* for you, but it wasn't!" he said with an inviting grin.

Mack excused himself and found the bathroom, where he washed his hands and his face and tried to collect himself.

7

GOD ON THE DOCK

*Let's pray that the human race never escapes Earth to
spread its iniquity elsewhere.*

—C. S. Lewis

Mack stood in the bathroom, looking into the mirror
while wiping his face dry with a towel. He was searching
for some sign of insanity in those eyes staring back at
him. Was this real? Of course not, it was impossible. But
then . . . He reached out his hand and slowly touched the
mirror. Maybe this was a hallucination being brought on by
all his grief and despair. Maybe it was a dream, and he was
asleep somewhere, maybe in the shack freezing to death?
Maybe . . . Suddenly, a terrible crash broke into his reverie. It
came from the direction of the kitchen, and Mack froze. For
a moment there was dead silence, and then, unexpectedly, he
heard uproarious laughter. Curious, he exited the bathroom
and poked his head through the doorway of the kitchen.

Mack was shocked at the scene in front of him. It
appeared that Jesus had dropped a large bowl of some sort of
batter or sauce on the floor, and it was everywhere. It must
have landed close to Papa because the lower portion of her
skirt and bare feet were covered in the gooey mess. They were
laughing so hard that Mack didn't think they were breathing.
Sarayu said something about humans being clumsy, and all
three started roaring again. Finally, Jesus brushed past Mack

and returned a minute later with a large basin of water and towels. Sarayu had already started wiping the goop from the floor and cupboards, but Jesus went straight to Papa and, kneeling at her feet, began to wipe off the front of her clothes. He worked down to her feet and gently lifted one foot at a time, which he directed into the basin where he cleaned and massaged it.

"Ooooh, that feels soooo good!" exclaimed Papa as she continued her tasks at the counter.

As he leaned against the doorway watching, Mack was full of thoughts. So this was God in relationship? It was beautiful and so appealing. He knew that it didn't matter whose fault it was—the mess from some bowl that had been broken, that a planned dish would not be shared. Obviously, what was truly important here was the love they had for one another and the fullness it brought them. He shook his head. How different this was from the way he sometimes treated the ones he loved!

Supper was simple, but a feast nonetheless. Roast bird of some kind in an orangey/mangoey kind of sauce. Fresh vegetables spiced with who but God knew what, all fruity and gingery, tangy and peppery. Rice, the quality of which Mack had never before tasted, could have been a meal by itself. The only awkward part was at the very beginning when Mack, out of habit, bowed his head before he remembered where he was. He looked up to find the three of them all grinning at him. So, as nonchalantly as he could, he said, "Um, thank you all . . . Could I have a bit of that rice there?"

"Sure. We *were* going to have this incredible Japanese sauce, but greasy fingers over there"—Papa nodded toward Jesus—"decided to see if it would bounce."

"C'mon, now," Jesus responded in mock defense. "My hands were slippery. What can I say?"

Papa winked at Mack as she passed him the rice. "You just can't get good help around here." Everyone laughed.

Conversation seemed almost normal. Mack was asked

about each of the children, except Missy, and he talked about their various struggles and triumphs. When he spoke of his concerns for Kate, the three nodded with concerned expressions but offered him no counsel or wisdom. He also answered questions about his friends, and Sarayu seemed most interested in asking about Nan. Finally, Mack blurted out something that had been bothering him throughout the discussion.

"Now here I am telling you about my kids and my friends and about Nan, but you already know everything I am telling you, don't you? You're acting like it's the first time you've heard it."

Sarayu reached across the table and took his hand. "Mackenzie, remember our conversation earlier about limitation?"

"Our conversation?" He glanced over at Papa, who was nodding knowingly.

"You can't share with one and not share with us all," Sarayu said and smiled. "Remember that choosing to stay on the ground is a choice to facilitate a relationship, to honor it. Mackenzie, you do this yourself. You don't play a game or color a picture with a child to show your superiority. Rather, you choose to limit yourself so as to facilitate and honor that relationship. You will even lose a competition to accomplish love. It is not about winning and losing, but about love and respect."

"So when I am telling you about my children . . . ?"

"We have limited ourselves out of respect for you. We are not bringing to mind, as it were, our knowledge of your children. As we are listening to you, it is as if this is the first time we have known about them, and we take great delight in seeing them through your eyes."

"I like that," reflected Mack, sitting back in his chair.

Sarayu squeezed his hand and seemed to sit back. "I do too! Relationships are never about power, and one way to avoid the will to hold power over another is to choose to limit oneself—to serve. Humans often do this—in touching the infirm and sick, in serving the ones whose minds have left to wander, in relating to the poor, in loving the very old and the very young, or even in caring for the other who has assumed a position of power over them."

"Well spoken, Sarayu," said Papa, her face beaming with pride. "I'll take care of the dishes later. But first, I would like to have a time of devotion."

Mack had to suppress a snicker at the thought of God having devotions. Images of family devotions from his childhood came spilling into his mind, not exactly good memories. Often, it was a tedious and boring exercise in coming up with the right answers, or, rather, the same old answers to the same old Bible story questions, and then trying to stay awake during his father's excruciatingly long prayers. And when his father had been drinking, family devotions devolved into a terrifying minefield, where any wrong answer or inadvertent glance could trigger an explosion. He half expected Jesus to pull out a huge old King James Bible.

Instead, Jesus reached across the table and took Papa's hands in his, scars now clearly visible on his wrists. Mack sat transfixed as he watched Jesus kiss his Father's hands and then look deeply into his Father's eyes and finally say, "Papa, I loved watching you today as you made yourself fully available to take Mack's pain into yourself and then gave him space to choose his own timing. You honored him, and you honored me. To listen to you whisper love and calm into his heart was truly incredible. What a joy to watch! I love being your Son."

Although Mack felt as if he were intruding, no one else seemed concerned, and he really had no idea where he would have gone in any case. To be in the presence of such love expressed seemed to dislodge an inner emotional logjam, and while he didn't understand exactly what he felt—it was good. What was he witnessing? Something simple, warm, intimate, genuine; this was holy. Holiness had always been a cold and sterile concept to Mack, but *this* was neither. Concerned that any movement on his part might shatter the moment, he simply closed his eyes and folded his hands in front of him. Listening intently with his eyes shut, he heard Jesus move his chair. There was a pause before he spoke again.

"Sarayu," Jesus began softly and tenderly, "you wash, I'll dry."

Mack's eyes snapped open in time to see the two smiling broadly at each other, picking up the dishes, and disappearing into the kitchen. He sat for a few minutes, unsure about what to do. Papa had gone somewhere and now that the other two were busy with dishes . . . well, it was an easy decision. He picked up silverware and glasses and headed for the kitchen. As soon as he had put them down for Sarayu to wash, Jesus tossed him a dish towel and they both began drying.

Sarayu began humming the same evocative tune he'd heard earlier with Papa, and Jesus and Mack simply listened as they worked. More than once the melody stirred Mack deep inside, knocking again at the door. To him it sounded Gaelic, and he could almost hear breath-pipes in accompaniment. But as difficult as it was for Mack to stay and allow his emotions to well up so powerfully, the melody absolutely captured him. If he could just keep listening to her, he would be thrilled to do dishes the rest of his life.

Ten minutes or so later they were finished. Jesus kissed Sarayu on the cheek and she disappeared around the corner. He then turned and smiled at Mack. "Let's go out on the dock and look at the stars."

"What about the others?" Mack asked.

"I'm here," replied Jesus. "I'm always here."

Mack nodded. This presence-of-God thing, although hard to grasp, seemed to be steadily penetrating past his mind and into his heart. He let it go at that.

"C'mon," said Jesus, interrupting Mack's thoughts. "I know you enjoy looking at stars! Want to?" He sounded just like a child full of anticipation and expectancy.

"Yeah, I think so," answered Mack, realizing that the last

time he had done that was on the ill-fated camping trip with the kids. Maybe it was time to take a few risks.

He followed Jesus out the back door. In the waning moments of twilight, Mack could make out the rocky shore of the lake, not overgrown as he remembered, but beautifully kept and picture perfect. The nearby creek seemed to be humming some sort of musical tune. Protruding about fifty feet into the lake was a dock, and Mack could barely make out three canoes tied at intervals along its course. Night was falling quickly and the distant darkness was already thick with the sounds of crickets and bullfrogs. Jesus took his arm and led him up the path while his eyes adjusted, but already Mack was looking up into a moonless night at the wonder of the emerging stars.

They made their way three-quarters of the way up the dock and lay down on their backs looking up. The elevation of this place seemed to magnify the heavens, and Mack reveled in seeing stars in such numbers and clarity. Jesus suggested that they close their eyes for a few minutes, allowing the last effects of dusk to disappear for the night. Mack complied, and when he finally opened his eyes, the sight was so powerful that he experienced vertigo for a few seconds. He almost felt as if he were falling up into space, the stars racing toward him as if to embrace him. He lifted his hands, imagining that he could reach out and pluck diamonds, one by one, off a velvet-black sky.

"Wow!" he whispered.

"Incredible!" whispered Jesus, his head near Mack's in the darkness. "I never get tired of this."

"Even though *you* created it?" Mack asked.

"I created it as the Word, before the Word became flesh. So even though I created this, I see it now as a human. And I must say, it is impressive!"

"It certainly is." Mack was not sure how to describe what he felt, but as they continued to lie in silence, gazing into the celestial display, watching and listening, he knew in his heart that this too was holy. As they both watched in awestruck wonder, a shooting star would occasionally blaze a brief trail across the night blackness, causing one or the other to exclaim, "Did you see that? Awesome!"

After a particularly long silence, Mack spoke. "I feel more comfortable around you. You seem so different from the other two."

"How do you mean, different?" came his soft voice out of the darkness.

"Well . . ." Mack paused as he thought about it. "More real, or tangible. I don't know." He struggled with the words and Jesus lay quietly, waiting. "It's like I've always known you. But Papa isn't at all what I expected from God, and Sarayu, she's *way* out there."

Jesus chuckled in the dark. "Since I am human we have much in common to begin with."

"But I still don't understand . . ."

"I am the best way any human can relate to Papa or Sarayu. To see me is to see them. The love you sense from me is no different from how they love you. And believe me, Papa and Sarayu are just as real as I am, though, as you've seen, in far different ways."

"Speaking of Sarayu, is she the Holy Spirit?"

"Yes. She is creativity; she is action; she is the breathing of life; she is much more. She is *my* Spirit."

"And her name, Sarayu?"

"That is a simple name from one of our human languages. It means 'Wind,' 'a common wind,' actually. She loves that name."

"Hmm," grunted Mack. "Nothing too common about her!"

"True, that," responded Jesus.

"And the name Papa mentioned, Elo . . . El . . ."

"Elousia," the voice said reverently from the dark next to him. "That is a wonderful name. *El* is my name as Creator God, but *ousia* is 'being' or 'that which is truly real,' so the name means 'the Creator God who is truly real and the ground of all being.' Now that is also a beautiful name."

There was silence for a minute while Mack pondered what Jesus had said. "So then, where does that leave us?" He felt as if he were asking the question for the entire human race.

"Right where you were always intended to be. In the very center of our love and our purpose."

Again a pause, then, "I suppose I can live with that."

Jesus chuckled. "I am glad to hear that," he said, and they both laughed. Neither spoke for a time. Stillness had fallen like a blanket, and all Mack was really aware of was the sound of water lapping up against the dock. It was he who eventually broke the silence again.

"Jesus?"

"Yes, Mackenzie?"

"I am surprised by one thing about you."

"Really? What?"

"I guess I expected you to be more"—*be careful here, Mack*—"uh . . . well, humanly striking."

Jesus chuckled. "Humanly striking? You mean handsome." Now he was laughing.

"Well, I was trying to avoid that, but yes. Somehow I thought you'd be the ideal man, you know, athletic and overwhelmingly good-looking."

"It's my nose, isn't it?"

Mack didn't know what to say.

Jesus laughed. "I am Jewish, you know. My grandfather on my mother's side had a big nose. In fact, most of the men on my mom's side had big noses."

"I just thought you'd be better-looking."

"By whose standards? Anyway, once you really get to know me, it won't matter to you."

The words, though delivered kindly, stung. Stung what, exactly? Mack lay there a few seconds and realized that as much as he thought he knew Jesus, perhaps he didn't . . . not really. Maybe what he knew was an icon, an ideal, an image through which he tried to grasp a sense of spirituality, but not a real person. "Why is that?" he finally asked. "You said if I really knew you it wouldn't matter what you looked like."

"It is quite simple really. *Being* always transcends appearance—that which only seems to be. Once you begin to know the being behind the very pretty or very ugly face, as determined by your bias, the surface appearances fade away until they simply no longer matter. That is why Elousia is such a wonderful name. God, who is the ground of all being, dwells in, around, and through all things—ultimately emerging as the real—and any appearances that mask that reality will fall away."

Silence followed as Mack wrestled with what Jesus had said. He gave up after only a minute or two and decided to ask the riskier question.

"You said I don't really know you. It would be a lot easier if we could always talk like this."

"Admittedly, Mack, this is special. You were really stuck and we wanted to help you crawl out of your pain. But don't think that just because I'm not visible, our relationship has to be less real. It will be different, but perhaps even more real."

"How is that?"

"My purpose from the beginning was to live in you and you in me."

"Wait, wait. Wait a minute. How can that happen? If you're still fully human, how can you be inside me?"

"Astounding, isn't it? It's Papa's miracle. It is the power of Sarayu, my Spirit, the Spirit of God who restores the union that was lost so long ago. Me? I choose to live moment by moment fully human. I am fully God, but I am human to the core. Like I said, it's Papa's miracle."

Mack was lying in the darkness, listening intently. "Aren't you talking about a real indwelling, not just some positional, theological thing?"

"Of course," answered Jesus, his voice strong and sure.

"It's what everything is all about. The human, formed out of the physical material of creation, can once more be fully indwelt by spiritual life, my life. It requires that a very real dynamic and active union exists."

"That is almost unbelievable!" Mack exclaimed quietly. "I had no idea. I need to think more about this. But I might have a lot more questions."

"And we have your lifetime to sort through them." Jesus chuckled. "But enough of that for now. Let's get lost again in the starry night."

In the silence that followed, Mack simply lay still, allowing the immensity of space and scattered light to dwarf him, letting his perceptions be captured by starlight and the thought that everything was about him . . . about the human race . . . that all this was all for us. After what seemed like a long time, it was Jesus who broke into the quiet.

"I'll never get tired of looking at this. The wonder of it all—the 'wastefulness of creation,' as one of our brothers has called it. So elegant, so full of longing and beauty even now."

"You know," Mack responded, suddenly struck anew by the absurdity of his situation: where he was, the person next to him. "Sometimes you sound so . . . I mean, here I am, lying next to God Almighty, and you really sound so . . ."

"Human?" Jesus offered. "But ugly." And with that he began to chuckle, quietly and restrained at first, but after a couple of snorts, laughter simply started tumbling out. It was infectious, and Mack found himself swept along from somewhere deep inside. He had not laughed from down there in a long time. Jesus reached over and hugged him, shaking from his own spasms of mirth, and Mack felt more clean and alive and well than he had since . . . well, he couldn't remember when.

Eventually, they both calmed again and the night's quiet asserted itself once more. It seemed that even the frogs had called it quits. Mack lay there realizing that he was now feeling guilty about enjoying himself, about laughing, and even in the darkness he could feel *The Great Sadness* roll in and over him.

"Jesus?" he whispered as his voice choked. "I feel so lost."

A hand reached out and squeezed his and didn't let go. "I know, Mack. But it's not true. I am with you and I'm not lost. I'm sorry it feels that way, but hear me clearly: *you are not lost.*"

"I hope you're right," Mack said, his tension lessened by the words of his newfound friend.

"C'mon," said Jesus, standing up and reaching down for Mack. "You have a big day ahead of you. Let's get you to bed." He put his arm around Mack's shoulder and together they walked back toward the cabin.

Mack was suddenly exhausted. Today had been one long day. Maybe he would wake up at home in his own bed after a night of vivid dreaming, but somewhere inside he hoped he was wrong.

8

A Breakfast of Champions

*Growth means change and
change involves risk, stepping
from the known to the unknown.*

—Author Unknown

When he reached his room, Mack discovered that his clothes, which he had left back in the car, were either folded on top of the dresser or hung in the open closet. To his amusement he also found a Gideon's Bible in the nightstand. He opened the window wide to let the outside night flow freely in, something that Nan never tolerated at home because of her fear of spiders and anything else crawly and creepy. Snuggling like a small child deep inside the heavy down comforter, he had made it through only a couple of verses before the Bible somehow left his hand, the light somehow turned off, someone kissed him on the cheek, and he was lifting gently off the ground in a flying dream.

Those who have never flown this way might think those who believe they do rather daft, but secretly they are probably at least a little envious. He hadn't had a flying dream in years, not since *The Great Sadness* had descended, but tonight Mack flew high into the starlit night, the air clear and cool but not uncomfortable. He soared above lakes and rivers, crossing an ocean coast and a number of reef-rimmed islets.

As odd as it sounds, Mack had *learned* inside his dreams to fly like this: to lift off the ground supported by nothing—no wings, no aircraft of any sort, just himself. Beginning flights were usually limited to a few inches, due mostly to fear or, more accurately, a dread of falling. Stretching his flights to a foot or two and eventually higher increased his confidence, as did his discovery that crashing wasn't painful at all but only a slow-motion bounce. In time, he learned to ascend into the clouds, cover vast distances, and land gently.

As he soared at will over rugged mountains and crystal white seashores, reveling in the missed wonder of dream flight, suddenly something grabbed him by the ankle and tore him out of the sky. In a matter of seconds he was dragged from the heights and violently thrown face-first onto a muddy and deeply rutted road. Thunder shook the ground and rain instantly drenched him to the bone. And there it came again, lightning illuminating the face of his daughter as she soundlessly screamed "Daddy" and then turned to run into the darkness, her red dress visible only for a few brief flashes and then gone. He fought with all his strength to extricate himself from the mud and the water, succeeding only in being sucked deeper into its grasp. And just as he was being taken under he woke with a gasp.

With his heart racing and his imagination anchored in the nightmare's images, it took a few moments for Mack to realize it had only been a dream. But even as it faded from his consciousness, the emotions didn't go with it. The dream had provoked *The Great Sadness*, and before he could even get out of bed, he was once again fighting his way through the despair that had devoured too many of his days.

With a grimace he looked around the room in the dull gray of the growing dawn that snuck in around the window shades. This wasn't his bedroom; nothing looked or felt familiar. Where was he? *Think, Mack, think!* Then he remembered. He was still at the shack with those three interesting characters, all of whom thought they were God.

"This can't really be happening," Mack grunted as he pulled his feet out of bed and sat on its edge with his head in his hands. He thought back to the previous day and again entertained the fear that he was going crazy. As he had never been much of a touchy-feely person, Papa—whoever she was—made him nervous, and he had no idea what to make of Sarayu. He admitted to himself that he liked Jesus a lot, but he seemed the least godlike of the three.

He let out a deep, heavy sigh. And if God was really here, why hadn't he taken his nightmares away?

Sitting in a quandary, he decided, wasn't helping, so he found his way to the bathroom where, to his amusement, everything he needed for a shower had been carefully laid out for him. He took his time in the warmth of the water, took his time shaving, and, back in the bedroom, took his time dressing.

The penetrating and alluring aroma of coffee drew his eye to the steaming cup waiting for him on the end table by the door. Taking a sip, he opened the shades and stood looking out through his bedroom window onto the lake, which he'd glimpsed only as a shadow the night before.

It was perfect, smooth as glass, except for the occasional trout leaping after its breakfast, sending circles of miniature waves radiating across the deep blue surface until they were slowly absorbed back into the larger surface. He estimated the far side was about a half mile away. Dew sparkled everywhere, diamondlike tears of the early morning reflecting the sun's love.

The three canoes resting easily at intervals along the dock looked inviting, but Mack shrugged off the thought. Canoes were no longer a joy. Too many bad memories.

The dock reminded him of the night before. Had he really lain out there with the One who made the universe? Mack shook his head, dumbfounded. What was going on here? Who were they really and what did they want from him? Whatever it was, he was sure he didn't have it to give.

The smell of eggs and bacon mixed with something else curled into his room, interrupting his thoughts. Mack decided it was time to emerge and speak for his share. As he entered the main living area, he heard the sound of a familiar Bruce Cockburn tune drifting from the kitchen and the high-pitched voice of a black woman singing along rather well: "Oh, Love that fires the sun, keep me burning." Papa emerged with plates in each hand full of pancakes and fried potatoes and greens of some sort. She was dressed in a long-flowing African-looking garment, complete with a vibrant multicolored headband. She looked radiant—almost glowing.

"You know," she exclaimed, "I love that child's songs! I am especially fond of Bruce, you know." She looked over at Mack, who was just sitting down at the table.

Mack nodded, his appetite increasing by the second.

"Yup," she continued, "and I know you like him too."

Mack smiled. It was true. Cockburn had been a family favorite for years, first his, then his and Nan's, and then each of the children to one degree or another.

"So, honey," Papa said, continuing busily with whatever she was doing, "how were your dreams last night? Dreams are sometimes important, you know. They can be a way of openin' up the window and lettin' the bad air out."

Mack knew this was an invitation to unlock the door to his terrors, but at the moment he wasn't ready to invite her into that hole with him. "I slept fine, thank you," he responded and then quickly changed the subject. "Is he your favorite? Bruce, I mean?"

She stopped and looked at him. "Mackenzie, I have no favorites. I am just especially fond of him."

"You seem to be especially fond of a lot of people," Mack observed with a suspicious look. "Are there any you are *not* especially fond of?"

She lifted her head and rolled her eyes as if she were

mentally going through the catalog of every being ever created. "Nope, I haven't been able to find any. Guess that's jes' the way I is."

Mack was interested. "Do you ever get mad at any of them?"

"Sho 'nuff! What parent doesn't? There is a lot to be mad about in the mess my kids have made and in the mess they're in. I don't like a lot of the choices they make, but that anger—especially for me—is an expression of love all the same. I love the ones I am angry with just as much as those I'm not."

"But—" Mack paused. "What about your wrath? It seems to me that if you're going to pretend to be God Almighty, you need to be a lot angrier."

"Do I now?"

"That's what I think. Weren't you always running around killing people in the Bible? You just don't seem to fit the bill."

"I understand how disorienting all this must be for you, Mack. But the only one pretending here is you. I am what I am. I'm not trying to fit anyone's bill."

"But you're asking me to believe that you're God, and I just don't see . . ." Mack had no idea how to finish his sentence, so he just gave up.

"I'm not asking you to believe anything, but I will tell you that you're going to find this day a lot easier if you simply accept what is, instead of trying to fit it into your preconceived notions."

"But if you are God, aren't you the One spilling out great bowls of wrath and throwing people into a burning lake of fire?" Mack could feel his deep anger emerging again, pushing out the questions in front of it, and he was a little chagrined at his own lack of self-control. But he asked anyway, "Honestly, don't you enjoy punishing those who disappoint you?"

At that, Papa stopped her preparations and turned toward Mack. He could see a deep sadness in her eyes. "I am not who you think I am, Mackenzie. I don't need to punish people for sin. Sin is its own punishment, devouring you from the inside. It's not my purpose to punish it; it's my joy to cure it."

"I don't understand."

"You're right. You don't," she said with a smile still sad around its edges. "But then again, we're not done yet."

Just then Jesus and Sarayu entered laughing through the back door, involved in their own conversation. Jesus came in dressed much as he had the day before, just jeans and a light blue button-down shirt that made his dark brown eyes stand out. Sarayu, on the other hand, was clothed in something so fine and lacy that it fairly flowed at the slightest breeze or spoken word. Rainbow patterns shimmered and reshaped with her every gesture. Mack wondered if she ever completely stopped moving. He rather doubted it.

Papa leaned down to eye level with Mack. "You raise some important questions, and we'll get around to them, I promise. But now let's enjoy breakfast together."

Mack nodded, again a little embarrassed as he turned his attention to the food. He was hungry anyway, and there was plenty to eat.

"Thank you for breakfast," he told Papa while Jesus and Sarayu were taking their seats.

"What?" she said in mock horror. "You aren't even going to bow your head and close your eyes?" She began walking toward the kitchen, grumbling as she went. "Tsk, tsk, tsk. What is the world coming to? You're welcome, honey," she said as she waved over her shoulder. She returned a moment later with still another bowl of steaming something that smelled wonderful and inviting.

They passed the food to one another, and Mack was spellbound watching and listening as Papa joined in the conversation Jesus and Sarayu were having. It had something to do with reconciling an estranged family, but it wasn't *what* they were talking about that captured Mack, it was *how* they related. He had never seen three people share with such simplicity and beauty. Each seemed totally aware of the others rather than of himself.

"So, what do you think, Mack?" Jesus asked, gesturing toward him.

"I have no idea what you're talking about," said Mack with his mouth half full of the very tasty greens. "But I love the way you do it."

"Whoa," said Papa, who had returned from the kitchen with yet another dish. "Take it easy on those greens, young man. Those things can give you the trots if you ain't careful."

"All right, I'll try to remember," Mack said as he reached for the dish in her hand. Then turning back to Jesus he added, "I love the way you treat each other. It's certainly not how I expected God to be."

"How do you mean?"

"Well, I know that you are one and all, and that there are three of you. But you respond with such graciousness to each other. Isn't one of you more the boss than the other two?"

The three looked at one another as if they had never thought of such a question.

"I mean," Mack hurried on, "I have always thought of God the Father as sort of being the boss and Jesus as the one following orders, you know, being obedient. I'm not sure how the Holy Spirit fits in exactly. He . . . I mean, she . . . uh . . ." Mack tried not to look at Sarayu as he stumbled for words. "Whatever—the Spirit always seemed kind of a . . . uh . . ."

"A free spirit?" offered Papa.

"Exactly—a free spirit, but still under the direction of the Father. Does that make sense?"

Jesus looked over at Papa, obviously trying with some difficulty to maintain the perception of a very serious exterior. "Does that make sense to you, Abba? Frankly, I haven't a clue what this man is talking about."

Papa scrunched up her face as if exerting great concentration. "Nope, I have been trying to make head or tail out of it, but sorry, he's got me lost."

"You know what I am talking about." Mack was a little frustrated. "I am talking about who's in charge. Don't you have a chain of command?"

"Chain of command? That sounds ghastly!" Jesus said.

"At least binding," Papa added as they both started laughing, and then Papa turned to Mack and sang, "Though chains be of gold, they are chains all the same."

"Now don't concern yourself with those two," Sarayu interrupted, reaching out her hand to comfort and calm him. "They're just playing with you. This is actually a subject of interest among us."

Mack nodded, relieved and a little chagrined that he had again allowed himself to lose his composure.

"Mackenzie, we have no concept of final authority among us, only unity. We are in a *circle* of relationship, not a chain of command or 'great chain of being,' as your ancestors termed it. What you're seeing here is relationship without any overlay of power. We don't need power over the other because we are always looking out for the best. Hierarchy would make no sense among us. Actually, this is your problem, not ours."

"Really? How so?"

"Humans are so lost and damaged that to you it is almost incomprehensible that people could work or live together without someone being in charge."

"But every human institution that I can think of, from political to business, even down to marriage, is governed by this kind of thinking. It is the web of our social fabric," Mack asserted.

"Such a waste!" said Papa, picking up the empty dish and heading for the kitchen.

"It's one reason why experiencing true relationship is so difficult for you," Jesus added. "Once you have a hierarchy you need rules to protect and administer it, and then you need law and the enforcement of the rules, and you end up with some kind of chain of command or a system of order that destroys relationship rather than promotes it. You rarely see or experience relationship apart from power. Hierarchy imposes laws and rules and you end up missing the wonder of relationship that we intended for you."

"Well," said Mack sarcastically, sitting back in his chair, "we sure seem to have adapted pretty well to it."

Sarayu was quick to reply, "Don't confuse adaptation with intention, or seduction with reality."

"So then—uh, could you please pass me a bit more of those greens? So then we've been seduced into this pre-occupation with authority?"

"In a sense, yes!" responded Papa, passing Mack the platter of greens but not letting go until he pulled twice. "I'm just looking out for you, son."

Sarayu continued, "When you chose independence over relationship, you became a danger to one another. Others became objects to be manipulated or managed for your own happiness. Authority, as you usually think of it, is merely the excuse the strong ones use to make others conform to what they want."

"Isn't it helpful in keeping people from fighting endlessly or getting hurt?"

"Sometimes. But in a selfish world it is also used to inflict great harm."

"But don't you use it to restrain evil?"

"We carefully respect your choices, so we work within your systems even while we seek to free you from them," Sarayu continued. "Creation has been taken down a very different path than we desired. In your world the value of the individual is constantly weighed against the survival of the system, whether political, economic, social, or religious—any system, actually. First one person, and then a few, and finally even many are easily sacrificed for the good and ongoing existence of that system. In one form or another this lies behind every struggle for power, every prejudice, every war, and every abuse of relationship. The 'will to power and independence' has become so ubiquitous that it is now considered *normal*."

"It's not?"

"It *is* the human paradigm," added Papa, having returned with more food. "It is like water to fish, so prevalent that it goes unseen and unquestioned. It *is* the matrix; a diabolical scheme in which you are hopelessly trapped even while completely unaware of its existence."

Jesus picked up the conversation. "As the crowning glory of creation, you were made in our image, unencumbered by structure and free to simply 'be' in relationship with me and one another. If you had truly learned to regard one another's concerns as significant as your own, there would be no need for hierarchy."

Mack sat back in his chair, staggered by the implications of what he was hearing. "So are you telling me that whenever we humans protect ourselves with power . . ."

"You are yielding to the matrix, not to us," finished Jesus.

"And now," Sarayu interjected, "we have come full circle, back to one of my initial statements: you humans are so lost and damaged that to you it is almost incomprehensible that relationship could exist apart from hierarchy. So you think that God must relate inside a hierarchy as you do. But we do not."

"But how could we ever change that? People will just use us."

"They most likely will. But we're not asking you to do it with others, Mack. We're asking you to do it with us. That's the only place it can begin. We won't use you."

"Mack," said Papa with an intensity that caused him to listen very carefully, "we want to share with you the love and joy and freedom and light that we already know within ourselves. We created you, the human, to be in face-to-face relationship with us, to join our circle of love. As difficult as it will be for you to understand, everything that has taken place is occurring exactly according to this purpose, without violating choice or will."

"How can you say that with all the pain in this world, all the wars and disasters that destroy thousands?" Mack's voice quieted to a whisper. "And what is the value in a little girl being murdered by some twisted deviant?" There it was again, the question that lay burning a hole in his soul. "You may not cause those things, but you certainly don't stop them."

"Mackenzie," Papa answered tenderly, seemingly not offended in the least by his accusation, "there are millions of reasons to allow pain and hurt and suffering rather than to eradicate them, but most of those reasons can be understood only within each person's story. I am not evil. You are the ones who embrace fear and pain and power and rights so readily in your relationships. But your choices are also not stronger than my purposes, and I will use every choice you make for the ultimate good and the most loving outcome."

"You see," explained Sarayu, "broken humans center their lives around things that seem good to them but will neither fill them nor free them. They are addicted to power, or the illusion of security that power offers. When a disaster happens, those same people will turn against the false powers they trusted. In their disappointment, either they become softened toward me or they become bolder in their independence. If you could only see how all of this ends and what we will achieve without the violation of one human will—then you would understand. One day you will."

"But the cost!" Mack was staggered. "Look at the cost—all the pain, all the suffering, everything that is so terrible and evil." He paused and looked down at the table. "And look what it has cost you. Is it worth it?"

"Yes!" came the unanimous, joyful response.

"But how can you say that?" Mack blurted. "It all sounds like the end justifies the means, that to get what you want you will go to any length, even if it costs the lives of billions of people."

"Mackenzie." It was the voice of Papa again, especially gentle and tender. "You really don't understand yet. You try to make sense of the world in which you live based on a very small and incomplete picture of reality. It is like looking at a parade through the tiny knothole of hurt, pain, self-centeredness, and power and believing you are on your own and insignificant. All of these thoughts contain powerful lies. You see pain and death as ultimate evils and God as the ultimate betrayer, or perhaps, at best, as fundamentally untrustworthy. You dictate the terms and judge my actions and find me guilty.

"The real underlying flaw in your life, Mackenzie, is that you don't think I am good. If you knew I was good and that everything—the means, the ends, and all the processes of individual lives—is all covered by my goodness, then while you might not always understand what I am doing, you would trust me. But you don't."

"I don't?" asked Mack, but it was not really a question. It was a statement of fact, and he knew it. The others seemed to know it too, and the table remained silent.

Sarayu spoke. "Mackenzie, you cannot produce trust, just as you cannot 'do' humility. It either is or is not. Trust is the fruit of a relationship in which you know you are loved. Because you do not know that I love you, you *cannot* trust me."

Again there was silence, and finally Mack looked up at Papa and spoke. "I don't know how to change that."

"You can't, not alone. But together we will watch that change take place. For now I just want you to be with me and discover that our relationship is not about performance or your having to please me. I'm not a bully, not some self-centered demanding little deity insisting on my own way. I am good, and I desire only what is best for you. You cannot find that through guilt or condemnation or coercion, only through a relationship of love. And I do love you."

Sarayu stood up from the table and looked directly at

Mack. "Mackenzie," she offered, "if you care to, I would like you to come and help me in the garden. There are things I need to do there before tomorrow's celebration. We can continue relevant elements of this conversation there. Please?"

"Sure," responded Mack and excused himself from the table. "One last comment," he added, turning back. "I just can't imagine any final outcome that would justify all this."

"Mackenzie." Papa rose out of her chair and walked around the table to give him a big squeeze. "We're not justifying it. We are redeeming it."

9

A LONG TIME AGO, IN A GARDEN FAR, FAR AWAY

Even should we find another Eden,
we would not be fit to enjoy it perfectly nor stay in it forever.

—Henry Van Dyke

Mack followed Sarayu as best he could out the back door and down the walkway past the row of firs. To walk behind such a being was like tracking a sunbeam. Light seemed to radiate through her and then reflect her presence in multiple places at once. Her nature was rather ethereal, full of dynamic shades and hues of color and motion. *No wonder so many people are a little unnerved at relating to her,* Mack thought. *She obviously is not a being who is predictable.*

Mack concentrated instead on staying to the walkway. As he rounded the trees, he saw for the first time a magnificent garden and orchard somehow contained within a plot of land hardly larger than an acre. For whatever reason, Mack had expected a perfectly manicured and ordered English garden. This was not that!

It was chaos in color. His eyes tried unsuccessfully to find some order in this blatant disregard for certainty. Dazzling sprays of flowers were blasted through patches of randomly planted vegetables and herbs, vegetation the likes of which

Mack had never seen. It was confusing, stunning, and incredibly beautiful.

"From above it's a fractal," Sarayu said over her shoulder with an air of pleasure.

"A what?" asked Mack absentmindedly, his mind still trying to grapple with and control the pandemonium of sight and the movements of hues and shades. Every step he took changed whatever patterns he for an instant thought he had seen, and nothing was like it had been.

"A fractal . . . something considered simple and orderly that is actually composed of repeated patterns no matter how magnified. A fractal is almost infinitely complex. I love fractals, so I put them everywhere."

"Looks like a mess to me," muttered Mack under his breath.

Sarayu stopped and turned to Mack, her face glorious. "Mack! Thank you! What a wonderful compliment!" She looked around at the garden. "That *is* exactly what this is—a mess. But"—she looked back at Mack and beamed—"it's still a fractal too."

Sarayu walked straight to a certain herb plant, plucked some heads off it, and turned to Mack.

"Here," she said, her voice sounding more like music than anything else. "Papa wasn't kidding at breakfast. You'd better chew on these greens for a few minutes. It will counteract the natural 'movement' of the ones you overindulged in earlier, if you know what I mean."

Mack chuckled as he accepted and carefully began to chew. "Yeah, but those greens tasted so good!" His stomach had begun to roll a little, and being kept off balance by the verdant wildness he had stepped into was not helping. The flavor of the herb was not distasteful: a hint of mint and some other spices he had probably smelled before but couldn't identify. As they walked, the growling in his stomach slowly began to subside, and he relaxed. He didn't realize he had been clenching.

Without speaking a word, he tried to follow Sarayu from place to place within the garden but found himself easily distracted by the blends of colors: currant and vermillion reds, tangerine and chartreuse divided by platinum and fuchsia, as well as innumerable shades of greens and browns. It was all wonderfully bewildering and intoxicating.

Sarayu seemed to be intently focused on a particular task. But like her name, she wafted about like a playful eddying wind, and he never quite knew which way she was blowing. He found it rather difficult to keep up with her. It reminded him of trying to follow Nan in a mall.

She moved through the garden snipping off various flowers and herbs and handing them to Mack to carry. The makeshift bouquet grew quite large, a pungent mass of perfume. The mixtures of aromatic spices were unlike anything he had ever smelled, and they were so strong he could almost taste them.

They deposited the final bouquet inside the door of a small garden shop that Mack had not noticed before, buried as it was in a thicket of wild growth including vines and what Mack thought were weeds.

"One task done," Sarayu announced, "and one to go." She handed Mack a shovel, rake, scythe, and pair of gloves and floated out and down a particularly overgrown path that seemed to go in the general direction of the far end of the garden. Along the way, she would occasionally slow to touch this plant or that flower, all the while humming the haunting tune that Mack had been captivated by the evening before. He followed obediently, carrying the tools he had been given and trying to keep her in sight while wondering at his surroundings.

When she stopped, Mack almost ran into her, distracted as he was looking around. Somehow she had changed and was now dressed in work clothes: jeans with wild designs, a work shirt, and gloves. They were in an area that could have been an orchard, but not really. Regardless, the place where they stood was an open spot surrounded on three sides by peach and cherry trees, and in the middle was a cascade of purple and yellow flowered bushes that almost took his breath away.

"Mackenzie." She pointed directly at the incredible purple and yellow patch. "I would like your help clearing this entire plot of ground. There is something very special that I want to plant here tomorrow, and we need to get it ready." She looked at Mack and reached for the scythe.

"You can't be serious! This is so gorgeous and in such a secluded spot."

But Sarayu didn't seem to notice. Without further explanation, she turned and began destroying the artistic display of flowers. She cut cleanly, seemingly without any effort.

Mack shrugged, donned his gloves, and began raking into piles the havoc she was wreaking. He struggled to keep up. It might not be a strain for her, but for him it was labor. Twenty minutes later the plants were all cut off at the roots, and the plot looked like a wound in the garden. Mack's forearms were etched with cut marks from the branches he had piled in one spot. He was out of breath and sweating, glad to be finished. Sarayu stood over the plot, examining their handiwork.

"Isn't this exhilarating?" she asked.

"I've been exhilarated in better ways," Mack retorted sarcastically.

"Oh, Mackenzie, if you only knew. It's not the work, but the purpose that makes it special. And," she said, smiling at him, "it's the only kind I do."

Mack leaned on his rake and looked around the garden and then at the red welts on his arms. "Sarayu, I know you are the Creator, but did you make the poisonous plants, stinging nettles, and mosquitoes too?"

"Mackenzie," responded Sarayu, seeming to move in tandem with the breezes, "a created being can only take what already exists and from it fashion something different."

"So, you are saying that you . . ."

". . . created everything that actually exists, including what you consider the bad stuff," Sarayu finished for him. "But when I created it, it was only good, because that is just the way I am." She seemed to almost billow into a curtsy before resuming her task.

"But," Mack continued, not satisfied, "then why has so much of the 'good' gone 'bad'?"

Now Sarayu paused before answering. "You humans, so little in your own eyes. You are truly blind to your own place in the creation. Having chosen the ravaged path of independence, you don't even comprehend that you are dragging the entire creation along with you." She shook her head and the wind sighed through the trees nearby. "So very sad, but it won't be this way forever."

They enjoyed a few moments of silence as Mack looked back toward the various plants that he could see from where they were standing. "So, are there plants in this garden that are poisonous?" he asked.

"Oh, yes!" exclaimed Sarayu. "They are some of my favorites. Some are even dangerous to the touch, like this one." She reached for a nearby bush and snapped off something that looked like a dead stick with only a few tiny leaves budding from the stem. She handed it to Mack, who raised both hands to avoid touching it.

Sarayu laughed. "I am here, Mack. There are times when it is safe to touch, and times when precautions must be taken. That is the wonder and adventure of exploration, a piece of what you call science—to discern and discover what we have hidden for you to find."

"So why did you hide it?" Mack inquired.

"Why do children love to hide and seek? Ask any person who has a passion to explore and discover and create. The choice to hide so many wonders from you is an act of love that is a gift inside the process of life."

Mack gingerly reached out and took the poisonous twig. "If you had not told me this was safe to touch, would it have poisoned me?"

"Of course! But if I direct you to touch, that is different. For any created being, autonomy is lunacy. Freedom involves trust and obedience inside a relationship of love. So, if you are not hearing my voice, it would be wise to take the time to understand the nature of the plant."

"So why create poisonous plants at all?" Mack queried, handing back the twig.

"Your question presumes that poison is bad, that such creations have no purpose. Many of these so-called bad plants, like this one, contain incredible properties for healing or are necessary for some of the most magnificent wonders when combined with something else. Humans have a great capacity for declaring something good or evil, without truly knowing."

Obviously the short break, which had been for Mack's sake, was over and Sarayu thrust a hand shovel at Mack, picking up the rake. "To prepare this ground, we must dig up the roots of all the wonderful growth that was here. It is hard work, but well worth it. If the roots are not here, then they cannot do what comes naturally and harm the seed we will plant."

"Okay," Mack grunted as they both got down on their knees alongside the freshly cleared plot. Sarayu was somehow able to reach deep under the ground and find the ends of the roots, bringing them effortlessly to the surface. She left the shorter ones for Mack, who used the hand shovel to dig under and pull them up. They then shook the dirt from the roots and threw them onto one of the piles that Mack had earlier raked together.

"I'll burn those later," she said.

"You were talking earlier about humans declaring good and evil without knowledge?" Mack asked, shaking another root free from its dirt.

"Yes. I was specifically talking about the tree of the knowledge of good and evil."

"*The* tree of the knowledge of good and evil?" asked Mack.

"Exactly!" she stated, seeming to almost expand and contract for emphasis while she worked. "And now, Mackenzie, you are beginning to see why eating the deadly fruit of that tree was so devastating to your race."

"I've never given it much thought, really," said Mack, intrigued by the direction their chat was taking. "So was there really an actual garden? I mean, Eden and all that?"

"Of course. I told you I have a thing for gardens."

"That's going to bother some people. There are lots of people who think it was only a myth."

"Well, their mistake isn't fatal. Rumors of glory are often hidden inside what many consider myths and tales."

"Oh, I've got some friends who are not going to like this," Mack observed as he wrestled with a particularly stubborn root.

"No matter. I myself am very fond of them."

"I'm so surprised," Mack said a little sarcastically, then smiled in her direction. "Okay, then." He drove his shovel into the dirt, grabbing the root above it with his hand. "So tell me about the tree of the knowledge of good and evil."

"This is what we were talking about at breakfast," she responded. "Let me begin by asking *you* a question. When something happens to you, how do *you* determine whether it is good or evil?"

Mack thought for a moment before answering. "Well, I haven't really thought about that. I guess I would say that something is good when I like it—when it makes me feel good or gives me a sense of security. Conversely, I'd call evil something that causes me pain or costs me something I want."

"So it is pretty subjective then?"

"I guess it is."

"And how confident are you in your ability to discern what indeed is good for you, or what is evil?"

"To be honest," said Mack, "I tend to sound justifiably angry when somebody is threatening my 'good,' you know, what I think I deserve. But I'm not really sure I have any logical ground for deciding what is actually good or evil, except how something or someone affects me." He paused to rest and catch his breath a moment. "All this sounds quite self-serving and self-centered, I suppose. And my track record isn't very encouraging either. Some things I initially thought were good turned out to be horribly destructive, and some things that I thought were evil, well, they turned out—"

Sarayu interrupted. "Then it is *you* who determines good and evil. You become the judge. And to make things more confusing, that which you determine to be good will change over time and circumstance. And then, beyond that and even worse, there are billions of you, each determining what is good and what is evil. So when your good and evil clash with your neighbor's, fights and arguments ensue and even wars break out."

The colors moving within Sarayu were darkening as she spoke, blacks and grays merging and shadowing the rainbow hues. "And if there is no reality of good that is absolute, then you have lost any basis for judging. It is just language, and one might as well exchange the word *good* for the word *evil*."

"I can see where that might be a problem," Mack agreed.

"A problem?" Sarayu almost snapped as she stood up and faced him. She was disturbed, but he knew that it was not directed at him. "Indeed! The choice to eat of that tree tore the universe apart, divorcing the spiritual from the physical. They died, expelling in the breath of their choice the very breath of God. I would say that is a problem!"

In the intensity of her speaking, Sarayu had risen slowly off the ground, but now as she settled back, her voice came quiet but distinct. "That was a great sorrow day."

Neither of them spoke for almost ten minutes while they worked. As he continued digging up roots and throwing them into the pile, Mack busily worked in his mind to untangle the implications of what she had said. Finally he broke the silence.

"I can see now," confessed Mack, "that I spend most of my time and energy trying to acquire what I have determined to be good, whether it's financial security or health or retirement or whatever. And I spend a huge amount of energy and worry fearing what I've determined to be evil." Mack sighed deeply.

"Such truth in that," said Sarayu gently. "Remember this.

It allows you to play God in your independence. That's why a part of you prefers not to see me. And you don't need me at all to create your list of good and evil. But you do need me if you have any desire to stop such an insane lust for independence."

"So there is a way to fix it?" asked Mack.

"You must give up your right to decide what is good and evil on your own terms. That is a hard pill to swallow— choosing to live only in me. To do that, you must know me enough to trust me and learn to rest in my inherent goodness."

Sarayu turned toward Mack; at least that was his impression. "Mackenzie, *evil* is a word we use to describe the absence of good, just as we use the word *darkness* to describe the absence of light or *death* to describe the absence of life. Both evil and darkness can be understood only in relation to light and good; they do not have any actual existence. I am light and I am good. I am love and there is no darkness in me. Light and Good actually exist. So, removing yourself from me will plunge you into darkness. Declaring independence will result in evil because apart from me, you can draw only upon yourself. That is death because you have separated yourself from me: Life."

"Wow!" Mack exclaimed, sitting back for a moment. "That really helps. But I can also see that giving up my independent right is not going to be an easy process. It could mean that—"

Sarayu interrupted his sentence again. "That in one instance, the good may be the presence of cancer or the loss of income—or even a life."

"Yeah, but tell that to the person with cancer or the father whose daughter is dead," Mack said, a little more sarcastically than he had intended.

"Oh, Mackenzie," reassured Sarayu. "Don't you think we have them in mind as well? Each of them was the center of another story that is untold."

"But—" Mack could feel his control getting away as he

drove his shovel in hard—"Didn't Missy have a right to be protected?"

"No, Mack. A child is protected because she is loved, not because she has a right to be protected."

That stopped him. Somehow, what Sarayu had just been saying seemed to turn the whole world upside down, and he was struggling to find some footing. Surely there were some rights that he could legitimately hold on to.

"But what about—"

"Rights are where survivors go, so that they won't have to work out relationships," she cut in.

"But if I gave up—"

"Then you would begin to know the wonder and adventure of living in me," she said, interrupting him again.

Mack was getting frustrated. He spoke louder, "But don't I have the right to—"

"To complete a sentence without being interrupted? No, you don't. Not in reality. But as long as you think you do, you will surely get ticked off when someone cuts you off, even if it is God."

He was stunned and stood up, staring at her, not knowing whether to rage or laugh. Sarayu smiled at him. "Mackenzie, Jesus didn't hold on to any rights. He willingly became a servant and lives out of his relationship to Papa. He gave up everything, so that by his dependent life he opened a door that would allow you to live free enough to give up your rights."

At that moment, Papa emerged down the walkway carrying two paper sacks. She was smiling as she approached.

"Well, you two are having a good conversation, I assume?" She winked at Mack.

"The best!" exclaimed Sarayu. "And guess what? He called our garden a mess—isn't that perfect?"

They both beamed broadly at Mack, who still wasn't absolutely sure he wasn't being played with. His anger was subsiding, but he could still feel the burning in his cheeks. The other two seemed to take no notice.

Sarayu reached up and kissed Papa on the cheek. "As always, your timing is perfect. Everything that I needed Mackenzie to do here is finished." She turned to him. "Mackenzie, you are such a delight! Thank you for all your hard work!"

"I didn't do that much, really," he said apologetically. "I mean, look at this mess." His gaze moved over the garden that surrounded them. "But it really is beautiful, and full of you, Sarayu. Even though it seems like lots of work still needs to be done, I feel strangely at home and comfortable here."

The two looked at each other and grinned.

Sarayu stepped toward him until she had invaded his personal space. "And well you should, Mackenzie, because this garden is your soul. This mess is *you*! Together, you and I, we have been working with a purpose in your heart. And it is wild and beautiful and perfectly in process. To you it seems like a mess, but I see a perfect pattern emerging and growing and alive—a living fractal."

The impact of her words almost crumbled all of Mack's reserve. He looked again at their garden—his garden—and it really was a mess, but incredible and wonderful at the same time. And beyond that, Papa was here and Sarayu loved the mess. It was almost too much to comprehend, and once again his carefully guarded emotions threatened to spill over.

"Mackenzie, Jesus would like to take you for a walk, if you want to go. I packed you a picnic lunch in case you get a little hungry. It'll tide you over till teatime."

As Mack turned to accept the lunch bags, he felt Sarayu slip by, kissing his cheek as she passed, but he didn't see her go. As with the wind he thought he could see her path, the plants bending in turn as if in worship. When he turned back, Papa was also gone, so he headed toward the workshop to see if he could find Jesus. It seemed they had an appointment.

10

WADE IN THE WATER

New world—big horizon
Open your eyes and see it's true
New world—across the frightening
Waves of blue

—David Wilcox

Jesus finished sanding the last corner of what looked like a casket sitting on a table in the workshop. He ran his fingers along the smooth edge, nodded with satisfaction, and put the sandpaper down. He walked out the door, brushing the powder off his jeans and shirt as Mack approached.

"Hey there, Mack! I was just putting some finishing touches on my project for tomorrow. Would you like to go for a walk?"

Mack thought about their time last night under the stars. "If you're going, I'm more than willing," he responded. "Why do you all keep talking about tomorrow?"

"It's a big day for you, one of the reasons you are here. Let's go. There's a special place I want to show you on the other side of the lake, and the panorama is beyond description. You can even see some of the higher peaks from over there."

"Sounds great!" responded Mack enthusiastically.

"It looks like you have our lunches, so we're ready to go."

Instead of angling off to one side of the lake or the other, where Mack suspected a trail might be, Jesus headed straight for the dock. The day was bright and beautiful. The sun was warm to the skin but not too much so, and a fresh-scented breeze softly and lovingly caressed their faces.

Mack next assumed that they would be taking one of the canoes nestled against the dock pylons, and he was surprised when Jesus didn't hesitate as he passed the third and last of them, heading directly for the end of the pier. Reaching the end of the dock, he turned to Mack and grinned.

"After you," he said with a mock flourish and bow.

"You're kidding, right?" sputtered Mack. "I thought we were going for a walk, not a swim."

"We are. I just thought going across the lake would take less time than going around it."

"I'm not that great a swimmer, and besides, the water looks pretty damn cold," complained Mack. He suddenly realized what he had said and felt his face flush. "Uh, I mean darn, pretty darn cold." He looked up at Jesus with a frozen grimace on his face, but the other man seemed to be actually enjoying Mack's discomfort.

"Now," said Jesus, folding his arms, "we both know that you are a very capable swimmer, once a lifeguard if I remember right. And the water is cold. And it's deep. But I'm not talking about swimming. I want to walk across with you."

What Jesus had been suggesting, Mack finally allowed into his consciousness. He was talking about walking *on* the water. Jesus, anticipating his hesitation, asserted, "C'mon, Mack. If Peter can do it . . ."

Mack laughed, more out of nerves than anything. To be sure, he asked one more time, "You want me to walk *on* the water to the other side—that is what you are saying, right?"

"You're a quick one, Mack. Nobody's gonna slide anything past you, that's for sure. C'mon, it's fun!" He laughed.

Mack walked to the edge of the dock and looked down. The water lapped only about a foot below where he stood, but it might as well have been a hundred feet. The distance looked enormous. To dive in would have been easy, he had done that a thousand times—but how do you step off a dock onto water? Do you jump as if you are landing on concrete, or do you step over the edge as if you are getting out of a boat? He looked back at Jesus, who was still chuckling.

"Peter had the same problem: how to get out of the boat. It's just like stepping off a one-foot-high stair. Nothing to it."

"Will my feet get wet?" queried Mack.

"Of course, water is still wet."

Again Mack looked down at the water and back at Jesus. "Then why is this so hard for me?"

"Tell me what you are afraid of, Mack."

"Well, let me see. What am I afraid of?" began Mack. "Well, I am afraid of looking like an idiot. I am afraid that you are making fun of me and that I will sink like a rock. I imagine that—"

"Exactly," Jesus interrupted. "You imagine. Such a powerful ability, the imagination! That power alone makes you so like us. But without wisdom, imagination is a cruel taskmaster. If I may prove my case, do you think humans were designed to live in the present or the past or the future?"

"Well," said Mack, hesitating, "I think the most obvious answer is that we were designed to live in the present. Is that wrong?"

Jesus chuckled. "Relax, Mack. This is not a test, it's a conversation. You are exactly correct, by the way. But now tell me, where do *you* spend most of your time in your mind, in your imagination: in the present, in the past, or in the future?"

Mack thought for a moment before answering. "I suppose I would have to say that I spend very little time in the present. I spend a big piece in the past, but most of the rest of the time, I am trying to figure out the future."

"Not unlike most people. When I dwell with you, I do so in the present—I live in the present. Not the past, although much can be remembered and learned by looking back, but only for a visit, not an extended stay. And for sure, I do not dwell in the future you visualize or imagine. Mack, do you realize that your imagination of the future, which is almost always dictated by fear of some kind, rarely, if ever, pictures me there with you?"

Again Mack stopped and thought. It was true. He spent a lot of time fretting and worrying about the future, and in his imagination it was usually pretty gloomy and depressing, if not outright horrible. And Jesus was also correct in saying that in Mack's thoughts of the future, God was always absent.

"Why do I do that?" asked Mack.

"It is your desperate attempt to get some control over something you can't. It is impossible for you to take power over the future because it isn't even real, nor will it ever be real. You try to play God, imagining the evil that you fear becoming reality, and then you try to make plans and contingencies to avoid what you fear."

"Yeah, that's basically what Sarayu was saying," responded Mack. "So why do I have so much fear in my life?"

"Because you don't believe. You don't know that we love you. The person who lives by his fears will not find freedom in my love. I am not talking about rational fears regarding legitimate dangers, but imagined fears, and especially the projection of those into the future. To the degree that those fears have a place in your life, you neither believe I am good nor know deep in your heart that I love you. You sing about it, you talk about it, but you don't know it."

Mack looked down once more at the water and breathed a huge sigh of the soul. "I have so far to go."

"Only about a foot, it looks to me." Jesus laughed, placing his hand on Mack's shoulder. It was all he needed and Mack stepped off the dock. In order to try to see the water as solid and not be deterred by its motion, he looked up at the far shore and held the lunch bags high just in case.

The landing was softer than he had thought it would be.

His shoes were instantly wet, but the water did not come up even to his ankles. The lake was still moving all around him, and he almost lost his balance because of it. It was strange. When he looked down, it seemed that his feet were on something solid but invisible. He turned to find Jesus standing next to him, holding his own shoes and socks in one hand and smiling.

He laughed. "We always take off our shoes and socks before we do this."

Mack shook his head, laughing as he sat back on the edge of the dock. "I think I will anyway." He took them off, wrung out his socks, and then rolled up his pant legs, just to be sure.

They started off with footwear and lunch bags in hand and walked toward the opposite shore, about a half mile distant. The water felt cool and refreshing and sent chills up his spine. Walking on the water with Jesus seemed like the most natural way to cross a lake, and Mack was grinning ear to ear just thinking about what he was doing. He would occasionally look down to see if he could see any lake trout.

"This is utterly ridiculous and impossible, you know!" he finally exclaimed.

"Of course," assented Jesus, grinning back at him.

They rapidly reached the far shore and Mack could hear the sound of rushing water growing louder, but he couldn't see its source. Twenty yards from the shore he stopped. To their left and behind a high rock ridge he could see it, a beautiful waterfall spilling over a cliff's edge and dropping at least a hundred feet into a pool at the canyon floor. There it became a large creek that probably joined the lake beyond where Mack could see. Between them and the waterfall was an expanse of mountain meadow, filled with blooming wildflowers haphazardly strewn and seeded by the wind. It was all stunning, and Mack stood for a moment breathing it in. An image of Missy flashed in his mind but didn't settle.

A pebbled beach awaited their approach, and behind it

a backdrop of rich and dense forest rose up to the base of a mountain, crested by the whiteness of freshly fallen snow. Slightly to their left, at the end of a small clearing and just to the other side of a small babbling brook, a trail disappeared quickly into the wooded darkness. Mack stepped off the water and onto the small rocks, gingerly making his way toward a log that had fallen. There he sat down and again wrung out his socks, placing them and his shoes to dry in the near-noon sun.

Only then did he look up and across the lake. The beauty was staggering. He could make out the shack, where smoke leisurely rose from the redbrick chimney as it nestled against the greens of the orchard and forest. But dwarfing it all was a massive range of mountains that hovered above and behind, like sentinels standing guard. Mack simply sat, Jesus next to him, and inhaled the visual symphony.

"You do great work!" he said softly.

"Thank you, Mack, and you've seen so little. For now most of what exists in the universe will be seen and enjoyed only by me, like special canvasses in the back of an artist's studio, but one day . . . And can you imagine this scene if the earth were not at war, striving so hard just to survive?"

"And you mean what, exactly?"

"Our earth is like a child who has grown up without parents, having no one to guide and direct her." As Jesus spoke, his voice intensified in subdued anguish. "Some have attempted to help her, but most have simply tried to use her. Humans, who have been given the task to lovingly steer the world, instead plunder her, with no consideration other than their immediate needs. And they give little thought to their own children, who will inherit their lack of love. So they use her and abuse her with little consideration, and then when she shudders or blows her breath, they are offended and raise their fists at God."

"You're an ecologist?" Mack said, half as an accusation.

"This blue-green ball in black space, filled with beauty even now, battered and abused and lovely," Jesus quoted.

"I know that song. You must care deeply about the creation." Mack smiled.

"Well, this 'blue-green ball in black space' belongs to me," Jesus stated emphatically.

After a moment, they opened their lunches together. Papa had filled the sacks with sandwiches and treats, and both ate heartily. Mack munched on something that he liked, but he couldn't quite decide if it was animal or vegetable. He thought it might be better not to ask.

"So why don't you fix it?" Mack asked, munching on his sandwich. "The earth, I mean."

"Because we gave it to you."

"Can't you take it back?"

"Of course we could, but then the story would end before it was consummated."

Mack gave Jesus a blank look.

"Have you noticed that even though you call me 'Lord' and 'King,' I have never really acted in that capacity with you? I've never taken control of your choices or forced you to do anything, even when what you were about to do was destructive or hurtful to yourself and others."

Mack looked back at the lake before responding. "I would have preferred that you did take control at times. It would have saved me and people I care about a lot of pain."

"To force my will on you," Jesus replied, "is exactly what love does not do. Genuine relationships are marked by submission even when your choices are not helpful or healthy.

"That's the beauty you see in my relationship with Abba and Sarayu. We are indeed submitted to one another and have always been so and always will be. Papa is as much submitted to me as I to him, or Sarayu to me, or Papa to her. Submission is not about authority and it is not obedience; it is all about relationships of love and respect. In fact, we are submitted to you in the same way."

Mack was surprised. "How can that be? Why would the God of the universe want to be submitted to me?"

"Because we want you to join us in our circle of relationship. I don't want slaves to my will; I want brothers and sisters who will share life with me."

"And that's how you want us to love one another, I suppose? I mean between husbands and wives, parents and children. I guess in any relationship?"

"Exactly! When I am your life, submission is the most natural expression of my character and nature, and it will be the most natural expression of your new nature within relationships."

"And all I wanted was a God who will just fix everything so no one gets hurt." Mack shook his head at the realization. "But I'm not very good at relationship stuff, not like Nan."

Jesus finished the last bite of his sandwich and, closing his lunch bag, placed it down next to him on the log. He wiped off a couple of crumbs that still adhered to his mustache and short beard. Then, grabbing a nearby stick, he began to doodle in the sand as he continued. "That's because, like most men, you find what you think of as fulfillment in your achievements, and Nan, like most women, finds it in relationships. It's more naturally her language." Jesus paused to watch an osprey dive into the lake not fifty feet from them and slowly take flight again, talons gripping a large lake trout still struggling to escape.

"Does that mean I'm hopeless? I really want what the three of you share, but I have no idea how to get there."

"There's a lot in your way right now, Mack, but you don't have to keep living with it."

"I know that's truer now that Missy's gone, but it has never been easy for me."

"You're not just dealing with Missy's murder. There's a larger twisting that makes sharing life with us difficult. The world is broken because in Eden you abandoned relationship with us to assert your own independence. Most men have expressed it by turning to the work of their hands and the sweat of their brows to find their identity, value, and security.

By choosing to declare what's good and evil, you seek to determine your own destiny. It was this turning that has caused so much pain."

Jesus braced himself with the stick to stand and paused while Mack finished his last bite and stood to join him. Together they began walking along the lakeshore. "But that isn't all. The woman's desire—and the word is actually her *turning*—so the woman's turning was not to the works of her hands but to the man, and his response was to rule 'over' her, to take power over her, to become the ruler. Before the choosing, she found her identity, her security, and her understanding of good and evil only in me, as did man."

"No wonder I feel like a failure with Nan. I can't seem to be that for her."

"You weren't made to be. And in trying you'll only be playing God."

Mack reached down, picked up a flat stone, and skipped it across the lake. "Is there any way out of this?"

"It is so simple, but never easy for you: by *re-turning*. By turning back to me. By giving up your ways of power and manipulation and just coming back to me." Jesus sounded as if he was pleading. "Women in general will find it difficult to turn from a man and stop demanding that he meets their needs, provides security, and protects their identity, and return to me. Men in general find it very hard to turn from the works of their hands, their own quests for power and security and significance, and return to me."

"I've always wondered why men have been in charge," Mack pondered. "Males seem to be the cause of so much of the pain in the world. They account for most of the crimes, and many of those are perpetrated against women and"—he paused—"children."

"Women," Jesus continued as he picked up a stone and skipped it, "turned from us to another relationship, while men turned to themselves and the ground. The world in many ways would be a much calmer and gentler place if women ruled. There would have been far fewer children sacrificed to the gods of greed and power."

"Then they would have fulfilled *that* role better."

"Better, maybe, but it still wouldn't have been enough. Power in the hands of independent humans, be they men or women, does corrupt. Mack, don't you see how filling roles is the opposite of relationship? We want male and female to be counterparts, face-to-face equals, each unique and different, distinctive in gender but complementary, and each empowered uniquely by Sarayu, from whom all true power and authority originate. Remember, I am not about performance and fitting into man-made structures; I am about being. As you grow in relationship with me, what you do will simply reflect who you really are."

"But you came in the form of a man. Doesn't that say something?"

"Yes, but not what many have assumed. I came as a man to complete a wonderful picture in how we made you. From the first day we hid the woman within the man, so that at the right time we could remove her from within him. We didn't create man to live alone; she was purposed from the beginning. By taking her out of him, he birthed her in a sense. We created a circle of relationship, like our own, but for humans. She, out *of* him, and now all the males, including me, birthed through her, and all originating, or birthed, from God."

"Oh, I get it," Mack said, stopping in mid-throw. "If the female had been created first, there would have been no circle of relationship, and thus no possibility of a fully equal face-to-face relationship between the male and the female. Right?"

"Exactly right, Mack." Jesus looked at him and grinned. "Our desire was to create a being that had a fully equal and powerful counterpart, the male and the female. But your independence with its quest for power and fulfillment actually destroys the relationship your heart longs for."

"There it is again," Mack said, sifting through the rocks to find the flattest stone. "It always comes back to power and how opposite that is from the relationship you have with the other two. I'd love to experience that, with you and with Nan."

"That's why we're here."

"I wish she were too."

"Oh, what could have been," Jesus mused.

Mack had no idea what he meant.

They were quiet for a few minutes, except for some grunting as rocks were thrown and the sounds they made skipping across the water.

Jesus stopped just as he was about to throw a rock. "One last thing that I want you to remember about this conversation, Mack, before you go." He tossed the rock.

Mack looked up, surprised. "Before I go?"

Jesus ignored his question. "Mack, just like love, submission is not something that you can do, especially not on your own. Apart from my life inside you, you can't submit to Nan, or your children, or anyone else in your life, including Papa."

"You mean," Mack quipped, "that I can't just ask, 'What would Jesus do?'"

Jesus chuckled. "Good intentions; bad idea. Let me know how it works for you, if that's the way you choose to go." He paused and grew sober. "Seriously, my life was not meant to be an example to copy. Being my follower is not trying to 'be like Jesus,' it means your independence is killed. I came to give you life, real life, my life. We will come and live our life inside you, so that you begin to see with our eyes, and hear with our ears, and touch with our hands, and think like we do. But we will never force that union on you. If you want to do your thing, have at it. Time is on our side."

"This must be the dying daily that Sarayu was talking about," said Mack and nodded.

"Speaking of time," said Jesus, turning and pointing at

the path that led into the forest at the end of the clearing, "you have an engagement. Follow that path and enter where it ends. I'll wait for you here."

As much as he wanted to, Mack knew that it would be no use to try to continue the conversation. In thoughtful silence he put on his socks and shoes. They were not totally dry by this time, but not too uncomfortable. Standing up without another word, he squished his way toward the end of the beach, stopped for a minute to look once more at the waterfall, jumped over the little brook, and entered the woods to find a well-maintained and marked path.

11

HERE COME DA JUDGE

Whoever undertakes to set himself up as a judge of Truth and Knowledge
is shipwrecked by the laughter of the gods.

—Albert Einstein

Oh my soul . . . be prepared for him
who knows how to ask questions.

—T. S. Eliot

Mack followed the trail that wound past the waterfall, away from the lake, and through a dense patch of cedar trees. It took less than five minutes to reach an impasse. The path took him directly to a rock face, the faint outline of a door barely visible on the surface. Obviously he was meant to enter, so he hesitantly reached out and pushed. His hand simply penetrated the wall as if it weren't there. Mack continued to move cautiously forward until his entire body passed through what appeared to be the solid stone exterior of the mountain. It was thick black within and he could see nothing.

Taking a deep breath and with his hands outstretched in front of him, he ventured a couple of small steps into the inky darkness and stopped. Fear seized him as he tried to breathe, unsure whether or not to continue. As his stomach clenched he felt it again: *The Great Sadness* settling on his shoulders with its full weight, almost suffocating him. He desperately wanted to back out into the light, but in the end he believed that Jesus would not have sent him in here without a good purpose. He pressed in farther.

Slowly his eyes recovered from the shock of moving from daylight into such deep shadows, and a minute later they adjusted enough to make out a single passageway curving off to his left. As he followed it, the brightness at the entrance behind him faded and was replaced by a faint luminosity reflecting off the walls from somewhere ahead.

Within a hundred feet, the tunnel turned abruptly to his left and Mack found himself standing at the edge of what he assumed was a huge cavern, although initially it seemed to be only a vast empty space. The illusion was magnified by the only light present, a dim radiance that encircled him but dissipated within ten feet in every direction. Beyond that he could see nothing, only inky blackness. The air in the place felt heavy and oppressive, with an attending chill that fought to take his breath away. He looked down and was relieved to see a faint reflection off a surface—not the dirt and rock of the tunnel, but a floor, smooth and dark like polished mica.

Bravely taking a step forward, he noticed that the light-circle moved with him, illuminating a little more of the area ahead. Feeling more confident, he began to slowly and deliberately walk in the direction he had been facing, focusing on the floor for fear it might at any moment drop away beneath him. He was so intent on watching his feet that Mack blundered into an object in front of him and almost fell.

It was a chair, a comfortable-looking wooden chair in the middle of . . . nothing. Mack quickly decided to sit and wait. As he did, the light that had assisted him continued to move forward as if he had kept walking. Directly in front of him, he now could make out an ebony desk of considerable size, completely bare. And then he jumped when the light coalesced on one spot, and he finally saw *her*. Behind the desk sat a tall, beautiful, olive-skinned woman with chiseled Hispanic features, clothed in a dark-colored flowing robe. She sat as straight and regal as a high court judge. She was stunning.

She is *beauty*, he thought. *Everything that sensuality strives to be, but falls painfully short.* In the dim light it was difficult to see where her face began, as her hair and robe framed and merged into her visage. Her eyes glinted and glistened as if they were portals into the vastness of the starry night sky, reflecting some unknown light source within her.

He dared not speak, afraid that his voice would simply be swallowed up in the intensity of the room's focus on her. He thought, *I'm Mickey Mouse about to speak to Pavarotti.* The thought made him smile. As if somehow sharing a simple delight in the grotesqueness of that image, she smiled back, and the place noticeably brightened. That was all it took for Mack to understand that he was expected and welcomed here. She looked strangely familiar, as if he might have known or glimpsed her somewhere in the past, only he knew that he had never truly seen or met her before.

"May I ask . . . If I may . . . I mean, who are you?" Mack fumbled, his voice sounding every bit to him like Mickey's, barely leaving an impression on the stillness of the room but then lingering like the shadow of an echo.

She ignored his query. "Do you understand why you are here?" Like a breeze sweeping away the dust, her voice gently ushered his question out of the room.

Mack could almost feel her words rain down on his head and melt into his spine, sending delicious tingles everywhere. He shivered and decided that he never wanted to speak again. He only wanted her to talk, to speak to him or to anyone, just as long as he could be present. But she waited.

"*You* know," he said quietly, his own voice suddenly so rich and resonant that Mack was tempted to look behind him to see who had spoken. Somehow he knew that what he had said was the truth . . . it simply sounded like it. "I have no idea," he added, fumbling again and turning his gaze toward the floor. "No one told me."

"Well, Mackenzie Allen Phillips," she said with a laugh, causing him to look up quickly, "I am here to help you."

If a rainbow makes a sound, or a flower as it grows, that was the sound of her laughter. It was a shower of light, an invitation to talk, and Mack chuckled along with her, not even knowing or caring why.

Soon again there was silence and her face, though remaining soft, took on a fiery intensity, as if she was able to peer deep inside of him, past the pretenses and facades, down to the places that are rarely, if ever, spoken of.

"Today is a very serious day with very serious consequences." She paused, as if to add weight to her already tangibly heavy words. "Mackenzie, you are here, in part, because of your children, but you are also here for—"

"My children?" Mack interrupted. "What do you mean, I'm here because of my children?"

"Mackenzie, you love your children in a way that your own father was never able to love you and your sisters."

"Of course I love my children. Every parent loves their children," Mack asserted. "But why does that have anything to do with why I'm here?"

"In some sense every parent does love their children," she responded, ignoring his second question. "But some parents are too broken to love them well and others are barely able to love them at all; you should understand that. But you, you do love your children well—very well."

"I learned much of that from Nan."

"We know. But you did learn, didn't you?"

"I suppose I did."

"Among the mysteries of a broken humanity, that too is rather remarkable: to learn, to allow change." She was as calm as a windless sea. "So then, Mackenzie, may I ask which of your children you love the most?"

Mack smiled inside. As the kids had come along, he had wrestled to answer this very question. "I don't love any one of them more than any of the others. I love each of them differently," he said, choosing his words carefully.

"Explain that to me, Mackenzie," she said with interest.

"Well, each one of my children is unique. And that uniqueness and special personhood calls out a unique response from me." Mack settled back into his chair. "I remember after Jon, my first, was born. I was so captivated by the wonder of who this little life was that I actually worried about whether I would have anything left to love a second child with. But when Tyler came along, it was as if he brought with him a special gift for me, a whole new capacity to love him specially. Come to think of it, it's like when Papa says she is especially fond of someone. When I think of each of my children individually, I find that I am especially fond of each one."

"Well said, Mackenzie!" Her appreciation was tangible, but then she leaned forward slightly, her tone still soft but serious. "But what about when they do not behave, or they make choices other than those you would want them to make, or they are just belligerent and rude? What about when they embarrass you in front of others? How does that affect your love for them?"

Mack responded slowly and deliberately, "It doesn't, really." He knew that what he was saying was true, even if Katie didn't believe it sometimes. "I admit that it does affect me and sometimes I get embarrassed or angry, but even when they act badly, they are still my sons and my daughter, they are still Josh and Kate, and they will be forever. What they do might affect my pride, but not my love for them."

She sat back, beaming. "You are wise in the ways of real love, Mackenzie. So many believe that it is love that grows, but it is the *knowing* that grows and love simply expands to contain it. Love is just the skin of knowing. Mackenzie, you love your children, whom you know so well, with a wonderful and real love."

A little embarrassed at her praise, Mack looked down. "Well, thanks, but I'm not that way with very many other people. My love tends to be pretty conditional most of the time."

"But it's a start, isn't it, Mackenzie? And you didn't move beyond your father's inability on your own—it was God and you together who changed you to love this way. And now you love your children much the way Father loves his."

Mack could feel his jaw involuntarily clench as he listened, and he felt the anger once more begin to rise. What should have been a reassuring commendation seemed more like a bitter pill that he now refused to swallow. He tried to relax to cover his emotions, but by the look in her eyes, he knew it was too late.

"Hmmmm," she mused. "Something I said bother you, Mackenzie?"

Her gaze now made him uncomfortable. He felt exposed.

"Mackenzie," she encouraged, "is there something you would like to say?"

The silence left by her question now hung in the air. Mack struggled to retain his composure. He could hear his mother's advice ringing in his ears: "If you don't have anything nice to say, better to not speak at all."

"Uh . . . well, no! Not really."

"Mackenzie," she prompted, "this is not a time for your mother's common sense. This is a time for honesty, for truth. You don't believe that Father loves his children very well, do you? You don't truly believe that God is good, do you?"

"Is Missy his child?" Mack snapped.

"Of course!" she answered.

"Then no!" he blurted, rising to his feet. "I don't believe that God loves all of his children very well!"

He had said it, and now his accusation echoed off whatever walls surrounded the chamber. While Mack stood there, angry and ready to explode, the woman remained calm and unchanging in her demeanor. Slowly she rose from her high-backed chair, moving silently behind it and motioning him toward it. "Why don't you sit here?"

"Is that what honesty gets you, the hot seat?" he muttered, but he didn't move, he simply stared back at her.

"Mackenzie." She remained standing behind her chair. "Earlier I began to tell you why you are here today. Not only are you here because of your children, but you are here for judgment."

As the word echoed in the chamber, panic rose inside Mack like a swelling tide and slowly he sank into his chair. Instantly he felt guilty as memories spilled through his mind like rats fleeing the rising flood. He gripped the arms of his chair, trying to find some balance in the onslaught of images and emotions. His failures as a human being suddenly loomed large, and in the back of his mind he could almost hear a voice intoning his catalog of sins, his dread deepening as the list grew longer and longer. He had no defense. He was lost and he knew it.

"Mackenzie—" she began, only to be interrupted.

"Now I understand. I'm dead, aren't I? That's why I can see Jesus and Papa, 'cause I'm dead." He sat back and looked up into the darkness, feeling sick to his stomach. "I can't believe it! I didn't even feel anything." He looked at the woman who patiently watched him. "How long have I been dead?" he asked.

"Mackenzie," she began, "I am sorry to disappoint you, but you have not yet fallen asleep in your world, and I believe that you have mis—"

Again, Mack cut her off. "I'm not dead?" Now he was incredulous and rose again to his feet. "You mean all this is real and I'm still alive? But I thought you said I came here for judgment."

"I did," she stated matter-of-factly, a look of amusement on her face. "But Macken—"

"Judgment? And I'm not even dead?" A third time he stopped her, processing what he'd heard, anger replacing his panic. "This hardly seems fair!" He knew his emotions were not helping. "Does this happen to other people—getting judged, I mean, before they're even dead? What if I change? What if I do better the rest of my life? What if I repent? What then?"

"Is there something you wish to repent of, Mackenzie?" she asked, unfazed by his outburst.

Mack slowly sat back down. He looked at the smooth surface of the floor and then shook his head before answering. "I wouldn't know where to begin," he mumbled. "I'm quite a mess, aren't I?"

"Yes, you are." Mack looked up and she smiled back. "You are a glorious, destructive mess, Mackenzie, but you are not here to repent, at least not in the way you understand. Mackenzie, you are not here to be judged."

"But," he said, "I thought you said that I was . . ."

"Here for judgment?" She remained cool and placid as a summer breeze as she finished his question. "I did. But *you* are not on trial here."

Mack took a deep breath, relieved at her words.

"*You* will be the judge!"

The knot in his stomach returned as he realized what she had said. Finally, he dropped his eyes to the chair that stood waiting for him. "What? Me? I'd rather not." He paused. "I don't have any ability to judge."

"Oh, that is not true," returned the quick reply, tinged now with a hint of sarcasm. "You have already proven yourself very capable, even in our short time together. And besides, you have judged many throughout your life. You have judged the actions and even the motivations of others, as if you somehow knew what those were in truth. You have judged the color of skin and body language and body odor. You have judged history and relationships. You have even judged the value of a person's life by the quality of your concept of beauty. By all accounts, you are quite well practiced in the activity."

Mack felt shame reddening his face. He had to admit he had done an awful lot of judging in his time. But he was no different from anyone else, was he? Who doesn't jump to conclusions about others from the way they impact us? There it was again—his self-centered view of the world

From left to right: Nan Phillips (Radha Mitchell), Mack Phillips (Sam Worthington), Missy Phillips (Amelie Eve), Josh Phillips (Gage Munroe), and Kate Phillips (Megan Charpentier) in THE SHACK. *Motion Picture Artwork © 2016 Summit Entertainment, LLC. All Rights Reserved. Credit: Jake Giles Netter.*

Mack Phillips (Sam Worthington, left), Missy Phillips (Amelie Eve, center), and Kate Phillips (Megan Charpentier, right) in THE SHACK. *Motion Picture Artwork © 2016 Summit Entertainment, LLC. All Rights Reserved. Credit: Jake Giles Netter.*

Mack Phillips (Sam Worthington) and Missy Phillips (Amelie Eve) in THE SHACK. *Motion Picture Artwork © 2016 Summit Entertainment, LLC. All Rights Reserved. Credit: Jake Giles Netter.*

Amelie Eve stars as Missy Phillips in THE SHACK. *Motion Picture Artwork © 2016 Summit Entertainment, LLC. All Rights Reserved. Credit: Jake Giles Netter.*

Sam Worthington stars as Mack Phillips in THE SHACK. *Motion Picture Artwork © 2016 Summit Entertainment, LLC. All Rights Reserved. Credit: Jake Giles Netter.*

Tim McGraw stars as Willie in THE SHACK. *Motion Picture Artwork © 2016 Summit Entertainment, LLC. All Rights Reserved. Credit: Jake Giles Netter.*

Radha Mitchell stars as Nan Phillips in THE SHACK. *Motion Picture Artwork © 2016 Summit Entertainment, LLC. All Rights Reserved. Credit: Jake Giles Netter.*

Papa (Octavia Spencer) and Young Mack Phillips (Carson Reaume) in THE SHACK. *Motion Picture Artwork © 2016 Summit Entertainment, LLC. All Rights Reserved. Credit: Jake Giles Netter.*

Mack Phillips (Sam Worthington, left) and Jesus (Avraham Aviv Alush, right) in THE SHACK. *Motion Picture Artwork © 2016 Summit Entertainment, LLC. All Rights Reserved. Credit: Jake Giles Netter.*

Octavia Spencer stars as Papa in THE SHACK. *Motion Picture Artwork © 2016 Summit Entertainment, LLC. All Rights Reserved. Credit: Jake Giles Netter.*

Sumire stars as Sarayu in THE SHACK. *Motion Picture Artwork © 2016 Summit Entertainment, LLC. All Rights Reserved. Credit: Jake Giles Netter.*

Mack Phillips (Sam Worthington) and Papa (Octavia Spencer) in THE SHACK. *Motion Picture Artwork © 2016 Summit Entertainment, LLC. All Rights Reserved. Credit: Jake Giles Netter.*

Avraham Aviv Alush stars as Jesus in THE SHACK. *Motion Picture Artwork © 2016 Summit Entertainment, LLC. All Rights Reserved. Credit: Jake Giles Netter.*

Papa (Octavia Spencer) and Mack Phillips (Sam Worthington) in THE SHACK. *Motion Picture Artwork © 2016 Summit Entertainment, LLC. All Rights Reserved. Credit: Jake Giles Netter.*

Josh Phillips (Gage Monroe, left), Sophia (Alice Braga, center), and Kate Phillips (Megan Charpentier, right) in THE SHACK. *Motion Picture Artwork © 2016 Summit Entertainment, LLC. All Rights Reserved. Credit: Jake Giles Netter.*

Nan Phillips (Radha Mitchell) and Mack Phillips (Sam Worthington) in THE SHACK. *Motion Picture Artwork © 2016 Summit Entertainment, LLC. All Rights Reserved. Credit: Jake Giles Netter.*

around him. He looked up and saw her peering intently at him and quickly looked down again.

"Tell me," she inquired, "if I may ask, on what criteria do you base your judgments?"

Mack looked up and tried to meet her gaze but found that when he looked directly at her, his thinking wavered. To peer into her eyes and keep a train of coherent and logical thought seemed impossible. He had to look away and into the darkness of the corner of the room, hoping to collect himself.

"Nothing that seems to make much sense at the moment," he finally admitted, his voice faltering. "I confess that when I made those judgments I felt quite justified, but now . . ."

"Of course you did." She said it like a statement of fact, like something routine, not playing for even a moment upon his evident shame and distress. "Judging requires that you think yourself superior over the one you judge. Well, today you will be given the opportunity to put all your ability to use. Come on," she said, patting the back of the chair. "I want you to sit here. Now."

Hesitantly but obediently he walked toward her and the waiting chair. With each step he seemed to grow smaller or they both grew larger, he couldn't tell which. He crawled up on the chair and felt childish with the massive desktop in front of him and his feet barely touching the floor. "And . . . just what will I be judging?" he asked, turning to look up at her.

"Not what." She paused and moved to the side of the desk. "Whom."

His discomfort was growing in leaps and bounds, and sitting in an oversized, regal chair didn't help. What right did he have to judge anyone? Sure, in some measure he probably was guilty of judging almost everyone he had met and many he had not. Mack knew he was thoroughly guilty of being self-centered. How dare *he* judge anyone else? All his judgments had been superficial, based on appearance and actions, things easily interpreted by whatever state of mind or prejudice supported the need to exalt himself, to feel safe, or to belong. He also knew that he was starting to panic.

"Your imagination," she said, interrupting his train of thought, "is not serving you well at this moment."

No kidding, Sherlock, is what he thought, but all that came out of his mouth was a weak "I really can't do this."

"Whether you can or cannot is yet to be determined," she said with a smile. "And my name is not Sherlock."

Mack was grateful for the darkened room that hid his embarrassment. The silence that followed seemed to hold him captive for much longer than the few seconds it actually took to find his voice and finally ask the question: "So, who is it that I am supposed to judge?"

"God"—she paused—"and the human race." She said it as if it was of no particular consequence. The words simply rolled off her tongue, as if this were a daily occurrence.

Mack was dumbfounded. "You have got to be kidding!" he exclaimed.

"Why not? Surely there are many people in your world you think deserve judgment. There must be at least a few who are to blame for so much of the pain and suffering. What about the greedy who feed off the poor of the world? What about the ones who sacrifice their young children to war? What about the men who beat their wives, Mackenzie? What about the fathers who beat their sons for no reason but to assuage their own suffering? Don't they deserve judgment, Mackenzie?"

Mack could sense the depths of his unresolved anger rising like a flood of fury. He sank back into the chair, trying to maintain his balance against an onslaught of images, but he could feel his control ebbing away. His stomach knotted as he clenched his fists, his breathing coming short and quick.

"And what about the man who preys on innocent little girls? What about him, Mackenzie? Is that man guilty? Should he be judged?"

"Yes!" screamed Mack. "Damn him to hell!"

"Is he to blame for your loss?"

"Yes!"

"What about his father, the man who twisted his son into a terror, what about him?"

"Yes, him too!"

"How far do we go back, Mackenzie? This legacy of brokenness goes all the way back to Adam—what about him? But why stop there? What about God? God started this whole thing. Is God to blame?"

Mack was reeling. He didn't feel like a judge at all, but rather the one on trial.

The woman was unrelenting. "Isn't this where you are stuck, Mackenzie? Isn't this what fuels *The Great Sadness*? That God cannot be trusted? Surely, a father like you can judge *the* Father!"

Again his anger rose like a towering flame. He wanted to lash out, but she was right and there was no point in denying it.

She continued, "Isn't that your just complaint, Mackenzie? That God has failed you, that he failed Missy? That before the creation, God knew that one day your Missy would be brutalized, and still he created? And then he *allowed* that twisted soul to snatch her from your loving arms when he had the power to stop him. Isn't God to blame, Mackenzie?"

Mack was looking at the floor, a flurry of images pulling his emotions in every direction. Finally he said it, louder than he intended, and pointed his finger right at her: "Yes! God is to blame!" The accusation hung in the room as the gavel fell in his heart.

"Then," she said with finality, "if you are able to judge God so easily, you certainly can judge the world." Again she spoke without emotion. "You must choose two of your children to spend eternity in God's new heavens and new earth, but only two."

"What?" he erupted, turning to her in disbelief.

"And you must choose three of your children to spend eternity in hell."

Mack couldn't believe what he was hearing and started to panic.

"Mackenzie." Her voice now came as calm and wonderful as he had first heard it. "I am only asking you to do something that you believe God does. He knows every person ever conceived, and he knows them so much more deeply and clearly than you will ever know your own children. He loves each one according to his knowledge of the being of that son or daughter. You believe he will condemn most to an eternity of torment, away from his presence and apart from his love. Is that not true?"

"I suppose I do. I've just never thought about it like this." He was stumbling over his words in his shock. "I just assumed that somehow God could do that. Talking about hell was always sort of an abstract conversation, not about anyone that I truly . . ." Mack hesitated, realizing that what he was about to say would sound ugly. "Not about anyone that I truly cared about."

"So you suppose, then, that God does this easily, but you cannot? Come now, Mackenzie. Which three of your five children will you sentence to hell? Katie is struggling with you the most right now. She treats you badly and has said hurtful things to you. Perhaps she is the first and most logical choice. What about her? You are the judge, Mackenzie, and you must choose."

"I don't want to be the judge," he said, standing up. Mack's mind was racing. This couldn't be real. How could God ask him to choose among his own children? There was no way he could sentence Katie, or any of his other children, to an eternity in hell just because she had sinned against him. Even if Katie or Josh or Jon or Tyler committed some heinous crime, he still wouldn't do it. He couldn't! For him, it wasn't about their performance; it was about his love for them.

"I can't do this," he said softly.

"You must," she replied.

"I can't do this," he said louder and more vehemently.

"You must," she said again, her voice softer.

"I . . . will . . . not . . . do . . . this!" Mack yelled, his blood boiling hot inside him.

"You must," she whispered.

"I can't. I can't. I won't!" he screamed, and now the words and emotions came tumbling out. The woman just stood watching and waiting. Finally he looked at her, pleading with his eyes. "Could I go instead? If you need someone to torture for eternity, I'll go in their place. Would that work? Could I do that?" He fell at her feet, crying and begging now. "Please let me go for my children. Please, I would be happy to . . . Please, I am begging you. Please . . . Please . . ."

"Mackenzie, Mackenzie," she whispered, and her words came like a splash of cool water on a brutally hot day. Her hands gently touched his cheeks as she lifted him to his feet. Looking at her through blurring tears, he could see that her smile was radiant. "Now you sound like Jesus. You have judged well, Mackenzie. I am so proud of you!"

"But I haven't judged anything," Mack offered in confusion.

"Oh, but you have. You have judged them worthy of love, even if it costs you everything. That is how Jesus loves." When he heard the words he thought of his new friend waiting by the lake. "And now you know Papa's heart," she added, "who loves all her children perfectly."

Immediately Missy's image flashed in his mind and he found himself bristling. Without thinking he lifted himself back onto the chair.

"What just happened, Mackenzie?" she asked.

He saw no use in trying to hide it. "I understand Jesus' love, but God is another story. I don't find them to be alike at all."

"You haven't enjoyed your time with Papa?" she asked, surprised.

"No, I love Papa, whoever she is. She's amazing, but she's not anything like the God I've known."

"Maybe your understanding of God is wrong."

"Maybe. I just don't see how God loved Missy perfectly."

"So the judgment continues?" she said with a sadness in her voice.

That made Mack pause, but only for a moment. "What am I supposed to think? I just don't understand how God could love Missy and let her go through that horror. She was innocent. She didn't do anything to deserve that."

"I know."

Mack continued, "Did God use her to punish me for what I did to my father? That isn't fair. She didn't deserve this. Nan didn't deserve this." Tears streamed down his face. "I might have, but they didn't."

"Is that who your God is, Mackenzie? It is no wonder you are drowning in your sorrow. Papa isn't like that, Mackenzie. She's not punishing you, or Missy, or Nan. This was not her doing."

"But she didn't stop it."

"No, she didn't. She doesn't stop a lot of things that cause her pain. Your world is severely broken. You demanded your independence, and now you are angry with the One who loved you enough to give it to you. Nothing is as it should be, as Papa desires it to be, and as it will be one day. Right now your world is lost in darkness and chaos, and horrible things happen to those she is especially fond of."

"Then why doesn't she do something about it?"

"She already has . . ."

"You mean what Jesus did?"

"Haven't you seen the wounds on Papa too?"

"I didn't understand them. How could she . . ."

"For love. She chose the way of the cross, where mercy triumphs over justice because of love. Would you instead prefer she'd chosen justice for everyone? Do you want justice, 'Dear Judge'?" And she smiled as she said it.

"No, I don't," he said as he lowered his head. "Not for me, and not for my children."

She waited.

"But I still don't understand why Missy had to die."

"She didn't have to, Mackenzie. This was no plan of Papa's. Papa has never needed evil to accomplish her good purposes. It is you humans who have embraced evil, and Papa has responded with goodness. What happened to Missy was the work of evil, and no one in your world is immune from it."

"But it hurts so much. There must be a better way."

"There is. You just can't see it now. Return from your independence, Mackenzie. Give up being her judge and know Papa for who she is. Then you will be able to embrace her love in the midst of your pain, instead of pushing her away with your self-centered perception of how you think the universe should be. Papa has crawled inside of your world to be with you, to be with Missy."

Mack stood up from the chair. "I don't want to be a judge anymore. I really do want to trust Papa." Unnoticed by Mack, the room lightened yet again as he moved around the table toward the simple chair where it all began. "But I'll need help."

She reached out and hugged Mack. "Now that sounds like the start of the trip home, Mackenzie. It certainly does."

The quiet of the cavern was suddenly broken by the sound of children's laughter. It seemed to be coming through one of the walls, which Mack could now clearly see as the room continued to brighten. As he stared in that direction, the stone surface grew increasingly translucent and daylight filtered into the cave. Startled, Mack peered through the haze and finally could make out the vague shapes of children playing in the distance.

"Those sound like *my* kids!" Mack exclaimed, his mouth open in astonishment. Moving to the wall, the mist parted as if someone had drawn a curtain, and he was unexpectedly looking out across a meadow, back toward the lake. In front of him loomed the backdrop of high snow-covered mountains,

perfect in their majesty, dressed in heavily wooded forests.
And nestled at their feet, he could clearly see the shack,
where he knew Papa and Sarayu would be waiting for him.
A large stream tumbled out of nowhere directly in front of
him and flowed into the lake alongside fields of high country
flowers and grasses. The sounds of birds were everywhere
and the sweet scent of summer hung rich in the air.

All this Mack saw, heard, and smelled in an instant, but
then his gaze was drawn to movement, to the group playing
along an eddy near where the stream flowed into the lake less
than fifty yards away. He saw his children there—Jon, Tyler,
Josh, and Kate. But wait! There was another!

He gasped, trying to focus more intently. Moving
toward them, he pushed up against an unseen force as if
the stone wall were still invisibly in front of him. Then it
became clear. "Missy!" There she was, kicking her bare feet
in the water. As if she heard him, Missy broke from the group
and came running down the trail that ended directly in front
of him.

"Oh, my God! Missy!" he yelled and tried to move forward, through the veil that held them separate. To his con-
sternation, he ran into a power that would not allow him
to get closer, as if some magnetic force increased in direct
opposition to his effort, deflecting him back into the room.

"She cannot hear you."

Mack didn't care. "Missy!" he screamed. She was so close.
The memory that he had been trying so hard not to lose but
had felt slowly slipping away now snapped back. He looked
for some kind of handhold, as if he could pry whatever it was
open and find some way to get through to his daughter. But
there was nothing.

Meanwhile, Missy had arrived and stood directly in front
of him. Her gaze was clearly not at him, but at something
that was in between, larger and obviously visible to her but
not to him.

Mack finally quit fighting the force field and half turned

to the woman. "Can she see me? Does she know that I'm here?" he asked desperately.

"She knows that you are here, but she cannot see you. From her side, she is looking at the beautiful waterfall and nothing more. But she knows you are behind it."

"Waterfalls!" Mack exclaimed, laughing to himself. "She just can't get enough of waterfalls!" Now Mack focused on her, trying to memorize again every detail of her expression and hair and hands. As he did so, Missy's face erupted in a huge smile, dimples standing out. In slow motion, with great exaggeration, he could see her mouth the words, "It's okay, I"—and now she signed the words—"love you."

It was too much and Mack wept for joy. Still he couldn't stop looking at her, watching her through his own cascading waterfall. To be this close again was painful, to see her standing in that Missy way, with one leg forward and a hand on her hip, wrist inward. "She's really okay, isn't she?"

"More than you know. This life is only the anteroom of a greater reality to come. No one reaches their potential in your world. It's only preparation for what Papa had in mind all along."

"Can I get to her? Maybe just one hug, and a kiss?" he begged quietly.

"No. This is the way she wanted it."

"She wanted it this way?" Mack was confused.

"Yes. She is a very wise child, our Missy. I am especially fond of her."

"Are you sure she knows I am here?"

"Yes, I am sure," she assured Mack. "She has been very excited for this day, to play with her brothers and sister, and to be near you. She very much would have liked her mother to be here too, but that will wait for another time."

Mack turned toward the woman. "Are my other children really here?"

"They are here, but they aren't. Only Missy is truly here. The others are dreaming, and each will have a vague memory of this—some in greater detail than others, but none fully or completely. This is a very peaceful time of sleep for each of them, except Kate. This dream will not be easy for her. Missy, though, is fully awake."

Mack watched every move his precious Missy was making. "Has she forgiven me?" he asked.

"Forgiven you for what?"

"I failed her," he whispered.

"It would be her nature to forgive, if there were anything to forgive, which there is not."

"But I didn't stop him from taking her. He took her while I wasn't paying attention . . ." His voice trailed off.

"If you remember, you were saving your son. Only you, in the entire universe, believe that somehow you are to blame. Missy doesn't believe that, neither does Nan or Papa. Perhaps it's time to let that go—that lie. And Mackenzie, even if you had been to blame, her love is much stronger than your fault could ever be."

Just then someone called Missy's name and Mack recognized the voice. She shrieked with delight and started to run back toward the others. Abruptly she stopped and ran back to her daddy. She made a big embrace as if she were hugging him and, with eyes closed, exaggerated a kiss. From behind the barrier he hugged her back. For a moment she stood completely still, as if knowing she was giving him a gift for his memory, waved, turned, and raced back to the others.

And now Mack could clearly see the voice that had called his Missy. It was Jesus, playing in the middle of his children. Without hesitation Missy leaped into his arms. He swung her around twice before putting her back on her feet, and then everyone laughed before hunting for smooth stones to skip across the surface of the lake. The voicing of their joy was a symphony to Mack's ears, and as he watched, his tears flowed freely.

Suddenly, without warning, water roared down from above, directly in front of him, and obliterated all the sights and sounds of his children. Instinctively, he jumped back. He now realized that the walls of the cave had dissolved around him, and he was standing in a grotto behind the waterfall.

Mack felt the woman's hands on his shoulders.

"Is it over?" he asked.

"For now," she replied tenderly. "Mackenzie, judgment is not about destruction, but about setting things right."

Mack smiled. "I don't feel stuck anymore."

She steered him gently toward the side of the waterfall until he could once again see Jesus on the shore, still skipping stones. "I think someone is waiting for you."

Her hands softly squeezed and then left his shoulders, and Mack knew without looking that she was gone. After carefully climbing over slippery boulders and across wet rocks, he found a way around the edge of the falls, then through the refreshing mist of tumbling water and back into daylight.

Exhausted but deeply fulfilled, Mack paused and closed his eyes for a moment, trying to etch the details of Missy's presence indelibly into his mind, hoping that in the days to come he would be able to bring back every moment with her, every nuance and movement.

And suddenly he missed Nan so very, very much.

12

IN THE BELLY OF THE BEASTS

*Men never do evil so completely and cheerfully
as when they do it from religious conviction.*

—Blaise Pascal

Once abolish the God and the government becomes the God.

—G. K. Chesterton

As Mack made his way down the trail toward the lake, he suddenly realized that something was missing. His constant companion, *The Great Sadness*, was gone. It was as if it had been washed away in the mists of the water- fall as he emerged from behind its curtain. Its absence felt odd, perhaps even uncomfortable. For the past years it had defined for him what was normal, but now, unexpectedly, it had vanished. *Normal is a myth*, he thought to himself.

The Great Sadness would not be part of his identity any longer. He knew now that Missy wouldn't care if he refused to put it on. In fact, she wouldn't want him to huddle in that shroud and would likely grieve for him if he did. He won- dered who he would be now that he was letting all that go— to walk into each day without the guilt and despair that had sucked the colors of life out of everything.

As he entered the clearing, he saw Jesus still waiting, still skipping stones.

"Hey, I think my best was thirteen skips," he said as he laughed and walked to meet Mack. "But Tyler beat me by three and Josh threw one that skipped so fast we all lost count." As they hugged, Jesus added, "You have special kids, Mack. You and Nan have loved them very well. Kate is struggling, as you know, but we're not done there."

The very ease and intimacy with which Jesus talked about his children touched him deeply. "Then they're gone?"

Jesus pulled back and nodded. "Yes, back to their dreams, except Missy, of course."

"Is she . . . ?" Mack began.

"She was overjoyed to have been this close to you, and she's thrilled knowing you are better."

Mack struggled to maintain his composure. Jesus understood and changed the subject.

"So, how was your time with Sophia?"

"Sophia? Ahh, so that's who she is!" exclaimed Mack. Then a perplexed look came across his face. "But doesn't that make four of you? Is she God too?"

Jesus laughed. "No, Mack. There are only three of us. Sophia is a personification of Papa's wisdom."

"Oh, like in Proverbs, where wisdom is pictured as a woman calling out in the streets, trying to find anyone who'll listen to her?"

"That's her."

"But"—Mack paused as he bent to untie the laces of his shoes—"she seemed so real."

"Oh, she's quite real," responded Jesus. He then looked around as if to see if anyone was watching and whispered, "She's part of the mystery surrounding Sarayu."

"I love Sarayu," Mack exclaimed as he stood, somewhat surprised at his own transparency.

"Me too!" Jesus stated with emphasis. They walked back to the shore and silently stood looking across at the shack.

"It was terrible and it was wonderful, my time with Sophia." Mack finally answered the question Jesus had asked earlier. He suddenly realized that the sun was still high in the sky. "Exactly how long have I been gone?"

"It's been less than fifteen minutes, so not long," Jesus replied. At Mack's look of bewilderment, he added, "Time with Sophia is not like normal time."

"Huh," grunted Mack. "I doubt if anything with her is normal."

"Actually"—Jesus started to speak but paused to throw one last skipping stone—"with her, everything is normal and elegantly simple. Because you are so lost and independent you bring to her many complications, and as a result you find even her simplicity profound."

"So, I'm complex and she's simple. Whew! My world *is* upside down." Mack had already sat down on a log and was taking off his shoes and socks for the walk back. "Can you tell me this? Here it is the middle of the day, and my children were here in their dreams? How does that work? Is any of this real? Or am I just dreaming too?"

Again Jesus laughed. "As far as how all this works? Don't ask, Mack. It's a little heady—something to do with time-dimensional coupling. More of Sarayu's stuff. Time, as you know it, presents no boundaries to the One who created it. You can ask her, if you like."

"Nah, I think I'll wait on that one. I was just curious." He chuckled.

"But as for 'Is any of this real?' Far more real than you can imagine." Jesus paused for a moment to get Mack's full attention. "A better question might be, 'What is real?'"

"I'm beginning to think that I have no idea," Mack offered.

"Would all this be any less 'real' if it were inside a dream?"

"I think I'd be disappointed."

"Why? Mack, there is far more going on here than you have the ability to perceive. Let me assure you, all of this is very much real, far more real than life as you've known it."

Mack hesitated but then decided to take the risk and ask. "There is one thing still bothering me, about Missy."

Jesus walked over and sat next to him on the log. Mack leaned over and put his elbows on his knees, staring past his hands and down at the pebbles near his feet. Finally he said, "I keep thinking about her, alone in that truck, so terrified . . ."

Jesus reached over and put his hand on Mack's shoulder and squeezed. Gently he said, "Mack, she was never alone. I never left her; we never left her, not for one instant. I could no more abandon her, or you, than I could abandon myself."

"Did she know you were there?"

"Yes, Mack, she did. Not at first—the fear was overwhelming and she was in shock. It took hours to get up here from the campsite. But as Sarayu wrapped herself around her, Missy settled down. The long ride actually gave us a chance to talk."

Mack was trying to take all of this in. He could no longer speak.

"She may have been only six years old, but Missy and I are friends. We talk. She had no idea what was going to happen. She was actually more worried about you and the other kids, knowing you couldn't find her. She prayed for you, for your peace."

Mack wept, fresh tears rolling down his cheeks. This time, he didn't mind. Jesus gently pulled him into his arms and held him.

"Mack, I don't think you want to know all the details. I'm sure they won't help you. But I can tell you there was not a moment that we were not with her. She knew my peace, and you would have been proud of her. She was so brave!"

The tears flowed freely now, but even Mack noticed this time it was different. He was no longer alone. Without embarrassment he wept onto the shoulder of this man he had grown to love. With each sob he felt the tension drain away, replaced by a deep sense of relief. Finally, he took a deep breath and blew it out as he lifted his head.

Then, without another word, he stood up, slung his shoes over one shoulder, and simply walked into the water.

Although he was a little surprised when his first step found the lake bottom up to his ankles, he didn't care. He stopped, rolled up his pant legs above the knees just to be sure, and took another step into the shockingly cold water. This one took him up to midcalf, and the next up to just below his knees, his feet still on the lake bottom. He looked back to see Jesus standing on the shore with his arms folded across his chest, watching him.

Mack turned and looked toward the opposite shore. He wasn't sure why it wasn't working this time, but he was determined to press on. Jesus was there, so he had nothing to worry about. The prospect of a long and cold swim was not too thrilling, but Mack was sure he could make it across if he had to.

Thankfully, when he took his next step, instead of going deeper he rose up a little, and with each succeeding stride he came up even more until he was on top of the water once again. Jesus joined him and they both continued walking toward the shack.

"This always works better when we do it together, don't you think?" Jesus asked, smiling.

"Still more to learn, I guess." Mack returned his smile. It didn't matter to him, he realized, whether he had to swim the distance or walk on water, as wonderful as the latter was. What mattered was that Jesus was with him. Perhaps he was beginning to trust him after all, even if it was only in baby steps.

"Thank you for being with me, for talking to me about Missy. I haven't really talked about that with anyone. It just felt so huge and terrifying. It doesn't seem to hold the same power now."

"The darkness hides the true size of fears and lies and regrets," Jesus explained. "The truth is they are more shadow than reality, so they seem bigger in the dark. When the light shines into the places where they live inside you, you start to see them for what they are."

"But why do we keep all that crap inside?" Mack asked.

"Because we believe it's safer there. And, sometimes, when you're a kid trying to survive, it really is safer there. Then you grow up on the outside, but on the inside you're still that kid in the dark cave surrounded by monsters, and out of habit you keep adding to your collection. We all collect things we value, you know?"

This made Mack smile. He knew Jesus was referring to something Sarayu had said about collecting tears. "So, how does that change, you know, for somebody who's lost in the dark like me?"

"Most often, pretty slowly," Jesus answered. "Remember, you can't do it alone. Some folks try with all kinds of coping mechanisms and mental games. But the monsters are still there, just waiting for the chance to come out."

"So what do I do now?"

"What you're already doing, Mack—learning to live loved. It's not an easy concept for humans. You have a hard time sharing anything." He chuckled and continued, "So, yes, what we desire is for you to 're-turn' to us, and then we come and make our home inside you, and then we share. The friendship is real, not merely imagined. We're meant to experience this life, your life, together, in a dialogue, sharing the journey. You get to share in our wisdom and learn to love with our love, and we get . . . to hear you grumble and gripe and complain, and . . ."

Mack laughed out loud and pushed Jesus sideways.

"Stop!" Jesus yelled and froze where he stood. At first Mack thought he might have offended him, but Jesus was looking intently into the water. "Did you see him? Look, here he comes again."

"What?" Mack stepped closer and shielded his eyes to try to see what Jesus was looking at.

"Look! Look!" shouted Jesus in a hushed sort of way. "He's a beauty! Must be almost two feet long!" And then Mack saw him, a huge lake trout gliding by only a foot or two beneath the surface, seemingly oblivious to the commotion he was causing above him.

"I've been trying to catch him for weeks, and here he comes just to bait me," he said with a laugh. Mack watched, amazed, as Jesus started to dodge this way and that, trying to keep up with the fish, and finally gave up. He looked at Mack, excited as a little kid. "Isn't he great? I'll probably never catch him."

Mack was bewildered by the whole scene. "Jesus, why don't you just command him to ... I don't know, jump into your boat or bite your hook? Aren't you the Lord of creation?"

"Sure," said Jesus, leaning down and running his hand over the water. "But what would be the fun in that, eh?" He looked up and grinned.

Mack didn't know whether to laugh or cry. He realized how much he had come to love this man, this man who was also God.

Jesus stood back up and together they continued their meandering toward the dock. Mack ventured another question. "Can I ask, why didn't you tell me about Missy earlier, like last night, or a year ago, or ... ?"

"Don't think we didn't try. Have you noticed that in your pain you assume the worst of me? I've been talking to you for a long time, but today was the first time you could hear it, and all those other times weren't a waste either. Like little cracks in the wall, one at a time but woven together, they prepared you for today. You have to take the time to prepare the soil if you want it to embrace the seed."

"I'm not sure why we resist it, resist *you* so much," Mack mused. "It seems kind of stupid now."

"It's all part of the timing of grace, Mack," Jesus continued. "If the universe contained only one human being, timing would be rather simple. But add just one more, and, well, you know the story. Each choice ripples out through time and relationships, bouncing off other choices. And out of what seems to be a huge mess, Papa weaves a magnificent tapestry. Only Papa can work all this out, and she does it with grace."

"So I guess all I can do is follow her," Mack concluded.

"Yup, that's the point. Now you're beginning to understand what it means to be truly human."

They reached the end of the dock and Jesus leaped up onto it, turning to help Mack. Together they sat down at its end and dangled their bare feet in the water, watching the mesmerizing effects of the wind on the surface of the lake. Mack was the first to break the silence.

"Was I seeing heaven when I was seeing Missy? It looked a lot like here."

"Well, Mack, our final destiny is not the picture of heaven that you have stuck in your head—you know, the image of pearly gates and streets of gold. Instead, it's a new cleansing of this universe, so it will indeed look a lot like here."

"Then what's with the pearly-gates-and-gold stuff?"

"That stuff, my brother," Jesus began, lying back on the dock and closing his eyes against the warmth and brightness of the day, "is a picture of me and the woman I'm in love with."

Mack looked at him to see if he was joking, but it was obvious he wasn't.

"It is a picture of my bride, the church: individuals who together form a spiritual city with a living river flowing through the middle, and on both shores trees growing with fruit that will heal the hurts and sorrows of the nations. And this city is always open, and each gate into it is made of a single pearl . . ." He opened one eye and looked at Mack. "That would be me!" He saw Mack's question and explained, "Pearls, Mack. The only precious stone made by pain, suffering, and—finally—death."

"I get it. You are the way in, but—" Mack paused, searching for the right words. "You're talking about the church as this woman you're in love with; I'm pretty sure I haven't met her." He turned away slightly. "She's not the place I go on Sundays," Mack said, more to himself than to Jesus, unsure if that was safe to say out loud.

"Mack, that's because you're seeing only the institution, a man-made system. That's not what I came to build. What I see are people and their lives, a living, breathing community of all those who love me, not buildings and programs."

Mack was a bit taken aback to hear Jesus talking about church this way, but then again, it didn't really surprise him. It was a relief. "So how do I become part of that church?" he asked. "This woman you seem to be so gaga over."

"It's simple, Mack. It's all about relationships and simply sharing life. What we are doing right now—just doing this—and being open and available to others around us. My church is all about people, and life is all about relationships. *You* can't build it. It's my job, and I'm actually pretty good at it," Jesus said with a chuckle.

For Mack these words were like a breath of fresh air! Simple. Not a bunch of exhausting work and a long list of demands, and not sitting in endless meetings staring at the backs of people's heads, people he really didn't even know. Just sharing life.

"But, wait—" Mack had a jumble of questions starting to surface. Maybe he had misunderstood. This seemed *too* simple! Again he caught himself. Perhaps it was because humans are so utterly lost and independent that they take what is simple and make it complex? So he thought twice about messing with what he was beginning to understand. To begin asking his jumbled mess of questions at this moment felt like throwing a dirt clod into a little pool of clear water.

"Never mind" was all he said.

"Mack, you don't need to have it all figured out. Just be with me."

After a moment he decided to join Jesus, and he lay on his back next to him, shielding his eyes from the sun in order to watch the clouds sweeping away the early afternoon.

"Well, to be honest," he admitted, "I'm not too disappointed that the 'street of gold' thing isn't the big prize. It always sounded a little boring to me, and not nearly as wonderful as being out here with you."

Near quiet descended as Mack took in the moment. He could hear the hush of wind caressing trees and the laughter of the nearby creek as it spilled its way into the lake. The day was majestic, the take-your-breath-away surroundings incredible.

"I really do want to understand. I mean, I find you so different from all the well-intentioned religious stuff I'm familiar with."

"As well-intentioned as it might be, you know that religious machinery can chew up people!" Jesus said with a bite of his own. "An awful lot of what is done in my name has nothing to do with me and is often, even if unintentional, very contrary to my purposes."

"You're not too fond of religion and institutions?" Mack said, not sure if he was asking a question or making an observation.

"I don't create institutions—never have, never will."

"What about the institution of marriage?"

"Marriage is not an institution. It's a relationship." Jesus paused, his voice steady and patient. "Like I said, I don't create institutions; that's an occupation for those who want to play God. So no, I'm not too big on religion, and not very fond of politics or economics either." Jesus' visage darkened noticeably. "And why should I be? They are the man-created trinity of terrors that ravages the earth and deceives those I care about. What mental turmoil and anxiety does any human face that is not related to one of those three?"

Mack hesitated. He wasn't sure what to say. This all felt a little over his head.

Noticing that Mack's eyes were glazing over, Jesus downshifted. "Put simply, these terrors are tools that many use to prop up their illusions of security and control. People are afraid of uncertainty, afraid of the future. These institutions, these structures and ideologies, are all a vain effort to create some sense of certainty and security where there isn't any. It's all false! Systems cannot provide you security, only I can."

Whoa! was all Mack could think. The landscape of how he and just about everyone he knew had sought to manage and navigate their lives was being reduced to little more than rubble. "So . . ." Mack was still processing and not really coming up with much. "So?" He turned it back into a question.

"I don't have an agenda here, Mack. Just the opposite," Jesus said. "I came to give you life to the fullest. My life." Mack was still straining to understand. "The simplicity and purity of enjoying a growing friendship?"

"Uh, got it!"

"If you try to live this without me, without the ongoing dialogue of us sharing this journey together, it will be like trying to walk on the water by yourself. You can't! And when you try, however well intentioned, you're going to sink." Knowing full well the answer, Jesus asked, "Have you ever tried to save someone who was drowning?"

Mack's chest and muscles instinctively tightened. He didn't like remembering Josh and the canoe, and the sense of panic that suddenly rushed back from the memory.

"It's extremely hard to rescue someone unless he is willing to trust you."

"Yes, it sure is."

"That's all I ask of you. When you start to sink, let me rescue you."

It seemed like a simple request, but Mack was used to being the lifeguard, not the one drowning. "Jesus, I'm not sure I know how to—"

"Let me show you. Just keep giving me the little bit you have, and together we'll watch it grow."

Mack began to put on his socks and shoes. "Sitting here with you, in this moment, it doesn't seem that hard. But when I think about my regular life back home, I don't know how to keep it as simple as you're suggesting. I'm stuck in that same grasp for control everyone else is. Politics, economics, social systems, bills, family, commitments . . . it can all be a bit overwhelming. I don't know how to change it all."

"No one is asking you to," Jesus said tenderly. "That is Sara-yu's task, and she knows how to do it without brutalizing any-one. This whole thing is a process, not an event. All I want from you is to trust me with what little you can, and grow in loving people around you with the same love I share with you. It's not your job to change them, or to convince them. You are free to love without an agenda."

"That's what I want to learn."

"And you are." Jesus winked.

Jesus stood up and stretched, and Mack followed.

"I have been told so many lies," he admitted.

Jesus looked at him and then with one arm pulled Mack in and hugged him. "I know, Mack, so have I. I just didn't believe them."

Together they began the walk down the dock. As they approached the shore, they slowed again. Jesus put his hand on Mack's shoulder and gently turned him until they were face-to-face.

"Mack, the world system is what it is. Institutions, systems, ideologies, and all the vain, futile efforts of humanity that go with them are everywhere, and interaction with all of it is unavoidable. But I can give you freedom to overcome any system of power in which you find yourself, be it religious, economic, social, or political. You will grow in the freedom to be inside or outside all kinds of systems and to move freely between and among them. Together, you and I can be in it and not of it."

"But so many of the people I care about seem to be both in it and of it!" Mack was thinking of his friends, church people who had expressed love to him and his family. He knew they loved Jesus, but he also knew they were sold out to religious activity and patriotism.

"Mack, I love them. And you wrongly judge many of them. For those who are both in it and of it, we must find ways to love and serve them, don't you think?" asked Jesus. "Remember, the

184 • THE SHACK

people who know me are the ones who are free to live and love without any agenda."

"Is that what it means to be a Christian?" It sounded kind of stupid as Mack said it, but it was how he was trying to sum everything up in his mind.

"Who said anything about being a Christian? I'm not a Christian."

The idea struck Mack as odd and unexpected, and he couldn't keep himself from grinning. "No, I suppose you aren't."

They arrived at the door of the workshop. Again Jesus stopped. "Those who love me have come from every system that exists. They were Buddhists or Mormons, Baptists or Muslims; some are Democrats, some Republicans and many don't vote or are not part of any Sunday morning or religious institutions. I have followers who were murderers and many who were self-righteous. Some are bankers and bookies, Americans and Iraqis, Jews and Palestinians. I have no desire to make them Christian, but I do want to join them in their transformation into sons and daughters of my Papa, into my brothers and sisters, into my Beloved."

"Does that mean," said Mack, "that all roads will lead to you?"

"Not at all." Jesus smiled as he reached for the door handle to the shop. "Most roads don't lead anywhere. What it does mean is that I will travel any road to find you." He paused. "Mack, I've got some things to finish up in the shop, so I'll catch up with you later."

"Okay. What do you want me to do?"

"Whatever you want, Mack. The afternoon is yours." Jesus patted him on the shoulder and grinned. "One last thing: remember earlier when you thanked me for letting you see Missy? That was all Papa's idea." With that he turned and waved over his shoulder as he walked into the workshop.

Mack knew instantly what he wanted to do and headed for the shack to see if he could find Papa.

13

A MEETING OF HEARTS

Falsehood has an infinity of combinations,
but truth has only one mode of being.

—Jean-Jacques Rousseau

As Mack neared the cabin he could smell scones or muffins or something wonderful. It might have been only an hour since lunch due to Sarayu's time-dimensional thingy, but he felt as if he hadn't eaten in hours. Even if he had been blind he would have had no trouble finding his way to the kitchen. But when he came in the back door he was surprised and disappointed to discover the place empty. "Anyone here?" he called.

"I'm on the porch, Mack." Her voice came through the open window. "Grab yourself something to drink and come join me."

Mack poured himself some coffee and walked out onto the front porch. Papa was reclining in an old Adirondack chair, eyes closed, soaking in the sun. "What's this? God has time to catch a few rays? Don't you have anything better to do this afternoon?"

"Mack, you have no idea what I'm doing right now."

There was another chair on the opposite side, so he stepped over to it and as he sat down she opened one eye. Between them on a small end table sat a tray full of a rich-looking pastry with fresh butter and an array of jams and jellies.

"Wow, this smells great!" he exclaimed.

"Dive in. It's a recipe I borrowed from your own great-great-grandma. Made it from scratch too." She grinned.

Mack wasn't sure what "made it from scratch" might mean when God was saying it and decided to leave well enough alone. He picked up one of the scones and bit into it without anything on it. It was still warm from the oven and fairly melted in his mouth.

"Wow! That is good! Thank you!"

"Well, you'll have to thank your great-great-grandma when you see her."

"I'm rather hoping," Mack said between bites, "that won't be too soon."

"Wouldn't you like to know?" Papa said with a playful wink and then closed her eyes again.

As Mack ate another scone he groped for the courage to speak his heart. "Papa?" he said, and for the first time calling God "Papa" did not seem awkward to him.

"Yes, Mack?" she answered as her eyes opened and she smiled with delight.

"I've been pretty hard on you."

"Hmmmm, Sophia must've gotten to you."

"Did she ever! I had no idea I had presumed to be your judge. It sounds so horribly arrogant."

"That's because it was," Papa responded with a smile.

"I am so sorry. I really had no idea . . ." Mack shook his head sadly.

"But that is in the past now, where it belongs. I don't even want your sorrow for it, Mack. I just want us to grow on together without it."

"I want that too," Mack said, reaching for another scone. "Aren't you going to eat any of these?"

"Nah, you go ahead; you know how it is—start cookin' and tastin' this and that and before you know it, you've used up your whole appetite. You enjoy," Papa said and nudged the tray toward him.

He took another and sat back to savor it. "Jesus said it was your idea to give me some time with Missy this afternoon. I can't begin to find words to thank you for that!"

"Aww, you're welcome, honey. It gave me great joy too! I was so looking forward to puttin' you two together I could hardly stand it."

"I wish Nan could have been here for that."

"That would have made it perfect!" Papa agreed with excitement.

Mack sat in silence, unsure what she meant or how to respond.

"Isn't Missy special?" She shook her head back and forth. "My, my, my, I'm especially fond of that one."

"Me too!" Mack beamed and thought of his princess behind the waterfall. Princess? Waterfall? Wait a minute! Papa watched as the tumblers fell into place.

"Obviously you know about my daughter's fascination with waterfalls and especially the legend of the Multnomah princess."

Papa nodded.

"Is that what this is about? Did she have to die so you could change me?"

"Whoa there, Mack." Papa leaned forward. "That's not how I do things."

"But she loved that story so much."

"Of course she did. That's how she came to appreciate what Jesus did for her and the whole human race. Stories about a person willing to exchange his or her life for another's are a golden thread in your world, revealing both your need and my heart."

"But if she hadn't died, I wouldn't be here now . . ."

"Mack, just because I work incredible good out of unspeakable tragedies doesn't mean I orchestrate the tragedies. Don't ever assume that my using something means I caused it or that I needed it to accomplish my purposes. That will only lead you to false notions about me. Grace doesn't depend on suffering to exist, but where there is suffering you will find grace in many facets and colors."

"Actually, that's a relief. I couldn't bear to think that my pain might have cut short her life."

"She was not your sacrifice, Mack. She is and will always be your joy. That's enough purpose for her."

Mack settled back in his chair, surveying the view from the porch. "I feel so full!"

"Well, you've eaten most of the scones."

"That's not what I meant." He laughed. "And you know it. The world just looks a thousand times brighter and I feel a thousand times lighter."

"You are, Mack! It's not easy being the judge of the entire world." Papa's smile reassured Mack that this new ground was safe.

"Or judging you," he added. "I was quite a mess . . . worse off than I thought. I have totally misunderstood who you are in my life."

"Not totally, Mack. We've had some wonderful moments too. So let's not make more of it than it is."

"But I always liked Jesus better than you. He seemed so gracious and you seemed so . . ."

"Mean? Sad, isn't it? He came to show people who I am and most folks believe the qualities he portrayed were unique to him. They still play us off like good cop/bad cop most of the time, especially the religious folk. When they want people to do what they think is right, they need a stern God. When they need forgiveness, they run to Jesus."

"Exactly," Mack said with a point of his finger.

"But we were all in him. He reflected my heart exactly. I love you and invite you to love me."

"But why me? I mean, why Mackenzie Allen Phillips? Why do you love someone who is such a screwup? After all the things I've felt in my heart toward you and all the accusations I've made, why would you even bother to keep trying to get through to me?"

"Because that is what love does," answered Papa. "Remember, Mackenzie, I don't wonder what you will do or what choices you will make. I already know. Let's say, for example, I am trying to teach you how not to hide inside lies—hypothetically, of course," she said with a wink. "And let's say that I know it will take you forty-seven situations and events before you will actually hear me—that is, before you will hear clearly enough to agree with me and change. So when you don't hear me the first time, I'm not frustrated or disappointed, I'm thrilled. Only forty-six more times to go! And that first time will be a building block to construct a bridge of healing that one day—that today—you will walk across."

"Okay, now I'm feeling guilty," he admitted.

"Let me know how that works for you." Papa chuckled. "Seriously, Mackenzie, it's not about feeling guilty. Guilt'll never help you find freedom in me. The best it can do is make you try harder to conform to some ethic on the outside. I'm about the inside."

"But what you said, I mean, about hiding inside lies. I guess I've done that one way or another most of my life."

"Honey, you're a survivor. No shame in that. Your daddy hurt you something fierce. Life hurt you. Lies are one of the easiest places for survivors to run. They give you a sense of safety, a place where you have to depend only on yourself. But it's a dark place, isn't it?"

"So dark," Mack muttered with a shake of his head.

"But are you willing to give up the power and safety it promises you? That's the question."

"What do you mean?" asked Mack, looking up at her.

"Lies are a little fortress; inside them you can feel safe and powerful. Through your little fortress of lies you try to run your life and manipulate others. But the fortress needs walls, so you build some. These are the justifications for your lies. You know, like you are doing this to protect someone you love, to keep them from feeling pain. Whatever works, just so you feel okay about the lies."

"But the reason I didn't tell Nan about the note was because it would have caused her so much hurt."

"See? There you go, Mackenzie, justifying yourself. What you just said is a bold-faced lie, but you can't see it." She leaned forward. "Do you want me to tell you what the truth is?"

Mack knew Papa was going deep, and somewhere inside he was both relieved to be talking about this and tempted to almost laugh out loud. He was no longer embarrassed by it. "No-o-o-o." He drew his answer out slowly and smirked up at her. "But go ahead anyway."

She smiled back and then grew serious. "The truth is, Mack, the real reason you did not tell Nan was not because you were trying to save her from pain. The real reason was that you were afraid of having to deal with the emotions you might have encountered, both from her and in yourself. Emotions scare you, Mack. You lied to protect yourself, not her!"

He sat back. Papa was absolutely right.

"And furthermore," she continued, "such a lie is unloving. In the name of caring about her, your lie became an inhibitor in your relationship with her, and in her relationship with me. If you had told her, maybe she would be here with us now."

Papa's words hit Mack like a punch in the stomach. "You wanted her to come too?"

"That was your decision and hers, if she had ever been given the chance to make it. The point is, Mack, you don't know what would have happened because you were so busy 'protecting' Nan."

And again he was floundering in guilt. "So, what do I do now?"

"You tell her, Mackenzie. You face the fear of coming out of the dark and tell her, and you ask for her forgiveness and let her forgiveness heal you. Ask her to pray for you, Mack. Take the risks of honesty. When you mess up again, ask for forgiveness again. It's a process, honey, and life is real enough without having to be obscured by lies. And remember, I am bigger than your lies. I can work beyond them. But that doesn't make them right or stop the damage they do or the hurt they cause others."

"What if she doesn't forgive me?" Mack knew that this was indeed a very deep fear that he lived with. It felt safer to continue to throw new lies on the growing pile of old ones.

"Ah, that is the risk of faith, Mack. Faith does not grow in the house of certainty. I am not here to tell you that Nan will forgive you. Perhaps she won't or can't, but my life inside you will appropriate risk and uncertainty to transform you by your own choices into a truth teller, and that will be a miracle greater than raising the dead."

Mack sat back and let her words sink in. "Will you please forgive me?" Mack finally offered.

"Did that a long time ago, Mack. If you don't believe me, ask Jesus. He was there."

Mack took a sip of his coffee, surprised to find that it was still as hot as when he first sat down. "But I've tried pretty hard to lock you out of my life."

"People are tenacious when it comes to the treasure of their imaginary independence. They hoard and hold their sickness with a firm grip. They find their identity and worth in their brokenness and guard it with every ounce of strength they have. No wonder grace has such little attraction. In that sense you have tried to lock the door of your heart from the inside."

"But I didn't succeed."

"That's because my love is a lot bigger than your stupidity," Papa said with a wink. "I used your choices to work perfectly into my purposes. There are many folk like you, Mackenzie, who end up locking themselves into a very small place with a monster that will ultimately betray them, that will not fill or deliver what they thought it would. Imprisoned with such a terror, they once again have the opportunity to return to me. The very treasure they trusted in will become their undoing."

"So you use pain to force people back to you?" It was obvious Mack didn't approve.

Papa leaned forward and gently touched Mack's hand. "Honey, I also forgave you for even thinking I could be that way. I understand how difficult it is for you, so lost in your perceptions of reality and yet so sure of your own judgments, to even begin to perceive, let alone imagine, *who* real love and goodness are. True love never forces." She squeezed his hand and sat back.

"But if I understand what you're saying, the consequences of our selfishness are part of the process that brings us to the end of our delusions and helps us find you. Is that why you don't stop every evil? Is that why you didn't warn me that Missy was in danger or help us find her?" The accusing tone was no longer in Mack's voice.

"If only it were that simple, Mackenzie. Nobody knows what horrors I have saved the world from 'cause people can't see what never happened. All evil flows from independence, and independence is your choice. If I were to simply revoke all the choices of independence, the world as you know it would cease to exist and love would have no meaning. This world is not a playground where I keep all my children free from evil. Evil is the chaos of this age that you brought to me, but it will not have the final say. Now it touches everyone I love, those who follow me and those who don't. If I take away the consequences of people's choices, I destroy the possibility of love. Love that is forced is no love at all."

Mack rubbed his hands through his hair and sighed. "It's just so hard to understand."

"Honey, let me tell you one of the reasons that it makes no sense to you. It's because you have such a small view of what it means to be human. You and this creation are incredible, whether you understand that or not. You are wonderful beyond imagination. Just because you make horrendous and destructive choices does not mean you deserve less respect for what you inherently are—the pinnacle of my creation and the center of my affection."

"But—" Mack started.

"Also," she interrupted, "don't forget that in the midst of all your pain and heartache, you are surrounded by beauty, the wonder of creation, art, your music and culture, the sounds of laughter and love, of whispered hopes and celebrations, of new life and transformation, of reconciliation and forgiveness. These also are the results of your choices, and every choice matters, even the hidden ones. So whose choices should we countermand, Mackenzie? Perhaps I should never have created? Perhaps Adam should have been stopped before he chose independence? What about your choice to have another daughter, or your father's choice to beat his son? You demand your independence but then complain that I actually love you enough to give it to you."

Mack smiled. "I've heard that before."

Papa smiled back and reached for a piece of pastry. "I told you Sophia got to you.

"Mackenzie, my purposes are not for my comfort, or yours. My purposes are always and only an expression of love. I purpose to work life out of death, to bring freedom out of brokenness and turn darkness into light. What you see as chaos, I see as a fractal. All things must unfold, even though it puts all those I love in the midst of a world of horrible tragedies—even the one closest to me."

"You're talking about Jesus, aren't you?" Mack asked softly.

"Yup, I love that boy." Papa looked away and shook her head. "Everything's about him, you know. One day you folk will understand what he gave up. There are just no words."

Mack could feel his own emotions welling up. Something touched him deeply as he watched Papa talk about her Son. He hesitated to ask but finally broke into the silence.

"Papa, can you help me understand something? What exactly did Jesus accomplish by dying?"

She was still looking out into the forest. "Oh"—she waved her hand—"nothing much. Just the substance of everything that love purposed from before the foundations of creation," Papa stated matter-of-factly, then turned and smiled.

"Wow, that's a pretty broad brush. Could you bring it down a few notches?" asked Mack rather boldly, or so he thought after the words had left his mouth.

Papa, instead of being upset, beamed at him. "My, but aren't you getting uppity an' all? Give a man an inch and he thinks he's a ruler."

Mack returned the grin, but his mouth was full and he didn't say anything.

"Like I said, everything is about him. Creation and history are all about Jesus. He is the very center of our purpose, and in him we are now fully human, so our purpose and your destiny are forever linked. You might say that we have put all our eggs in the one human basket. There is no plan B."

"Seems pretty risky," Mack surmised.

"Maybe for you, but not for me. There has never been a question that what I wanted from the beginning, I will get." Papa sat forward and crossed her arms on the table. "Honey, you asked me what Jesus accomplished on the cross, so now listen to me carefully: through his death and resurrection, I am now fully reconciled to the world."

"The whole world? You mean those who believe in you, right?"

"The whole world, Mack. All I am telling you is that reconciliation is a two-way street, and I have done my part, totally, completely, finally. It is not the nature of love to force a relationship, but it is the nature of love to open the way."

At that, Papa stood up and gathered the dishes to take into the kitchen.

Mack shook his head and looked up. "So, I don't really understand reconciliation and I'm really scared of emotions. Is that about it?"

Papa didn't answer immediately but shook her head as she turned and walked away in the direction of the kitchen. Mack overheard her grunt and mutter, as if only to herself, "Men! Such idiots sometimes."

He couldn't believe it. "Did I hear God call me an idiot?" he called through the screen door.

He saw her shrug before disappearing around the corner, and then he heard her yell back in his direction, "If the shoe fits, honey. Yes, sir, if the shoe fits . . ."

Mack laughed and sat back. He felt finished. His brain tank was more than full, as was his stomach. He carried the rest of the dishes to the kitchen and placed the stack on the counter, kissed Papa on the cheek, and headed for the back door.

14

VERBS AND OTHER FREEDOMS

God is a verb.

—Buckminster Fuller

Mack stepped outside into the mid-afternoon sun. He felt an odd mixture of being wrung out like a rag and yet exhilaratingly alive. What an incredible day this had been and it was barely half over. For a moment he stood undecided before wandering down to the lake. When he saw the canoes tied up to the dock, he knew it would probably forever be bittersweet, but the thought of taking one out on the lake energized him for the first time in years.

Untying the last one at the end of the dock, he gingerly slid into it and began paddling toward the other side. For the next couple of hours he circled the lake, exploring its nooks and crannies. He found two rivers and a couple of creeks that either fed from above or emptied down toward the lower basins, and he discovered a perfect spot to drift and watch the waterfall. Alpine flowers blossomed everywhere, adding splashes of color to the landscape. This was the most calm and consistent sense of peace that Mack had felt in ages—if ever.

He even sang a few songs, a couple of old hymns and a couple of old folk songs, just because he wanted to. Singing was also something he had not done in a long time. Reaching back into the distant past, he began to voice the silly little song he used to sing to Kate: "K-K-K-Katie . . . beautiful Katie, You're the only one that I adore . . ." He shook his head as he thought about his daughter, so tough but so fragile; he wondered how he might find a way to reach her heart. He was no longer surprised how easily tears could come to his eyes.

At one point he turned to watch eddies and whorls made by the paddle blade and stern and when he turned back, Sarayu was sitting in the prow, looking at him. Her sudden presence made him jump.

"Geez!" he exclaimed. "You startled me."

"I am sorry, Mackenzie," she apologized, "but supper is almost ready, and it is time to invite you to make your way back to the shack."

"Have you been with me the entire time?" inquired Mack, a little ramped from the adrenaline rush.

"Of course. I am always with you."

"Then how come I didn't know it?" asked Mack. "Lately I've been able to tell when you're around."

"For you to know or not," she explained, "has nothing at all to do with whether I am actually here or not. I am always with you; sometimes I want you to be aware in a special way—more intentional."

Mack nodded that he understood and turned the canoe toward the distant shore and the shack. He now distinctly felt her presence in the tingle down his spine. They both smiled simultaneously.

"Will I always be able to see you or hear you like I do now, even if I'm back home?"

Sarayu smiled. "Mackenzie, you can always talk to me and I will always be with you, whether you sense my presence or not."

"I know that now, but how will I hear you?"

"You will learn to hear my thoughts in yours, Mackenzie," she reassured him.

"Will it be clear? What if I confuse you with another voice? What if I make mistakes?"

Sarayu laughed, the sound like tumbling water, only set to music. "Of course you will make mistakes; everybody makes mistakes, but you will begin to better recognize my voice as we continue to grow our relationship."

"I don't want to make mistakes," Mack grunted.

"Oh, Mackenzie," responded Sarayu, "mistakes are a part of life, and Papa works her purpose in them too." She was amused and Mack couldn't help but grin back. He could see her point well enough.

"This is so different from everything I've known, Sarayu. Don't get me wrong—I love what you all have given me this weekend. But I have no idea how to go back to my life. Somehow it seemed easier to live with God when I thought of him as the demanding taskmaster, or even to cope with the loneliness of *The Great Sadness*."

"You think so?" she asked. "Really?"

"At least then I seemed to have things under control."

"*Seemed* is the right word. What did it get you? *The Great Sadness* and more pain than you could bear, pain that spilled over even on those you care for the most."

"According to Papa, that's because I'm scared of emotions," he disclosed.

Sarayu laughed out loud. "I thought that little interchange was hilarious."

"I am afraid of emotions," Mack admitted, a bit perturbed that she seemed to make light of it. "I don't like how they feel. I've hurt others with them and I can't trust them at all. Did you create all of them or only the good ones?"

"Mackenzie." Sarayu seemed to rise up into the air. Mack still had a difficult time looking right at her, but with the late-afternoon sun reflecting off the water, it was even worse. "Emotions are the colors of the soul—they are spectacular and incredible. When you don't feel, the world becomes dull and colorless. Just think how *The Great Sadness* reduced the range of color in your life down to monotones and flat grays and blacks."

"So help me understand them," pleaded Mack.

"Not much to understand, actually. They just are. They are neither bad nor good; they just exist. Here is something that will help you sort this out in your mind, Mackenzie. *Paradigms power perception and perceptions power emotions.* Most emotions are responses to perception—what you think is true about a given situation. If your perception is false, then your emotional response to it will be false too. So check your perceptions, and beyond that check the truthfulness of your paradigms—what you believe. Just because you believe something firmly doesn't make it true. Be willing to reexamine what you believe. The more you live in the truth, the more your emotions will help you see clearly. But even then, you don't want to trust them more than me."

Mack allowed his paddle to turn in his hands as he let it play in the water's movements. "It feels like living out of relationship—you know, trusting and talking to you—is a bit more complicated than just following rules."

"What rules are those, Mackenzie?"

"You know, all the things the Scriptures tell us we should do."

"Okay . . ." she said with some hesitation. "And what might those be?"

"You know," he answered sarcastically. "About doing good things and avoiding evil, being kind to the poor, reading your Bible, praying, and going to church. Things like that."

"I see. And how is that working for you?"

He laughed. "Well, I've never done it very well. I have moments that aren't too bad, but there's always something I'm struggling with or feeling guilty about. I just figured I needed to try harder, but I find it difficult to sustain that motivation."

"Mackenzie!" she chided, her words flowing with affection. "The Bible doesn't teach you to follow rules. It is a picture of Jesus. While words may tell you what God is like and even what he may want from you, you cannot do any of it on your own. Life and living are *in him* and in no other. My goodness, you didn't think you could live the righteousness of God on your own, did you?"

"Well, I thought so, sorta . . ." he said sheepishly. "But you gotta admit, rules and principles are simpler than relationships."

"It is true that relationships are a whole lot messier than rules, but rules will never give you answers to the deep questions of the heart, and they will never love you."

Dipping his hand in the water, he played, watching the patterns his movements made. "I'm realizing how few answers I have . . . to anything. You know, you've turned me upside down or inside out or something."

"Mackenzie, religion is about having the right answers, and some of its answers are right. But I am about the process that takes you to the *living answer*, and once you get to him, he will change you from the inside. There are a lot of smart people who are able to say a lot of right things from their brains because they have been told what the right answers are, but they don't know me at all. So really, how can their answers be right even if they are right, if you understand my drift?" She smiled at her pun. "So even though they might be right, they are still wrong."

"I understand what you're saying. I did that for years after seminary. I had the right answers sometimes, but I didn't know you. This weekend, sharing life with you has been far more illuminating than any of those answers." They continued to move lazily with a current.

"So, will I see you again?" he asked hesitantly.

"Of course. You might see me in a piece of art, or music, or silence, or through people, or in creation, or in your joy and sorrow. My ability to communicate is limitless, living and transforming, and it will always be tuned to Papa's goodness and love. And you will hear and see me in the Bible in fresh ways. Just don't look for rules and principles; look for relationship—a way of coming to be with us."

"It still won't be the same as having you sit on the bow of my boat."

"No, it will be far better than you've yet known, Mackenzie. And when you finally sleep in this world, we'll have an eternity together—face-to-face."

And then she was gone. Although he knew that she was not really.

"So please, help me live in the truth," he said out loud. *Maybe that counts as prayer*, he thought.

ᏚᎡᏚᏚᎡ

When Mack entered the cabin he saw that Jesus and Sarayu were already there and seated at the table. Papa was busy as usual bringing platters of wonderful-smelling dishes, again only a few that Mack recognized, and even those he had to look at twice to make sure they were something he was familiar with. Conspicuously absent were any greens. He headed for the bathroom to clean up, and when he returned the other three had already begun to eat. He pulled up the fourth chair and sat down.

"You don't really have to eat, do you?" he asked as he began to ladle something into his bowl that resembled a thin seafood soup, with squid and fish and other more ambiguous delicacies.

"We don't have to do anything," Papa stated rather strongly.

"Then why do you eat?" Mack inquired.

"To be with you, honey. You need to eat, so what better excuse to be together?"

"Anyway, we all like to cook," added Jesus. "And I enjoy food—a lot. Nothing like a little shaomai, ugali, nipla, or kori bananje to make your taste buds happy. Follow that with some sticky toffee pudding or a tiramisu and hot tea. Yum! It doesn't get any better than that."

They all laughed and then busily resumed passing platters and helping themselves. As Mack ate, he listened to the banter among the three. They talked and laughed like old friends who knew one another intimately. As he thought about it, that was assuredly more true for his hosts than anyone inside or outside creation. He was envious of the carefree but respectful conversation and wondered what it would take to share that with Nan and maybe even with some friends.

Again Mack was struck by the wonder and sheer absurdity of the moment. His mind wandered through the incredible conversations that had involved him during the previous twenty-four hours. Wow! He had been here only one day? And what was he supposed to do with all this when he got back home? He knew that he would tell Nan everything. She might not believe him and not that he would blame her—he probably wouldn't believe any of it either.

As his mind picked up speed he felt himself withdrawing from the others. None of this could be real. He closed his eyes and tried to shut out the exchanges going on around him. Suddenly, it was dead silent. He slowly opened one eye, half expecting to be waking up at home. Instead, Papa, Jesus, and Sarayu were all staring at him with silly grins plastered to their faces. He didn't even try to explain himself. He knew that they knew.

Instead, he pointed to one of the dishes and asked, "Could I try some of that?" The interactions resumed and this time he listened. But again, he felt himself withdrawing. To counteract it, he decided to ask a question.

"Why do you love us humans? I suppose, I . . ." As he spoke he realized he hadn't formed his question very well. "I guess what I want to ask is, why do you love me, when I have nothing to offer you?"

"If you think about it, Mack," Jesus answered, "it should be very freeing to know that you can offer us nothing, at least not anything that can add or take away from who we are . . . That should alleviate any pressure to perform."

"And do you love your own children more when they perform well?" added Papa.

"No, I see your point." Mack paused. "But I do feel more fulfilled because they are in my life—do you?"

"No," said Papa. "We are already completely fulfilled within ourselves. You are designed to be in community as well, made as you are in our very image. So for you to feel that way about your children, or anything that 'adds' to you, is perfectly natural and right. Keep in mind, Mackenzie, that I am not a human being, not in my very nature, despite how we have chosen to be with you this weekend. I am truly human in Jesus, but I am a totally separate other in my nature."

"You do know—of course you do," Mack said apologetically, "that I can only follow that line of thought so far, and then I get lost and my brain turns to mush?"

"I understand," acknowledged Papa. "You cannot see in your mind's eye something you cannot experience."

Mack thought about that for a moment. "I guess so . . . Whatever . . . See? Mush."

When the others stopped laughing, Mack continued, "You know how truly grateful I am for everything, but you've dumped a whole lot in my lap this weekend. What do I do when I get back? What do you expect of me now?"

Jesus and Papa both turned to Sarayu, who had a forkful of something halfway to her mouth. She slowly put it back down on her plate and then answered Mack's confused look.

"Mack," she began, "you must forgive these two. Humans have a tendency to restructure language according to their independence and need to perform. So when I hear language abused in favor of rules over sharing life with us, it is difficult for me to remain silent."

"As it must," added Papa.

"So what exactly did I say?" asked Mack, now quite curious.

"Mack, go ahead and finish your bite. We can talk as you eat."

Mack realized that he too had a fork halfway to his mouth. He gratefully took the bite as Sarayu began to speak. As she did, she seemed to lift off her chair and shimmer with a dance of subtle hues and shades, and the room was faintly filling with an array of aromas, incenselike and heady.

"Let me answer that by asking you a question. Why do you think we came up with the Ten Commandments?"

Again Mack had his fork halfway to his mouth, but he took the bite anyway while he thought of how to answer Sarayu.

"I suppose, at least I have been taught, that it's a set of rules you expected humans to obey in order to live righteously in your good graces."

"If that were true, which it is not," Sarayu countered, "then how many do you think lived righteously enough to enter our good graces?"

"Not very many, if people are like me," Mack observed.

"Actually, only one succeeded—Jesus. He not only obeyed the letter of the Law but fulfilled the spirit of it completely. But understand this, Mackenzie—to do that he had to rest fully and dependently upon me."

"Then why did you give us those commandments?" asked Mack.

"Actually, we wanted you to give up trying to be righteous on your own. It was a mirror to reveal just how filthy your face gets when you live independently."

"But as I'm sure you know, there are many," responded Mack, "who think they are made righteous by following the rules."

"But can you clean your face with the same mirror that shows you how dirty you are? There is no mercy or grace in rules, not even for one mistake. That's why Jesus fulfilled all of it for you—so that it no longer has jurisdiction over you. And the Law that once contained impossible demands—'Thou shall not . . .'—actually becomes a promise we fulfill in you."

She was on a roll now, her countenance billowing and moving. "But keep in mind that if you live your life alone and independently, the promise is empty. Jesus laid the demand of the Law to rest; it no longer has any power to accuse or command. Jesus is both the promise and its fulfillment."

"Are you saying I don't have to follow the rules?" Mack had now completely stopped eating and was concentrating on the conversation.

"Yes. In Jesus you are not under any law. All things are lawful."

"You can't be serious! You're messing with me again," moaned Mack.

"Child," said Papa, "you ain't heard nuthin' yet."

"Mackenzie," Sarayu continued, "those who are afraid of freedom are those who cannot trust us to live in them. Trying to keep the Law is actually a declaration of independence, a way of keeping control."

"Is that why we like the Law so much—to give us some control?" asked Mack.

"It is much worse than that," resumed Sarayu. "It grants you the power to judge others and feel superior to them. You believe you are living to a higher standard than those you judge. Enforcing rules, especially in more subtle expressions like responsibility and expectation, is a vain attempt to create certainty out of uncertainty. And contrary to what you might think, I have a great fondness for uncertainty. Rules cannot bring freedom; they have only the power to accuse."

"Whoa!" Mack suddenly realized what Sarayu had said. "Are you telling me that responsibility and expectation are just another form of rules we are no longer under? Did I hear you right?"

"Yup," Papa affirmed. "Now we're in it—Sarayu, he is all yours!"

Mack ignored Papa, choosing instead to concentrate on Sarayu, which was no easy task.

Sarayu smiled at Papa and then back at Mack. She began to speak slowly and deliberately. "Mackenzie, I will take a verb over a noun anytime."

She stopped and waited. Mack wasn't at all sure about what he was supposed to understand by her cryptic remark and said the only thing that came to mind. "Huh?"

"I"—she opened her hands to include Jesus and Papa—"I am a verb. I am that I am. I will be who I will be. I am a verb! I am alive, dynamic, ever active, and moving. I am a being verb."

Mack still felt as if he had a blank stare on his face. He understood the words she was saying, but they just weren't connecting yet.

"And as my very essence is a verb," she continued, "I am more attuned to verbs than nouns. Verbs such as *confessing, repenting, living, loving, responding, growing, reaping, changing, sowing, running, dancing, singing,* and on and on. Humans, on the other hand, have a knack for taking a verb that is alive and full of grace and turning it into a dead noun or principle that reeks of rules—then something growing and alive dies. Nouns exist because there is a created universe and physical reality, but if the universe is only a mass of nouns, it is dead. Unless 'I am,' there are no verbs, and verbs are what makes the universe alive."

Mack was still struggling, although a glimmer of light seemed to begin to shine into his mind. "And this means what, exactly?"

Sarayu seemed unperturbed by his lack of understanding. "For something to move from death to life, you must introduce something living and moving into the mix. To move from something that is only a noun to something dynamic and unpredictable, to something living and present tense, is to move from Law to grace. May I give you a couple of examples?"

"Please do," assented Mack. "I'm all ears."

Jesus chuckled and Mack scowled at him before turning back to Sarayu. The faintest shadow of a smile crossed her face as she resumed.

"Then let's use your two words: *responsibility* and *expec-*

tation. Before your words became nouns, they were first my words, nouns with movement and experience buried inside them: the ability to respond and expect. My words are alive and dynamic—full of life and possibility; yours are dead, full of law and fear and judgment. That is why you won't find the word *responsibility* in the Scriptures."

"Oh, boy." Mack grimaced, beginning to see where this was going. "We sure seem to use it a lot."

"Religion must use law to empower itself and control the people needed in order to survive. I give you an ability to respond and your response is to be free to love and serve in every situation, and therefore each moment is different and unique and wonderful. Because I am your ability to respond, I have to be present in you. If I simply gave you a *responsibility*, I would not have to be with you at all. It would now be a task to perform, an obligation to be met, something to fail."

"Oh, boy, oh, boy," Mack said again, without much enthusiasm.

"Let's use the example of friendship and how removing the element of life from a noun can drastically alter a relationship. Mack, if you and I are friends, there is an expectancy that exists within our relationship. When we see each other or are apart, there is an expectancy of being together, of laughing and talking. That expectancy has no concrete definition; it is alive and dynamic and everything that emerges from our being together is a unique gift shared by no one else. But what happens if I change that expectancy to an *expectation*—spoken or unspoken? Suddenly, law has entered into our relationship. You are now expected to perform in a way that meets my expectations. Our living friendship rapidly deteriorates into a dead thing with rules and requirements. It is no longer about you and me, but about what friends are supposed to do, or the responsibilities of a good friend."

"Or," noted Mack, "the responsibilities of a husband, or a father, or an employee, or whatever. I get the picture. I would much rather live in expectancy."

"As I do," mused Sarayu.

"But," argued Mack, "if you didn't have expectations and responsibilities, wouldn't everything just fall apart?"

"Only if you are of the world, apart from me, and under the law. Responsibilities and expectations are the basis of guilt and shame and judgment, and they provide the essential framework that promotes performance as the basis for identity and value. You know well what it is like not to live up to someone's expectations."

"Boy, do I!" Mack mumbled. "It's not my idea of a good time." He paused briefly, a new thought flashing through his mind. "Are you saying you have no expectations of me?"

Papa now spoke up. "Honey, I've never placed an expectation on you or anyone else. The idea behind expectations requires that someone does not know the future or outcome and is trying to control behavior to get the desired result. Humans try to control behavior largely through expectations. I know you and everything about you. Why would I have an expectation other than what I already know? That would be foolish. And beyond that, because I have no expectations, you never disappoint me."

"What? You've never been disappointed in me?" Mack was trying hard to digest this.

"Never!" Papa stated emphatically. "What I do have is a constant and living expectancy in our relationship, and I give you an ability to respond to any situation and circumstance in which you find yourself. To the degree that you resort to expectations and responsibilities, to that degree you neither know me nor trust me."

"And," added Jesus, "to that degree you will live in fear."

Mack wasn't convinced. "But don't you want us to set priorities? You know: God first, then whatever, followed by whatever?"

"The trouble with living by priorities," Sarayu said, "is that everything is seen as a hierarchy, a pyramid, and you and I have already had that discussion. If you put God at the top, what does that really mean, and how much is enough? How much time do you give me before you can go on about the rest of your day, the part that interests you so much more?"

Papa again interrupted. "You see, Mackenzie, I don't just want a piece of you and a piece of your life. Even if you were able, which you are not, to give me the biggest piece, that is not what I want. I want all of you and all of every part of you and your day."

Jesus now spoke again. "Mack, I don't want to be first among a list of values; I want to be at the center of everything. When I live in you, then together we can live through everything that happens to you. Rather than the top of a pyramid, I want to be the center of a mobile, where everything in your life—your friends, family, occupation, thoughts, activities—is connected to me but moves with the wind, in and out and back and forth, in an incredible dance of being."

"And I," concluded Sarayu, "am the wind." She smiled and bowed.

There was silence while Mack collected himself. He had been gripping the edge of the table with both hands as if to hold on to something tangible in the face of such an onslaught of ideas and images.

"Well, enough of all this," stated Papa, getting up from her chair. "Time for some fun! You all go ahead while I put away the stuff that'll spoil. I'll take care of the dishes later."

"What about devotion?" asked Mack.

"Nothing is a ritual, Mack," said Papa, picking up a few platters of food. "So tonight, we are doing something different. You are going to enjoy this!"

As Mack stood up and turned to follow Jesus to the back door, he felt a hand on his shoulder and turned around. Sarayu was standing close, looking at him intently.

"Mackenzie, if you would allow me, I would like to give you a gift for this evening. May I touch your eyes and heal them, just for tonight?"

Mack was surprised. "I see well enough, don't I?"

"Actually," Sarayu said apologetically, "you see very little, even though for a human you see fairly well. But just for tonight, I would love you to see a bit of what we see."

"Then by all means," Mack agreed. "Please touch my eyes and more if you choose."

As she reached her hands toward him, Mack closed his eyes and leaned forward. Her touch was like ice, unexpected and exhilarating. A delicious shiver went through him and he reached up to hold her hands to his face. There was nothing there, so he slowly began to open his eyes.

15

A FESTIVAL OF FRIENDS

*You can kiss your family and friends good-bye and
put miles between you, but at the same time you carry them with
you in your heart, your mind, your stomach, because you do not
just live in a world but a world lives in you.*

—Frederick Buechner, *Telling the Truth*

When Mack opened his eyes he had to immediately shield them from a blinding light that overwhelmed him. Then he heard something.

"You will find it very difficult to look at me directly," said the voice of Sarayu, "or at Papa. But as your mind becomes accustomed to the changes, it will be easier."

He was standing right where he had closed his eyes, but the shack was gone, as were the dock and shop. Instead he was outside, perched on the top of a small hill under a brilliant but moonless night sky. He could see that the stars were in motion, not hurriedly but smoothly and with precision, as if there were grand celestial conductors coordinating their movements.

Occasionally, as if on cue, comets and meteor showers would tumble through the starry ranks, adding variation to the flowing dance. Then Mack saw some of the stars grow and change color as if they were turning nova or white dwarf. It was as if time itself had become dynamic and volatile, adding to the seemingly chaotic but precisely managed heavenly display.

He turned back to Sarayu, who still stood next to him. Although she was difficult to look at directly, as usual, he could now make out symmetry and colors embedded within patterns, as if miniature diamonds, rubies, sapphires, and gems of all colors had been sewn into a garment of light, which moved first in waves and then scattered as particulates.

"It is all so incredibly beautiful," he whispered, surrounded as he was by such a holy and majestic sight.

"Truly," said the voice of Sarayu from out of the light. "Now, Mackenzie, look around."

He did and gasped. Even in the darkness of the night everything had clarity and shone with halos of light in various hues and shades of color. The forest was itself afire with light and color, yet each tree was distinctly visible, each branch, each leaf. Birds and bats created a trail of colored fire as they flew or chased one another. He could even see that in the distance an army of creation was in attendance: deer, bear, mountain sheep, and majestic elk near the edges of the forest, and otter and beaver in the lake, each shining in its own colors and blaze. Myriads of little creatures scampered and darted everywhere, each alive within its own glory.

In a rush of peach and plum and currant flames, an osprey dove toward the surface of the lake but pulled up at the last instant to skim across its surface, sparks from its wings falling like snow into the waters as it passed. Behind it, a large rainbow-clothed lake trout burst through the surface as if to taunt a passing hunter and then dropped back in the midst of a splash of colors.

Mack felt larger than life, as if he were able to be present wherever he looked. Two bear cubs playing near the feet of their mother caught his eye, ochre, mint, and hazel tumbling as they rolled and laughed in their native tongue. From where he stood, Mack felt that he could reach out and touch them, and without thought he stretched out his arm. He drew it back, startled, as he realized that he too was ablaze. He looked at his hands, wonderfully crafted and clearly visible inside the cascading colors of light that seemed to glove them. He examined the rest of his body to find that light and color robed him completely: a clothing of purity that allowed him both freedom and propriety.

Mack realized also that he felt no pain, not even in his usually aching joints. In fact, he had never felt this well, this whole. His head was clear and he breathed deeply the scents and aromas of the night and of the sleeping flowers in the garden, many of which had begun to awaken to this celebration.

Delirious and delicious joy welled up inside him and he jumped, floating slowly up into the air, then returning gently to the ground. *So similar*, he thought, *to dream-flying*.

And then Mack saw the lights: single moving points emerging from the forest, converging upon the meadow below where he and Sarayu stood. He could see them now high up on the surrounding mountains, appearing and disappearing as they made their way toward them, down unseen paths and trails.

They broke into the meadow, an army of children. There were no candles—they themselves were lights. And within their own radiance, each was dressed in a distinctive garb that Mack imagined represented every tribe and tongue. He could identify only a few, but it didn't matter. These were the children of the earth, Papa's children. They entered with quiet dignity and grace, faces full of contentment and peace, young ones holding the hands of even younger ones.

For a moment Mack wondered if Missy might be there, and although he looked for a minute, he gave up. He settled within himself that if she were, and if she wanted to run to him, she would. The children had now formed a huge circle within the meadow, with a path left open from near where Mack stood into the very center. Little bursts of fire and light, like a stadium of slow-popping flashbulbs, ignited when the children would giggle or whisper. Even though Mack had no idea what was going on, they obviously did, and the anticipation was almost too much for them.

Emerging into the clearing behind them and forming another circle of larger lights were those Mack presumed to be adults like himself, colorfully brilliant and yet subdued.

Suddenly, Mack's attention was caught by an unusual motion. It appeared that one of the light beings in the outer circle was having some difficulty. Flashes and spears of violet and ivory would arch briefly into the night in their direction. As these retreated they were replaced by orchid, gold, and flaming vermillion, burning and brilliant sprays of radiance that burst out again toward them, flaming against the immediate darkness, only to subside and return to their source.

Sarayu chuckled.

"What's going on?" Mack whispered.

"There is a man here who is having some difficulty keeping in what he is feeling."

Whoever was struggling could not contain himself and was agitating some of the others nearby. The ripple effect was clearly visible as the flashing light extended into the surrounding ring of children. Those closest to the instigator seemed to be responding as color and light flowed from them toward him. The combinations that emerged from each were unique and seemed to Mack to contain a distinctive response to the one causing the commotion.

"I still don't understand," Mack whispered again.

"Mackenzie, the pattern of color and light is unique to each person; no two are alike and no pattern is ever the same twice. Here, we are able to *see* one another truly, and part of *seeing* means that individual personality and emotion are visible in color and light."

"This is incredible!" Mack exclaimed. "Then why are the children's colors mostly white?"

"As you near them you will see that they have many individual colors that have merged into white, which contains all. As they mature and grow to become who they really are, the colors they exhibit will become more distinctive, and unique hues and shades will emerge."

"Incredible!" was all Mack could think to say, and he looked more intently. He now noticed that behind the circle of adults, others had emerged, spaced equally around the entire perimeter. Taller flames, they seemed to blow with the wind currents and were a similar sapphire and aqua blue, with unique bits of other colors embedded in each one.

"Angels," answered Sarayu before Mack could ask. "Servants and watchers."

"Incredible!" Mack said a third time.

"There is more, Mackenzie, and this will help you understand the problem this particular one is having." She pointed in the direction of the ongoing commotion.

Even to Mack, it was obvious that the man, whoever he was, continued to have difficulty. Sudden and abrupt spears of light and color at times shot out even farther toward them.

"Not only are we able to see the uniqueness of one another in color and light, but we are able to respond through the same medium. But this response is very difficult to control, and it is usually not intended to be restrained as this one is attempting. It is most natural to let its expression just be."

"I don't understand." Mack hesitated. "Are you saying that we can respond to one another in colors?"

"Yes." Sarayu nodded, or at least Mack thought she did. "Each relationship between two persons is absolutely unique. That is why you cannot love two people the same. It simply is not possible. You love each person differently because of who they are and the uniqueness that they draw out of you. And the more you know another, the richer the colors of that relationship."

Mack was listening but still watching the display before them.

Sarayu continued, "Perhaps the best way you can understand is for me to give you a quick illustration. Suppose, Mack, that you are hanging out with a friend at your local coffee shop. You are focused on your companion, and if you had eyes to see, the two of you would be enveloped in an array of colors and light, which mark not only your uniqueness as individuals but also the uniqueness of the relationship between you and the emotions you'd be experiencing in that moment."

"But—" Mack began to ask, only to be cut off.

"But suppose," Sarayu went on, "that another person you love enters the coffee shop, and although you are wrapped up in the conversation with your first friend, you notice this other's entry. Again, if you had eyes to see the greater reality, here is what you would witness: as you continued your current conversation, a unique combination of color and light would leave you and wrap itself around the one who had just entered, representing you in another form of loving and greeting that one. And one more thing, Mackenzie: it is not only visual but sensual as well. You can feel, smell, and even taste that uniqueness."

"I love that!" Mack exclaimed. "But except for that one over there"—he pointed in the direction of the agitated lights among the adults—"how are they all so calm? I would think there would be color everywhere. Don't they know each other?"

"They know one another very well, most of them, but they are here for a celebration that is not about them, nor about their relationships with one another, at least not directly," Sarayu explained. "They are waiting."

"For what?" Mack asked.

"You will see very soon," replied Sarayu, and it was obvious that she was not about to say any more on the matter.

"So then why"—Mack's attention had returned to the troublemaker—"why is that one having so much difficulty and why does he seem focused on us?"

"Mackenzie," Sarayu said gently, "he is not focused on us, he is focused on you."

"What?" Mack was dumbfounded.

"The one having so much trouble containing himself— that one—is your father."

A wave of emotions, a mixture of anger and longings, washed over Mack, and as if on cue his father's colors burst from across the meadow and enveloped him. He was lost in a wash of ruby and vermillion, magenta and violet, as the light and color whirled around and embraced him. And somehow, in the middle of the exploding storm, he found himself running across the meadow to find his father, running toward the source of the colors and emotions. He was a little boy wanting his daddy, and for the first time he was not afraid. He was running, not caring for anything but the object of his heart, and he found him. His father was on his knees awash in light, tears sparkling like a waterfall of diamonds and jewels into the hands that covered his face.

"Daddy!" yelled Mack, and he threw himself onto the man who could not even look at his son. In the howl of wind and flame, Mack took his father's face in his two hands, forcing his dad to look him in the face so he could stammer the words he had always wanted to say: "Daddy, I'm so sorry! Daddy, I love you!" The light of his words seemed to blast darkness out of his father's colors, turning them bloodred. They exchanged sobbing words of confession and forgiveness, as a love greater than either one healed them.

Finally, they were able to stand together, a father holding his son as he had never been able to before. It was then that Mack noticed the swell of a song that washed over them both as it penetrated the holy place where he stood with his father. With arms around each other they listened, unable to speak through the tears, to the song of reconciliation that lit the night sky. An arching fountain of brilliant color began among the children, especially those who had suffered the greatest, and then rippled as if passed from one to the next by the wind, until the entire field was flooded with light and song.

Mack somehow knew that this was not a time for conversation and that his time with his father was quickly passing. He sensed that by some mystery this was as much for his dad as it was for him. As for Mack, the new lightness he felt was euphoric. Kissing his father on the lips, he turned and made his way back to the small hill where Sarayu stood waiting for him. As he passed through the ranks of children, he could feel their touches and colors quickly embrace him and fall away. Somehow, he was already known and loved here.

When he reached Sarayu, she embraced him as well and he let her just hold him as he continued to cry. When he had regained some semblance of coherence, he turned to look back at the meadow, the lake, and night sky. A hush descended. The anticipation was palpable. Suddenly, to their right and from out of the darkness emerged Jesus, and pandemonium broke out. He was dressed in a simple brilliant white garment and wore on his head a simple gold crown, but he was every inch the King of the universe.

He walked the path that opened before him into the center—the center of all creation, the man who is God and the God who is man. Light and color danced and wove a tapestry of love for him to step on. Some were crying out words of love, while others simply stood with hands lifted up. Many of those whose colors were the richest and deepest were lying flat on their faces. Everything that had a breath sang out a song of unending love and thankfulness. Tonight the universe was as it was intended.

As Jesus reached the center he paused to look around. His gaze stopped on Mack standing on the small hill at the outer edge, and he heard Jesus whisper in his ear, "Mack, I am especially fond of you." That was all Mack could bear as he slumped to the ground, dissolving into a wash of joyful tears. He couldn't move, gripped as he was in Jesus' embrace of love and tenderness.

He then heard Jesus say clearly and loudly, but oh so gently and invitingly: "Come!" And they did, the children first and then the adults, each in turn for as long as they needed; to laugh and talk and embrace and sing with their Jesus. Time seemed to have completely stopped as the celestial dance and display continued. And each in turn then left, until none remained except the burning blue sentinels and the animals. Even these Jesus walked among, calling each by name until they and their young turned to make their way back to dens and nests and bedding pastures.

Mack stood motionless, trying to absorb this experience that was beyond his ability to capture. "I had no idea," he whispered, shaking his head and gazing into the distance. "Unbelievable!"

Sarayu laughed a shower of colors. "Just imagine, Mackenzie, if I had touched not only your eyes, but also your tongue and nose and ears."

Finally, they were alone once more. The wild, haunting cry of a loon echoing across the lake seemed to signal the end of the celebration, and the sentinels vanished in unison. The only sound remaining was a chorus of crickets and frogs resuming their own songs of worship from out of the water's edge and surrounding meadows. Without a word, the three turned and walked back toward the shack, which had again become visible to Mack. Like a curtain being drawn across his eyes, he was suddenly blind again; his vision returned to normal. He felt a loss and a longing, and even a little sad, until Jesus came alongside and took his hand, squeezing it to let Mack know that everything was as it should be.

16

A MORNING OF SORROWS

An infinite God can give all of Himself to each of His children.
He does not distribute Himself that each may have a part,
but to each one He gives all of Himself as fully as if
there were no others.

—A. W. Tozer

It seemed that he had only just entered a deep sleep of dreamless rest when Mack felt a hand shaking him awake.

"Mack, wake up. It's time for us to go." The voice was familiar, but deeper, as if he had just woken from sleep himself.

"Huh?" He groaned. "What time is it?" he mumbled as he tried to figure out where he was and what he was doing.

"It's time to go!" returned the whisper.

Although he didn't think that answered what he had been asking, he climbed out of the bed grumbling and fumbling until he found the lamp switch and snapped it on. It was blinding after the pitch dark, and it took another moment before he could pry one eye open and squint up at his early morning visitor.

The man standing next to him looked a bit like Papa; dignified, older, wiry, and taller than Mack. He had silver-white hair pulled back into a ponytail, matched by a gray-splashed mustache and goatee. Plaid shirt with sleeves rolled up, jeans, and hiking boots completed the outfit of someone ready to hit the trail. "Papa?" Mack asked.

"Yes, son."

Mack shook his head. "You're still messing with me, aren't you?"

"Always," he said with a warm smile and then answered Mack's next question before it was asked. "This morning you're going to need a father. C'mon now and let's get going. I have everything you need on the chair and table at the end of your bed. I'll meet you out in the kitchen where you can grab a bite to eat before we head out."

Mack nodded. He didn't bother to ask where they might be heading out to. If Papa had wanted him to know, he would have told him. He quickly dressed in perfectly fitting clothes, similar to what Papa was wearing, and donned a pair of hiking boots. After a quick stop in the bathroom to freshen up, he walked into the kitchen.

Jesus and Papa stood by the counter looking a lot more rested than Mack felt. He was about to speak when Sarayu entered through the back door with a large rolled-up pack. It looked like an elongated sleeping bag, bound tightly with a strap hooked to each end so it could be easily carried. She handed it to Mack and he could immediately smell a wonderful mixture of scents arising from the bundle. It was a blend of aromatic herbs and flowers that he thought he recognized. He could smell cinnamon and mint, along with salts and fruits.

"This is a gift, for later. Papa will show you how to use it." She smiled and hugged him. Or that was the only way he could describe it. It was just so hard to tell with her.

"You may carry it," added Papa. "You picked those with Sarayu yesterday."

"My gift will wait here until you return." Jesus smiled and also hugged Mack, only with him it felt like a hug.

The two left out the back and Mack was alone with Papa, who was busy scrambling a couple of eggs and frying two strips of bacon.

"Papa," Mack asked, surprised at how easy it had become to call him that, "aren't you eating?"

"Nothing is a ritual, Mackenzie. You need this, I don't." He smiled. "And don't wolf it down. We have plenty of time, and eating too fast is not good for your digestion."

Mack ate slowly and in relative silence, simply enjoying Papa's presence.

At one point Jesus poked his head into the dining area to inform Papa that he had put the tools they would need just outside the door. Papa thanked Jesus, who kissed him on the lips and left out the back door.

Mack was helping clean the few dishes when he said, "You really love him, don't you? Jesus, I mean."

"I know who you mean," Papa answered, laughing. He paused in the middle of washing the frying pan. "With all of my heart! I suppose there is something very special about an only begotten Son." Papa winked at Mack and continued. "That is part of the uniqueness in which I know him."

They finished the dishes and Mack followed Papa outside. Dawn was starting to break over the mountain peaks, the colors of early morning sunrise beginning to identify themselves against the ashy gray of the escaping night. Mack lifted Sarayu's gift and slung it over his shoulder. Papa handed him a small pick that was standing next to the door and lifted a pack onto his own back. He grabbed a shovel with one hand and a walking stick in the other and without a word headed past the garden and orchard in the general direction of the right side of the lake.

By the time they reached the trailhead there was enough light to navigate easily. Here Papa stopped and pointed his walking stick at a tree just off the path. Mack could barely make out that someone had marked the tree with a small red arc. It meant nothing to Mack, and Papa offered no explanation. Instead, he turned and started down the path, keeping an easy pace.

Sarayu's gift was relatively light for its size, and Mack used the handle end of the pick as a walking stick. The path took them across one of the creeks and deeper into the forest. Mack was grateful that his boots were waterproof when a misstep caused him to slip off a rock into ankle-deep water. He could hear Papa humming a tune as he walked, but he didn't recognize it.

As they hiked, Mack thought about the multitude of things he had experienced during the previous two days. The conversations with each of the three, alone and then together, the time with Sophia, the devotion he had been part of, looking at the night sky with Jesus, the walk across the lake. And then last night's celebration topped it off, including the reconciliation with his father—so much healing with so little spoken. It was hard to take it all in.

As he mulled it all over and considered what he had learned, Mack realized how many more questions he still had. Perhaps he would get a chance to ask some of them, but he sensed that now was not the time. He knew only that he would never be the same and wondered what these changes would mean for Nan and him and the kids, especially Kate.

But there was something that he still wanted to ask, and the issue kept gnawing at him as they walked. Finally, he broke the silence.

"Papa?"

"Yes, son."

"Sophia helped me understand a great deal about Missy yesterday. And it really helped talking to Papa. Uh, I mean, talking to you too." Mack felt confused, but Papa stopped and smiled as if he understood, so Mack continued. "Is it strange that I need to talk to you about it too? I mean, you are more of a father-father, if that makes any sense."

"I understand, Mackenzie. We are coming full circle. Forgiving your dad yesterday was a significant part of your being able to know me as Father today. You don't need to explain any further." Somehow Mack knew they were nearing the end of a long journey, and Papa was working to help him take the last few steps.

"There was no way to create freedom without a cost, as you know." Papa looked down, scars visible and indelibly written into his wrists. "I knew that my creation would rebel, would choose independence and death, and I knew what it would cost me to open a path of reconciliation. Your independence has unleashed what seems to you a world of chaos, random and frightening. Could I have prevented what happened to Missy? The answer is yes."

Mack looked up at Papa, his eyes asking the question that didn't need voicing. Papa continued, "First, by not creating at all, these questions would be moot. Or second, I could have chosen to actively interfere in her circumstance. The first was never a consideration, and the latter was not an option for purposes that you cannot possibly understand now. At this point, all I have to offer you as an answer are my love and goodness, and my relationship with you. I did not purpose Missy's death, but that doesn't mean I can't use it for good."

Mack shook his head sadly. "You're right. I don't grasp it very well. I think I see a glimpse for a second and then all the longing and loss I feel seems to rise up and tell me that what I thought I saw just couldn't be true. But I do trust you . . ." And suddenly, it was like a new thought, surprising and wonderful. "Papa, I *do* trust you!"

Papa beamed back at him. "I know, son, I know."

With that he turned and started back up the trail and Mack followed, his heart a little lighter and more settled. They soon began a relatively easy climb and the pace slowed. Occasionally, Papa would pause and tap a boulder or a large tree along the path, each time indicating the presence of the little red arc. Before Mack could ask the obvious question, Papa would turn and continue down the trail.

In time the trees began to thin out and Mack caught glimpses of shale fields where landslides had taken out sections of the forest some time before the trail had been built. They stopped once for a quick break, and Mack drank some of the cool water Papa had packed in canteens.

Shortly after their break, the path became steeper and the pace slowed even more. Mack guessed that they had been traveling almost two hours when they broke out of the tree line. He could see the path outlined against the mountainside ahead of them, but first they would have to traverse a large rock and boulder field.

Again Papa stopped and put down his pack, reaching inside for water.

"We are almost there, child," he stated, handing Mack the canteen.

"We are?" Mack inquired, looking again at the lonely and desolate rock field that lay ahead of them.

"Yes!" It was all Papa offered, and Mack wasn't sure he wanted to ask where exactly they almost were.

Papa chose a small boulder near the path and, placing his pack and shovel next to it, sat down. He appeared troubled. "I want to show you something that is going to be very painful for you."

"Okay." Mack's stomach started to churn as he put down his pick and swung Sarayu's gift across his lap and he sat down. The aromas, heightened by the morning sun, filled his senses with beauty and brought a measure of peace. "What is it?"

"To help you see it, I want to take away one more thing that darkens your heart."

Mack knew immediately what it was and, turning his gaze away from Papa, started boring a hole with his eyes into the ground between his feet.

Papa spoke gently and reassuringly. "Son, this is not about shaming you. I don't do humiliation, or guilt, or condemnation. They don't produce one speck of wholeness or righteousness, and that is why they were nailed into Jesus on the cross."

He waited, allowing that thought to penetrate and wash away some of Mack's sense of shame before continuing. "Today we are on a healing trail to bring closure to this part of your journey—not just for you, but for others as well.

Today, we are throwing a big rock into the lake, and the resulting ripples will reach places you would not expect. You already know what I want, don't you?"

"I'm afraid I do," Mack mumbled, feeling emotions rising as they seeped out of a locked room in his heart.

"Son, you need to speak it, to name it."

Now there was no holding back as hot tears poured down his face, and between sobs Mack cried, "Papa, how can I ever forgive that son of a bitch who killed my Missy? If he were here today, I don't know what I would do. I know it isn't right, but I want him to hurt like he hurt me . . . If I can't get justice, I still want revenge."

Papa simply let the torrent rush out of Mack, waiting for the wave to pass.

"Mack, for you to forgive this man is for you to release him to me and allow me to redeem him."

"Redeem him?" Again Mack felt the fire of anger and hurt. "I don't want you to redeem him! I want you to hurt him, to punish him, to put him in hell . . ." His voice trailed off.

Papa waited patiently for the emotions to ease.

"I'm stuck, Papa. I can't just forget what he did, can I?" Mack implored.

"Forgiveness is not about forgetting, Mack. It is about letting go of another person's throat."

"But I thought you forgot our sins."

"Mack, I am God. I forgot nothing. I know everything. So forgetting for me is the choice to limit myself. Son"— Papa's voice got quiet and Mack looked up at him, directly into his deep brown eyes—"because of Jesus, there is now no law demanding that I bring your sins back to mind. They are gone when it comes to you and me, and they run no interference in our relationship."

"But this man . . ."

"But he too is my son. I want to redeem him."

"So what then? I just forgive him and everything is okay, and we become buddies?" Mack stated softly but bitterly.

"You don't have a relationship with this man, at least not yet. Forgiveness does not establish relationship. In Jesus, I have forgiven all humans for their sins against me, but only some choose relationship. Mackenzie, don't you see that forgiveness is an incredible power—a power you share with us, a power Jesus gives to all he indwells so that reconciliation can grow? When Jesus forgave those who nailed him to the cross, they were no longer in his debt, nor mine. In my relationship with those men, I will never bring up what they did or shame or embarrass them."

"I don't think I can do this," Mack whispered.

"I want you to. Forgiveness is first for you, the forgiver," answered Papa, "to release you from something that will eat you alive, that will destroy your joy and your ability to love fully and openly. Do you think this man cares about the pain and torment you have gone through? If anything, he feeds on that knowledge. Don't you want to cut that off? And in doing so, you'll release him from a burden that he carries whether he knows it or not—acknowledges it or not. When you choose to forgive another, you love him well."

"I do not love him."

"Not today, you don't. But I do, Mack, not for what he's become, but for the broken child that has been twisted by his pain. I want to help you take on the nature that finds more power in love and forgiveness than hate."

"So, does that mean"—Mack was again a little angry at the direction of the conversation—"that if I forgive this man, then I let him play with Kate, or my first granddaughter?"

"Mackenzie." Papa was strong and firm. "I already told you that forgiveness does not create a relationship. Unless people speak the truth about what they have done and change their minds and behavior, a relationship of trust is not possible. When you forgive someone you certainly release him from judgment, but without true change, no real relationship can be established."

"So forgiveness does not require me to pretend what he did never happened?"

"How can you? You forgave your dad last night. Will you ever forget what he did to you?"

"I don't think so."

"But now you can love him in the face of it. His change allows for that. Forgiveness in no way requires that you trust the one you forgive. But should he finally confess and repent, you will discover a miracle in your own heart that allows you to reach out and begin to build between you a bridge of reconciliation. And sometimes—and this may seem incomprehensible to you right now—that road may even take you to the miracle of fully restored trust."

Mack slid to the ground and leaned back against the rock he had been sitting on. He studied the dirt between his feet. "Papa, I think I understand what you're saying. But it feels like if I forgive this guy he gets off free. How do I excuse what he did? Is it fair to Missy if I don't stay angry with him?"

"Mackenzie, forgiveness does not excuse anything. Believe me, the last thing this man is, is free. And you have no duty to justice in this. I will handle that. As for Missy, she has already forgiven him."

"She has?" Mack didn't even look up. "How could she?"

"Because of my presence in her. That's the only way true forgiveness is ever possible."

Mack felt Papa sit down next to him on the ground, but he still didn't look up. As Papa's arms enfolded Mack he began to cry. "Let it all out," he heard Papa whisper, and he finally was able to do just that. He closed his eyes as the tears poured out. Missy and her memories again flooded his mind: visions of coloring books and crayons and torn and bloody dresses. He wept until he had cried out all the darkness, all the longing, and all the loss, until there was nothing left.

With his eyes now closed, rocking back and forth, he pleaded, "Help me, Papa. Help me! What do I do? How do I forgive him?"

"Tell him."

Mack looked up, half expecting to see a man he had never met standing there.

"How, Papa?"

"Just say it out loud. There is power in what my children declare."

Mack began to whisper in tones at first halfhearted and stumbling, but then with increasing conviction, "I forgive you. I forgive you. I forgive you."

Papa held him close. "Mackenzie, you are such a joy."

When Mack finally collected himself, Papa handed him a wet cloth so he could wash his face. He then stood up, a little unsteady at first.

"Wow!" he said hoarsely, trying to find any word that might describe the emotional journey he had just waded through. He felt alive. He handed the kerchief back to Papa and asked, "So is it all right if I'm still angry?"

Papa was quick to respond. "Absolutely! What he did was terrible. He caused incredible pain to many. It was wrong, and anger is the right response to something that is so wrong. But don't let the anger and pain and loss you feel prevent you from forgiving him and removing your hands from around his neck."

Papa grabbed his pack and threw it on. "Son, you may have to declare your forgiveness a hundred times the first day and the second day, but the third day will be less and each day after, until one day you will realize that you have forgiven completely. And then one day you will pray for his wholeness and give him over to me so that my love will burn from his life every vestige of corruption. As incomprehensible as it sounds at this moment, you may well know this man in a different context one day."

Mack groaned. But as much as what Papa was saying caused his stomach to churn, in his heart he knew that it was the truth. Papa stood up and Mack turned toward the trail to return the way they had come.

"Mack, we are not done here," he stated.

Mack stopped and turned. "Really? I thought this was why you brought me here."

"I did, but I told you I had something to show you, something you have asked me to do. We are here to bring Missy home."

Suddenly it all made sense. He looked at Sarayu's gift and realized what it was for. Somewhere in this desolate landscape the killer had hidden Missy's body, and they had come to retrieve it.

"Thank you" was all he could say to Papa as once more a waterfall rolled down his cheeks as if from an endless reservoir. "I hate all this—this crying and blubbering like an idiot, all these tears," he moaned.

"Oh, child," spoke Papa tenderly. "Don't ever discount the wonder of your tears. They can be healing waters and a stream of joy. Sometimes they are the best words the heart can speak."

Mack pulled back and looked Papa in the face. Such pure kindness and love and hope and living joy he had never beheld. "But you promised that someday there will be no more tears. I'm looking forward to that."

Papa smiled, gently touched the backs of his fingers to Mack's face, and tenderly wiped his tear-tracked cheeks. "Mackenzie, this world is full of tears, but if you remember, I promised that it would be I who would wipe them from your eyes."

Mack managed a smile as his soul continued to melt and heal in the love of his Father.

"Here," Papa said and handed him a canteen. "Take a good swallow. I don't want you shriveling up like a prune before all this is over."

Mack couldn't help but laugh, which seemed so out of place, but then on second thought he knew it was perfect. It was a laugh of hope and restored joy . . . of the process of closure.

Papa led the way. Before leaving the main path and following a trail into the strewn mass of boulders, Papa paused and with his walking stick tapped a large boulder. He looked back at Mack and gestured to him that he should look more closely. There it was again, the same red arc. And now Mack realized the trail they were following had been marked by the man who had taken his daughter. As they walked, Papa now explained to Mack that no bodies had ever been found because this man would scout out places to hide them, sometimes months before he would kidnap the girls.

Halfway through the boulder field, Papa left the path and entered a maze of rocks and mountain walls, but not before once again pointing out the now familiar marking on a nearby rock face. Mack could see that unless people knew what they were looking for, the marks would easily go unnoticed. Ten minutes later, Papa stopped in front of a seam where two outcroppings met. There was a small pile of boulders at the base, one of them bearing the killer's symbol.

"Help me with these," he said to Mack as he began peeling the larger rocks away. "All this hides a cave entrance."

Once the covering rocks were removed, they picked and shoveled away at the hardened dirt and gravel that blocked the entrance. Suddenly, the remaining debris gave way and an opening into a small cave was visible; it was probably once the den of some hibernating animal. The stale odor of decay poured out and Mack gagged. Papa reached into the end of the roll Sarayu had given Mack and pulled out a bandanna-sized piece of linen from the end of it. He tied it around Mack's mouth and nose and immediately its sweet smell cut through the stench of the cave.

There was only enough space for them to crawl. Taking a powerful flashlight from his own pack, Papa wriggled into the cave first with Mack right behind, still carrying Sarayu's gift.

It took them only a few minutes to find their bittersweet treasure. On a small rock outcropping, Mack saw the body of what he assumed was his Missy; faceup, her body covered by a dirty and decaying sheet. He knew that, like an old glove without a hand to animate it, the real Missy wasn't there.

Papa unwrapped what Sarayu had sent with them and immediately the den filled with wonderful living aromas and scents. Even though the sheet under Missy's body was fragile, it held enough for Mack to lift her and place her in the midst of all the flowers and spices. Papa then tenderly wrapped her up and carried her to the entrance. Mack exited first and Papa passed their treasure to him. He stood up as Papa exited and pulled the pack over his shoulders. Not a word had been spoken except for Mack muttering occasionally under his breath, "I forgive you . . . I forgive you . . ."

Before they left the site, Papa picked up the rock with the red arc on it and laid it over the entrance. Mack noticed but didn't pay much attention, busy as he was with his own thoughts and tenderly holding the body of his daughter close to his heart.

17

CHOICES OF THE HEART

*Earth has no sorrow that
heaven cannot heal.*

—Thomas Moore, "Come Ye Disconsolate"

Even though Mack carried the burden of Missy's body back to the cabin, the time passed quickly. When they arrived at the shack, Jesus and Sarayu were waiting by the back door. Jesus gently relieved him of his burden and together they went to the shop where he had been working. Mack had not entered here since his arrival and was surprised at its simplicity. Light streaming through large windows caught and reflected wood dust still hanging in the air. The walls and workbenches, covered with all manner of tools, were organized to easily facilitate the shop's activities. This was clearly the sanctuary of a master craftsman.

Directly before them stood his work, a masterpiece of art in which to lay the remains of Missy. As Mack walked around the box he immediately recognized the etchings in the wood. On closer examination he discovered that details of Missy's life were carved into the wood. He found an engraving of Missy with her cat, Judas. There was another of Mack sitting in a chair reading Dr. Seuss to her. All the family was visible in scenes worked into the sides and top: Nan and Missy making cookies, the trip to Wallowa Lake with the tram ascending the mountain, and even Missy coloring at the camp table along with an accurate representation of the ladybug pin the killer had left behind. There was even a rendering of Missy standing and smiling as she looked into the waterfall, knowing her daddy was on the other side. Interspersed throughout were flowers and animals that were Missy's favorites.

Mack turned and hugged Jesus, and as they embraced, Jesus whispered into his ear, "Missy helped—she picked out what she wanted on it."

Mack's grip tightened. He couldn't let go for a long while.

"We have the perfect place prepared for her body," Sarayu said, sweeping past. "Mackenzie, it is in *our* garden."

With great care they gently placed the remains of Missy into the box, laying her on a bed of soft grasses and moss, and then filled it full with the flowers and spices from Sarayu's pack. Closing the lid, Jesus and Mack each easily picked up an end and carried it out, following Sarayu into the garden to the place in the orchard that Mack had helped clear. There, between cherry and peach trees, surrounded by orchids and daylilies, a hole had been dug right where Mack had uprooted the flowering shrub the day before. Papa was waiting for them. Once the crafted box was gently placed into the ground, Papa gave Mack a huge hug, which he returned in kind.

Sarayu stepped forward. "I," she said with a flourish and bow, "am honored to sing Missy's song, which she wrote just for this occasion."

And she began to sing, with a voice like an autumn wind: a sound of turning leaves and forests slowly slumbering, the tones of oncoming night and a promise of new days dawning. It was the haunting tune that he had heard her and Papa humming before, and Mack now listened to his daughter's words:

Breathe in me . . . deep
That I might breathe . . . and live
And hold me close that I might sleep
Soft held by all you give

Come kiss me, wind, and take my breath
Till you and I are one
And we will dance among the tombs
Until all death is gone

And no one knows that we exist
Wrapped in each other's arms
Except the One who blew the breath
That hides me safe from harm

Come kiss me, wind, and take my breath
Till you and I are one
And we will dance among the tombs
Until all death is gone

When she finished, there was silence; and then God, all three, simultaneously said, "Amen." Mack echoed the amen, picked up one of the shovels, and, with help from Jesus, began filling in the hole, covering the box in which Missy's body rested.

When the task was complete, Sarayu reached within her clothing and withdrew her small, fragile bottle. From it she poured out a few drops of the precious collection into her hand and began to carefully scatter Mack's tears onto the rich black soil under which Missy's body slept. The droplets fell like diamonds and rubies, and wherever they landed flowers instantly burst upward and bloomed in the brilliant sun. Sarayu then paused for a moment, looking intently at one pearl resting in her hand, a special tear, and then dropped it into the center of the plot. Immediately a small tree broke through the earth and began unbending itself from the spot, young and luxurious and stunning, growing and maturing until it burst into blossom and bloom. Sarayu then, in her whispery breeze-blown way, turned and smiled at Mack, who had been watching transfixed. "It is a tree of life, Mack, growing in the garden of your heart."

Papa came up next to him and put his arm over his shoulder. "Missy is incredible—you know that. Truly, she loves you."

"I miss her terribly . . . it still hurts so much."

"I know, Mackenzie. I know."

It was a little after noon, by the path of the sun, when the four left the garden and reentered the cabin. There was nothing prepared in the kitchen, nor was there any food on the dining table. Instead, Papa led them all into the living room, where on the coffee table sat a glass of wine and a loaf of freshly baked bread. They all sat down except Papa, who remained standing. He directed his words to Mack.

"Mackenzie," he began, "we have something for you to consider. While you have been with us, you have been healed much and have learned much."

"I think that's an understatement." Mack chuckled.

Papa smiled. "We are especially fond of you, you know. But here is the choice for you to make. You can remain with us and continue to grow and learn, or you can return to your other home, to Nan and to your children and friends. Either way, we promise to always be with you, although this way is a little more overt and obvious."

Mack sat back and thought about it. "What about Missy?" he asked.

"Well, if you choose to stay," Papa continued, "you will see her this afternoon. She will come too. But if you choose to leave this place, then you will be also choosing to leave Missy behind."

"This is not an easy choice," Mack said with a sigh. There was silence in the room for several minutes as Papa allowed Mack the space to struggle with his own thoughts and desires. Finally, Mack asked, "What would Missy want?"

"Although she would love to be with you today, she lives where there is no impatience. She does not mind waiting."

"I'd love to be with her." He smiled at the thought. "But this would be so hard on Nan and my other children. Let me ask you something. Is what I do back home important? Does it matter? I really don't do much other than working and caring for my family and friends—"

Sarayu interrupted him. "Mack, if anything matters then everything matters. Because you are important, everything you do is important. Every time you forgive, the universe changes; every time you reach out and touch a heart or a life, the world changes; with every kindness and service, seen or unseen, my purposes are accomplished and nothing will ever be the same again."

"Okay," Mack said with finality. "Then I'll go back. I don't think anyone will ever believe my story, but if I go back I know I can make some difference, no matter how little that difference might be. There are a few things I need, uh, want to do anyway." He paused and looked from one to the next, then grinned. "You know . . . "

They all laughed.

"And I really do believe that you will never leave me or abandon me, so I am not afraid to go back. Well, maybe a little."

"That," said Papa, "is a very good choice." He beamed at him, sitting down next to him.

Now Sarayu stood in front of Mack and spoke. "Mackenzie, now that you are going back, I have one more gift for you to take."

"What is it?" Mack asked, curious about anything that Sarayu might give.

"It is for Kate," she said.

"Kate?" exclaimed Mack, realizing that he still carried her as a burden in his heart. "Please, tell me."

"Kate believes that she is to blame for Missy's death."

Mack was stunned. What Sarayu had told him was so obvious. It made perfect sense that Kate would blame herself. She had raised the paddle that started the sequence of events that led to Missy's being taken. He couldn't believe the thought had never even crossed his mind. In one moment, Sarayu's words opened a new vista into Kate's struggle.

"Thank you so much!" he told her, his heart full of gratitude. Now he had to go back for sure, even if only for Kate. She nodded and smiled and sort of sat down. Finally, Jesus stood and reached up to one of the shelves to bring down Mack's little tin box. "Mack, I thought you might want this . . ."

Mack took it from Jesus and held it in his hands a moment. "Actually, I don't think I'm going to need this anymore," he said. "Can you keep it for me? All my best treasures are now hidden in you anyway. I want you to be my life."

"I am," said the clear and true voice of assurance.

ॐ

Without any ritual, without ceremony, they savored the warm bread and shared the wine and laughed about the stranger moments of the weekend. He knew it was over and time for him to head back and figure out how to tell Nan about everything.

He had nothing to pack. His few belongings that had appeared in his room were gone, presumably back in his car. He changed out of his hiking attire and put on the clothes that he had come in, freshly laundered and neatly folded. As he finished dressing he grabbed his coat off a wall hook, then took one last look around his room before heading out.

"God, the servant." He chuckled but then felt a welling-up again as the thought made him pause. "It is more truly God, my servant."

When Mack returned to the living room, the three were gone. A steaming cup of coffee waited for him by the fireplace. He hadn't had a chance to say good-bye, but as he thought about it, saying good-bye to God seemed a little silly. It made him smile. He sat down on the floor with his back to the fireplace and took a sip of the coffee. It was wonderful, and he could feel its warmth travel down his chest. Suddenly he was exhausted, the many emotions having taken their toll. As if his eyes had a will of their own, they closed, and Mack slipped softly and gently into a comforting sleep.

The next sensation he felt was cold, icy fingers reaching through his clothing and chilling his skin. He snapped awake and scrambled clumsily to his feet, his muscles sore and stiff from lying on the floor. Looking around he quickly saw that everything was back to the way it had been two days earlier, even down to the bloodstain near the fireplace where he had been sleeping.

He jumped up and ran out the battered door and onto the broken porch. The shack once again stood old and ugly, doors and windows rusted and broken. Winter covered the forest and the trail leading back to Willie's Jeep. The lake was barely visible through the surrounding vegetation of tangled briars and devil's club. Most of the dock had sunk and only a few of the larger pylons and attached sections were still standing. He was back in the real world. Then he smiled to himself. It was more likely he was back in the unreal world.

He pulled on his coat and tracked his way back to his car following his old footprints, which were still visible in the snow. As Mack reached the car a fresh, light snow began to fall. The drive back into Joseph was uneventful and he arrived in the dark of a winter's evening. He topped off his tank, grabbed a bite of bland-tasting food, and tried to call Nan unsuccessfully. She was probably on the road, he told himself, and cell coverage could be sketchy at best. Mack resolved to drive by the police station and see if Tommy was in, but after a slow loop revealed no activity inside, he decided against going in. How could he explain what had happened to Nan, let alone Tommy?

At the next crossroads the light turned red and he pulled to a stop. He was tired, but at peace and strangely exhilarated. He didn't think he would have any problem staying awake on the long ride home. He was anxious to get home to his family, especially Kate.

Lost in thought, Mack simply pulled through the intersection when the light turned green. He never even saw the other driver run the opposing red light. There was only a brilliant flash of light and then nothing, except silence and inky blackness.

In a split second Willie's red Jeep was destroyed, in minutes Fire and Rescue and the police arrived, and within hours Mack's broken and unconscious body was delivered by Life Flight to Emmanuel Hospital in Portland, Oregon.

18

OUTBOUND RIPPLES

Faith never knows where it is being led,
but it knows and loves the One who is leading.

—Oswald Chambers

And finally, as if from far away, he heard a familiar voice squeal in delight, "He squeezed my finger! I felt it! I promise!"

He couldn't even open his eyes to see, but he knew Josh was holding his hand. He tried to squeeze again, but the darkness overwhelmed him and he faded out. It took a full day for Mack to gain complete consciousness again. He could barely move another muscle in his body. Even the effort to lift a single eyelid seemed overwhelming, although doing so was rewarded with screams and shouts and laughter. One after another, a parade of people rushed up to his one barely open eye, as if they were looking into a deep dark hole containing some incredible treasure. Whatever they saw seemed to please them immensely, and off they would go to spread the news.

Some faces he recognized, but the ones he didn't, Mack soon learned, were those of his doctors and nurses. He slept often, but it seemed that every time he opened his eyes it would cause no little excitement. *Just wait until I can stick out my tongue*, he thought. *That will really get them.*

Everything seemed to hurt. He was now painfully aware when a nurse moved his body against his will, for physical therapy and to keep him from developing bedsores. It was apparently routine treatment for people who had been unconscious for more than a day or two, but knowing that didn't make it any more bearable.

At first Mack had no idea where he was or how he had ended up in such a predicament. He barely could keep track of *who* he was. The drugs didn't help, although he was grateful for the morphine taking the edge off his pain. Over the course of the next couple of days, his mind slowly cleared up and he began to get his voice back. A steady parade of family and friends came by to wish a speedy recovery or perhaps glean a little information, which wasn't forthcoming. Josh and Kate were regulars, sometimes doing homework while Mack snoozed, or answering his questions that for the first couple of days he asked again and again and again.

At some point Mack finally understood, even though he had been told many times, that he had been mostly unconscious for almost four days after a terrible accident in Joseph. Nan made it clear that he had a lot of explaining to do but was for the time being focused more on his recovery than her need for answers. Not that it mattered. His memory was in a fog, and though he could remember bits and pieces he couldn't pull them together to make any sense.

He vaguely remembered the drive to the shack, but things got sketchy beyond that. In his dreams the images of Papa, Jesus, Missy playing by the lake, Sophia in the cave, and the light and color of the festival in the meadow came back to him like shards from a broken mirror. Each was accompanied by waves of delight and joy, but he wasn't sure if they were real or hallucinations conjured up by collisions between some damaged or otherwise wayward neurons and the drugs coursing through his veins.

On the third afternoon after he had regained consciousness, he awoke to find Willie staring down at him, looking rather grumpy.

"You idiot!" Willie gruffed.

"Nice to see you too, Willie." Mack yawned.

"Where'd you learn to drive, anyway?" Willie ranted. "Oh, yeah, I remember, farm boy not used to intersections. Mack, from what I heard, you should have been able to smell that other guy's breath a mile away."

Mack lay there, watching his friend ramble on, trying to listen and comprehend every word, which he didn't.

"And now," Willie continued, "Nan's mad as a hornet and won't talk to me. She blames me for loaning you my Jeep and letting you go to the shack."

"So why did I go to the shack?" Mack asked, struggling to collect his thoughts. "Everything is fuzzy."

Willie groaned in desperation. "You have to tell her I tried to talk you out of it."

"You did?"

"Don't do this to me, Mack. I tried to tell you . . ."

Mack smiled as he listened to Willie rant. If he had few other memories, he did remember this man cared about him, and just having him near made him smile. Mack was suddenly startled to realize that Willie had leaned down very close to his face.

"Seriously, was *he* there?" he whispered, then quickly looked around to make sure no one was within earshot.

"Who?" whispered Mack. "And why are we whispering?"

"You know, God," Willie insisted. "Was he at the shack?"

Mack was amused. "Willie," he whispered, "it's not a secret. God is everywhere. So, I was at the shack."

"I know that, you pea brain," he stormed. "Don't you remember anything? You mean you don't even remember the *note*? You know, the one you got from Papa that was in your mailbox when you slipped on the ice and banged yourself up."

That's when the penny dropped and the disjointed story began to crystallize in Mack's mind. Everything suddenly made sense as his mind began connecting the dots and filling in the details—the note, the Jeep, the gun, the trip to the shack, and every facet of that glorious weekend. The images and memories began to flood back so powerfully that he felt as if they might pick him up and sweep him off his bed and out of this world. And as he remembered he began to cry, until tears were rolling down his cheeks.

"Mack, I'm sorry." Willie was now begging and apologetic. "What did I say?"

Mack reached up and touched his friend's face. "Nothing, Willie. I remember everything now. The note, the shack, Missy, Papa. I remember everything."

Willie didn't move, not sure what to think or say. He was afraid he had pushed his friend over the edge, the way he was rambling on about the shack and Papa and Missy. Finally he asked, "So, are you telling me that he was there? God, I mean?"

And now Mack was laughing and crying. "Willie, he was there! Oh, was he there! Wait till I tell you. You'll never believe it. Man, I'm not sure I do either." Mack stopped, lost in his memories for a moment. "Oh, yeah," he said at last. "He told me to tell you something."

"What? Me?" Mack watched as concern and doubt traded places on Willie's face. "So, what did he say?" Again he leaned forward.

Mack paused, grasping for the words. "He said, 'Tell Willie that I'm especially fond of him.'"

Mack stopped and watched his friend's face and jaw tighten and puddles of tears fill his eyes. His lips and chin quivered, and Mack knew his friend was fighting hard for control.

"I gotta go," he whispered hoarsely. "You'll have to tell me all about it later." And with that Willie simply turned and left the room, leaving Mack to wonder, and remember.

When Nan next came in she found Mack propped up in bed and grinning from ear to ear. He didn't know where to begin, so he let her talk first. She filled him in on some of the details he was still confused about, delighted that he was finally able to retain the information. He had been almost killed by a drunk driver and had undergone emergency surgery for various broken bones and internal injuries. There had been a great deal of concern that he might lapse into a long-term coma, but his waking had alleviated all the worry.

As she talked, Mack thought it indeed strange that he would get in an accident right after spending a weekend with God. *The seemingly random chaos of life*, wasn't that how Papa put it?

Then he heard Nan say the accident had happened on Friday night. "Don't you mean Sunday?" he asked.

"Sunday? Don't you think I'd know what night it was? It was Friday night when they flew you in here."

Her words confused him and for a moment he wondered if the events at the shack had been a dream after all. Perhaps it was one of those Sarayu time-warp displacement thingys, he assured himself.

When Nan finished recounting her side of the events, Mack began telling her all that had happened to him. But first, he asked for her forgiveness, confessing how and why he had lied to her. This surprised Nan, and she credited his new transparency to the trauma and morphine.

The full story of his weekend, or day as Nan kept reminding him, unfolded slowly, spread over a number of different tellings. Sometimes the drugs would get the better of him and he would slip off to dreamless sleep, occasionally mid-sentence. Initially, Nan focused on being patient and attentive, trying as best she could to suspend judgment but not seriously considering that his ravings were anything but remnants of neurological damage. But the vividness and depth of his memories touched her and slowly undermined her resolve to stay objective. There was life in what he was telling her, and she quickly understood that whatever had happened had greatly impacted and changed her husband.

Her skepticism eroded to the point where she agreed to find a way for her and Mack to have some time alone with

Kate. Mack would not tell her why and that made her nervous, but she was willing to trust him in the matter. Josh was sent on an errand, leaving just the three of them.

Mack reached out his hand and Kate took it. "Kate," he began, his voice still a little weak and raspy, "I want you to know that I love you with all my heart."

"I love you too, Daddy." Seeing him like this had evidently softened her a little.

He smiled and then grew serious again, still holding onto her hand.

"I want to talk to you about Missy."

Kate jerked back as if stung by a yellow jacket, her face turning dark. Instinctively she tried to pull her hand away, but Mack held tight, which took a considerable portion of his strength. She glanced around. Nan came up and put her arm around her. Kate was trembling. "Why?" she demanded in a whisper.

"Katie, it wasn't your fault."

Now she hesitated, almost as if she had been caught with a secret. "What's not my fault?"

Again, it took effort to get the words out, but she clearly heard. "That we lost Missy." Tears rolled down his cheeks as he struggled with those simple words.

Again she recoiled, turning away from him.

"Honey, no one blames you for what happened."

Her silence lasted only a few seconds longer before the dam burst. "But if I hadn't been careless in the canoe, you wouldn't have had to . . ." Her voice filled with self-loathing.

Mack interrupted with a hand on her arm. "That's what I'm trying to tell you, honey. It wasn't your fault."

Kate sobbed as her father's words penetrated her war-ravaged heart. "But I've always thought it was my fault. And I thought that you and Mom blamed me, and I didn't mean . . ."

"None of us meant for this to happen, Kate. It just happened, and we'll learn to live through it. But we'll learn together. Okay?"

Kate had no idea how to respond. Overwhelmed and sobbing, she broke free from her father's hand and rushed out of the room. Nan, with tears trailing down her cheeks, gave Mack a helpless but encouraging look and quickly left in pursuit of her daughter.

The next time Mack awoke, Kate was lying asleep next to him on the bed, snuggled up and safe. Evidently Nan had been able to help Kate work through some of her pain.

When Nan noticed that his eyes had opened, she quietly approached so as not to wake their daughter and kissed him. "I believe you," she whispered, and he nodded and smiled, surprised by how important that was to hear. It was probably the drugs that were making him so emotional, he thought.

⊱⊰⊱⊰⊱⊰

Mack improved rapidly over the next few weeks. Barely a month after he was discharged from the hospital, he and Nan called Joseph's newly appointed deputy sheriff, Tommy Dalton, to talk to him about the possibility of a hike back into the area beyond the shack. Since everything at the shack had reverted back to its original desolation, Mack had begun to wonder if Missy's body might still be in the cave. It could be tricky explaining to law enforcement how he knew where his daughter's body was hidden, but Mack was confident that one friend would give him the benefit of the doubt regardless of what happened.

Tommy was indeed gracious. Even after hearing the story of Mack's weekend, which he chalked up to the dreams and nightmares of a still-grieving father, he agreed to go back up to the shack. He wanted to see Mack anyway. Personal items had been salvaged from the wreckage of Willie's Jeep, and returning them was as good an excuse as any to spend some time together. So on a clear, crisp Saturday morning in early November, Willie drove Mack and Nan to Joseph in his new-used SUV where they met Tommy, and together the four headed into the Reserve.

Tommy was surprised to watch Mack walk past the shack and up to a tree near a trailhead. Just as he had explained to them on the drive up, Mack found and pointed to a red arc at the base of the tree. Still walking with a slight limp, he led them on a two-hour hike into the wilderness. Nan said not a word, but her face clearly revealed the intensity of emotions that she battled with each step. Along the way they continued to find the same red arc etched into trees and onto rock faces. By the time they arrived at a wide expanse of boulders, Tommy was becoming convinced, perhaps not of the veracity of Mack's wild story, but that they were surely following a carefully marked trail—one that could possibly have been left by Missy's killer. Without hesitation Mack turned directly into the maze of rocks and mountain walls.

They probably would never have found the exact spot if it hadn't been for Papa. Sitting at the top of a pile of stones in front of the cave was the rock with the red marking turned outward. To realize what Papa had done made Mack almost laugh out loud.

But they did find it, and when Tommy was fully convinced of what they were opening up, he made them stop. Mack understood why it was important and a little grudgingly agreed that they should reseal the cave to protect it. They would return to Joseph, where Tommy could notify forensic specialists and the proper law enforcement agencies. On the trip down, Tommy again listened to Mack's story, this time with a new openness. He also took the opportunity to coach his friend on the best ways to handle the grilling he would soon be getting. Even though Mack's alibi was flawless, there would still be serious questions.

The following day experts descended like buzzards, recovering Missy's remains and bagging the sheet along with whatever else they could find. It took only weeks after that to glean enough evidence to track down and arrest the Little Ladykiller. Learning from the clues the man had left for himself to find Missy's cave, authorities were able to locate and recover the bodies of the other little girls he had murdered.

AFTER WORDS

Well, there you have it—at least as it was told to me. I am sure there will be some who wonder whether everything really happened as Mack recalls it, or if the accident and morphine made him just a little bit loopy. As for Mack, he continues to live his normal productive life and remains adamant that every word of the story is true. All the changes in his life, he tells me, are enough evidence for him. *The Great Sadness* is gone, and he experiences most days with a profound sense of joy.

So the question I am faced with as I pen these words is, how do I end a tale like this? Perhaps I can do that best by telling you a little about how it has affected me. As I stated in the foreword, Mack's story changed me. I don't think that there is one aspect of my life, especially my relationships, that hasn't been touched deeply and altered in ways that truly matter. Do I think it's true? I want all of it to be true. Perhaps if some of it is not actually true in one sense, it is still true nonetheless—if you know what I mean. I guess you and Sarayu will have to figure that one out.

And Mack? Well, he's a human being who continues through a process of change like the rest of us. Only he welcomes it while I tend to resist it. I have noticed that he loves larger than most, is quick to forgive and even quicker to ask for forgiveness. The transformations in him have caused quite a ripple through his community of relationships—and not all of them easy. But I have to tell you that I've never been around another adult who lives life with such simplicity and joy. Somehow he has become a child again. Or maybe more accurately, he's become the child he never was allowed to be, abiding in simple trust and wonder. He embraces even the darker shades of life as part of some incredibly rich and profound tapestry crafted masterfully by invisible hands of love.

As I write this, Mack is testifying at the Ladykiller trial. He had hoped to visit with the accused but has not yet been granted permission. But he's determined to see him, even if it happens long after the verdict is rendered.

If you ever get a chance to hang out with Mack, you will soon learn that he's hoping for a new revolution, one of love and kindness—a revolution that revolves around Jesus and what he did for us all and what he continues to do in anyone who has a hunger for reconciliation and a place to call home. This is not a revolution that will overthrow anything, or if it does, it will do so in ways we could never contrive in advance. Instead, it will be the quiet daily powers of dying and serving and loving and laughing, of simple tenderness and unseen kindness, because *if anything matters, then everything matters.* And one day, when all is revealed, every one of us will bow our knees and confess in the power of Sarayu that Jesus is the Lord of all creation, to the glory of Papa.

Oh, one last note. I'm convinced that Mack and Nan still go up there sometimes, to the shack, you know, just to be alone. It wouldn't surprise me if he walks out to that old dock, takes off his shoes and socks, and, you know, puts his feet on the water just to see if . . . well, you know . . .

—Willie

Earth's crammed with heaven,
And every common bush afire with God,
But only he who sees takes off his shoes;
The rest sit round it and pluck blackberries.

—Elizabeth Barrett Browning

AUTHOR'S NOTE

It has been almost a decade since 11,000 copies of *The Shack* were drop-shipped to a home in California from a local printer. What began with fifteen copies printed at Office Depot, a Christmas gift for our six children, became an unanticipated phenomenon that caught everyone by surprise.

Three men together, Wayne Jacobsen, Brad Cummings, and Bobby Downes, wanted to see this story eventually come to life on the big screen, and it seemed prudent to first get it into print. After the early complete draft was ignored or turned down by twenty-six publishers, Wayne and Brad decided to establish their own publishing house, Windblown Media, with one initial title, *The Shack*. They each contributed a third of the original cost for the first print run and a friend of mine loaned me the rest.

I never intended on becoming a published author. I chalk up all this to God's kind sense of humor. My personal vision was to pay bills and help feed and clothe my family, and I was holding down three jobs simultaneously to do that. Some of the work was hard physical labor and other work was Internet-based, and while all of the jobs were low-paying, they provided "enough" to pay our rent and buy the basic necessities. We were content, something money can never purchase.

Wayne and Brad found a printer local to them, and in May 2007 the first copies were delivered to Brad's garage. He had volunteered to do most of the "heavy lifting," shipping out books at night as his days were filled with installing sprinkler systems into people's yards. Wayne, an author himself, in the flow of his own speaking and writing schedule, helped me better craft the story line during the two years of editing and rewriting. What happened next, none of us anticipated.

I certainly didn't. The goal was this: Windblown Media would sell the first shipment over the course of two years, working up to 100,000 copies over five years, at which point the three men anticipated that Hollywood would come knocking at their door regarding a movie.

It is largely true that ignorance is bliss. In retrospect, and after a steep learning curve, I now understand that our goal was naïve and incredibly optimistic—hardly realistic. I did not know at that time that the average successful book sells only around 3,000 copies during its entire existence and a novel with sales of 7,500 is a bestseller. We had 11,000 copies sitting in a garage with a website but no real promotion or marketing.

No matter. I was busy lifting sixty-pound buckets of turkey stuffing into hoppers at a food processing plant, shipping out soldering tips and cleaning toilets for a circuit board manufacturer's rep warehouse, and acting like a glorified disk jockey on the Internet assisting companies with their web conferencing.

Then things got wild and crazy. What was supposed to take two years happened in three and a half months. People would find the website and order a book. A few weeks later, they would return and order multiple copies or even cases. And I started getting emails from readers all over the world, messages that were wrenching and wonderful, beautiful and painful, telling me how this little book had intersected their lives at "just the right time." They would tell me moving and stunning stories of the transformational impact of the questions and conversation contained in *The Shack*.

Publishers, even some of those who had turned us down, and booksellers began contacting Brad and Wayne wanting to help in marketing, sales, and distribution. The term "wildfire" started showing up—an unanticipated anomaly that sets the landscape ablaze. In the first thirteen months, May 2007 through June 2008, Windblown Media spent less than $300 in marketing and advertising and shipped almost 1.1 million copies of *The Shack*. In June 2008, *The Shack* debuted on the *New York Times* bestseller list at #1, where it remained for 49 weeks in a row.

That should make you laugh. It certainly is no indication of our brilliance or acumen. This was a "God-thing." It was a combination of the mysteries of timing and our participation that cannot be replicated and would likely frustrate anyone who tried.

In the last years, *The Shack* has been translated into 50 languages and has sold at least 19 million copies worldwide, placing it (unofficially) in the top 100 fiction bestsellers of all time. And now it's a movie!

But it is the stories that have emerged around *The Shack*, *Cross Roads*, and now *EVE* that have so deeply touched me. Every human being is a story, and when we share the stories of our lives we are talking about Holy Ground, where the dust of creation meets with fire that refines, the activity of God in the wonder of our humanity. I think that is why we are born barefooted, because we are designed to walk on Holy Ground. Let me tell you just one story among the thousands I have been sent or told.

Most of *The Shack* movie was shot in southern British Columbia, the most western of Canadian provinces and home to my immediate family. Lionsgate, Gil Netter (the producer), and Stuart Hazeldine (the director) graciously invited me on two different occasions to spend a day on the set. The first time was on the very first day of filming, and I was asked if I would come and pray a blessing over the cast and crew. What a surreal day! I got to meet Mack, Nan, the kids, Willie, and the 50 or so crew and other personnel but Papa, Jesus, and Sarayu weren't there, at least not in any visible form.

The second invitation was near the end of the filming

schedule. I was asked if I could fly to BC on a Wednesday, spend Thursday at one of the locations, and fly out Friday. I didn't know which of the many sites it would be, what was being filmed, or who would be there. Movies are not shot in sequential order. It depends on actor and location availability as well as a myriad of other details. But who cares, right? This is so fun!

It took years, but I am now convinced in my heart and mind that God is good, all the time, and involved in the details of our lives, in ways mysterious—both gentle and confrontational, but like quantum realities, often behind the perceived and playing in the nudge, a hunch and idea that pops into our awareness. I believe that all human beings hear God for themselves, but it is in each person's unique language, often so normal to each of us that we discount it.

Minutes after I got the second invitation, the thought popped into my head (see, there it is), "Hmmm, I have been trying to meet Brad Jersak face to face, and he lives in southern BC...I wonder..." I had met Eden, his wife, but Brad had always been out of town. He is a theologian/speaker/writer and part of the faculty of a seminary in England, so I didn't even know if he was on the same continent at the time. I sent him an email telling him that I would be coming and wondered if he might have time to visit. I had just endorsed his latest book, and he had read the manuscript for *EVE*, so we had lots to talk about.

Ten minutes later he emailed back, "Could I pick you up from the Vancouver, BC, airport? We could have lunch, spend the afternoon, have supper with Eden, and I could drop you off at your hotel in the valley."

I checked with transport, and they were glad to save a four-hour round trip, so I emailed Brad with the good news.

Brad's next response was a stunner. He sent an email with a photo attached and wrote, "While we were emailing, I was walking in the woods up at Cultus Lake with one of my longtime best friends, Dwight, the man who first told me about *The Shack* and gave me my first copy back in 2008. He and his wife, Lorie, have a summer place and we are visiting with them, and just now Dwight and I stumbled onto this..." The photo was a selfie of Brad and Dwight in the woods, and a sign with one word and an arrow on it: "Shack." About two blocks from Dwight and Lorie's was one of the locations for the movie shoot and they hadn't even known.

"By the way," Brad continued, "*The Shack* had an enormous impact on Dwight and Lorie, and I was wondering if there would be any time while you are here that you could spend a few minutes with them. You need to know that three years ago, their youngest of five children, 16 years old, wasn't doing well and ended her life. Even though Lorie is a spiritual formations director, she is 'stuck' inside this Great Sadness, disheartened, deeply grieving, and sometimes furious at God. So is Dwight, but he thinks if he could read *The Shack* again, it would bring healing to his heart. He has been unable to get past Chapter One."

"We will find a way to make it happen," I wrote back. "I don't know where the location for the shoot will be the day I am there, or even what they are filming, but we will make time." Unanticipated, I had again stumbled onto Holy Ground, full of anguish and profound hurt. The loss between a parent and a child is the deepest place of wounding in the cosmos, and one that God shares with us. I immediately, with permission, sent the email thread to Gil and Stuart with a note, "This is the kind of story that happens around this book, and I wanted you to see this. This movie you are making matters, and has the potential to touch the precious places of the human soul and speak to the losses we all share together."

The following Wednesday, Brad picked me up at the airport, and we spent the day together and had supper with Eden before he dropped me at the hotel in Chilliwack. It was almost midnight before I received the "call sheet" for Thursday's shoot: Cultus Lake, two blocks from Dwight and Lorie's.

When I arrived on the set the next morning, I found Gil, Lani (Gil's wife who is a *Shack* evangelist), and Stuart.

"You remember that email I sent you," I said. "Would there be a possibility that my friends could come on set?"

Without hesitation, the answer was yes. I sent a text to Brad and twenty minutes later, Brad, Eden, Dwight, and Lorie arrived at the lake shore and were utterly embraced into the arms of this movie-making cast and crew, most who still have no idea of their story. They were friends and that was enough. I learned later that Lorie's therapist, John, had felt "nudged" to encourage her to spend some time with me and "be open" because "things can happen in the flash of an eye."

It was at this location that a complete reconstruction of the shack stood, one of three that they built and tore down depending on the part of the book they were filming. I still didn't know what scene would be shot, but it would be here at this refurbished, beautifully crafted cabin. The five of us were ushered into a mobile tent, in which the producer, director, and Lani had iconic director's chairs to watch on large screens the actual camera shots and listen with headphones to the actual recording as the actors played out their roles. There were five chairs with headsets waiting for us, and we settled in to watch.

You might not know this, but each scene in a movie is shot many times, with different camera angles, lighting, emphasis on words or actions by the actors, and so on. Later, all those takes are crafted into what the theater audience will one day watch, making the eventual cutting and editing an essential and critical part of the creative process.

For the next hour and a half, we watched this scene shot and reshot. Having spent a rough night in the shack, filled with nightmares, Mackenzie emerges onto the porch in the morning, looking disheveled and disoriented. Papa has breakfast waiting for him, and in silence Mack sits down but doesn't touch his food.

Papa, who tenderly acknowledges him and continues to talk, finally stops and says, "You know, Mackenzie. Part of your problem is that you don't believe that I am good, and until you believe that I am good, you will never trust me."

It is one of "those" moments, and you can see the struggle and controlled fury etched on Mackenzie's face. Finally, he spits out, "Why would I ever trust you? My daughter is dead!"

We sat, stunned. Of all the scenes, it's this one. I glance over at Dwight and Lorie, and tears are rolling down their faces. We are all crying. And they continue to sit there as we watch it over and over and over.

There is so much more that happened that day. We all got to meet Papa (Octavia Spencer), Jesus (Aviv Alush—an ethnic Jewish actor to play Jesus, what an idea) and Sarayu (Sumire), but beyond all of their embraces was the Relentless Affection of a God who is Good all the time and involved in the details of our lives.

That day changed us all, especially Lorie and Dwight. In a sense, the entire day was for them, God whispering that He knew both the pain and the sense of abandonment, but had never left and was "especially fond of them."

Consider the elements that had to be woven together: Where the movie was being shot, that I was invited on this particular day, that Brad was even in BC, that he and Dwight would be walking in the woods, that this was the scene to be shot, and beyond all of this, the intricate timing of each element. If you tell me this is only coincidence, I will tell you that coincidence has a Name.

As I was writing this, I got an email from Lorie. She wrote,

> I just woke up remembering Octavia pacing around the grounds near the lake being so mindful of her lines and putting so much effort into portraying her poignant part, and then sharing in my pain and

healing as she opened up with me about a loss of her own. I remember Sam Worthington coming to you in the director's tent humbly seeking your touch and inspiration and then calling out into the night air of the dock scene, almost in agony, as if speaking the message of his lines for that one person in ten who he so wanted to be sure "got it." Tears well as I recall the endless effort and earnest energies poured out that day so that I (and millions) would "get it." I truly hope billions of hearts receive from this movie the costly and yet free Amazing Grace that this powerful healing story sings to each of us in the Grand Embrace.

One day I asked our son, who is finishing a five-year Ph.D. in Statistics, about stories like this where the weaving of timing and events is beyond explanation, "Hey Chad, what are the odds of this happening?"

He grinned. "Dad, it's 100 percent."

"Of course." I laughed as the profound simplicity of what he was saying dawned on me. "Of course."

ACKNOWLEDGMENTS

I brought a stone to three friends. It was a chunk of boulder that I had carved out of the caves of my experience. These three, Wayne Jacobsen, Brad Cummings, and Bobby Downes, with great and careful kindness helped me chip away at that rock until we were able to see a wonder below its face.

Wayne was the first to see this story and went out of his way to encourage me to have it published. His enthusiasm brought in the others to refine the story and to prepare it to share with a wider audience, both in print and we hope in film. He and Brad bore the lion's share of work in the three major rewrites that brought this story to its final form, adding their insights into the ways in which God works and keeping the story true to Mack's pain and his healing. These two brought energy, creativity, and skill to the writing, and the quality of work that you now hold in your hands is due in large measure to their gifts and sacrifice. Bobby brought his unique background in filmmaking to help us collaborate on the story to tighten its flow and heighten its drama. You can visit Wayne at www.lifestream.org, Brad at www.thegodjourney.com, and Bobby at www.christiancinema.com. I am especially fond of each of you three! KMW!

Many have intersected this project and given time and heart to sand the surface or etch a design or voice an opinion, encouragement, or objection, leaving a piece of their lives inside this story and how it has unfolded. These include Marisa Ghiglieri and Dave Aldrich as design collaborators, and Kate Lapin and especially Julie Williams, who assisted with production. A number of friends took time from their schedules to prod and poke and help me edit, especially in the early rewrites. These include Australia Sue, brilliant Jim Hawley in Taiwan, and especially my cousin Dale Bruneski in Canada.

There is a host whose insight, perspective, companionship, and encouragement have mattered. Thanks to Larry Gillis in Hawaii, my buddy Dan Polk in DC, MaryKay and Rick Larson, Micheal and Renee Harris, Julie and Tom Rushton, and the Gunderson household in Boring, Oregon (that's a noun, not an adjective), along with the folk at DCS, my great friend Dave Sargent in Portland, the individuals and families of the northeast Portland community, and the Closner/Foster/Weston/Dunbar kinfolk in Estacada.

I am full of gratitude for the Warren clan (numbering around one hundred now), who helped Kim rescue me from the dark side, and my parents and Canadian family, the Youngs, Sparrows, Bruneskis, and others. I love you, Aunt Ruby; I know you've had a hard time of it lately. Also, I have no words to express my heart and love for Kim, my children, and our two incredible daughters-in-law, Courtney and Michelle, who are both bearing our first grandkids (yippee!).

Creative stimulation includes a number of old dead guys, like Jacques Ellul, George Macdonald, Tozer, Lewis, Gibran, the Inklings, and Søren Kierkegaard. But I am also grateful to writers and speakers like Ravi Zacharias, Malcolm Smith, Anne Lamott, Wayne Jacobsen, Marilynne Robinson, Donald Miller, and Maya Angelou, to name a few. Musical inspiration is eclectic, a smattering of U2, Dylan, Moby, Paul Colman, Mark Knopfler, James Taylor, Bebo Norman, Matt Wertz (you are something special), Nichole Nordeman, Amos Lee, Kirk Franklin, David Wilcox, Sarah McLachlan, Jackson Browne, the Indigo Girls, the Dixie Chicks, Larry Norman, and a whole lot of Bruce Cockburn.

Thank you, Anna Rice, for loving this story and penetrating it with your musical gift. You gave (me) us an incredible gift.

Most of us have our own grief, broken dreams, and damaged hearts, each of us our unique losses, our own "shack." I pray you find the same grace there that I did, and that the abiding presence of Papa, Jesus, and Sarayu will fill up your inside emptiness with joy unspeakable and full of glory.

Also by

WM. PAUL YOUNG

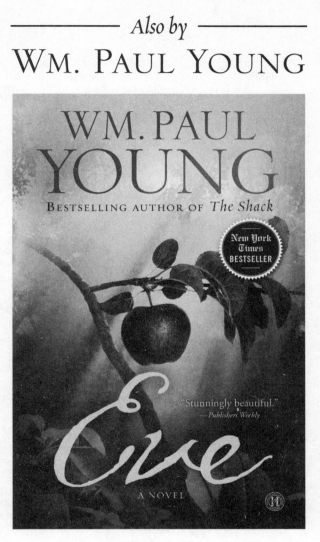

Pick up or download your copy today!

HOWARD BOOKS
AN IMPRINT OF SIMON & SCHUSTER, INC.
A CBS COMPANY

If you enjoyed *The Shack,* consider this
bestselling novel...

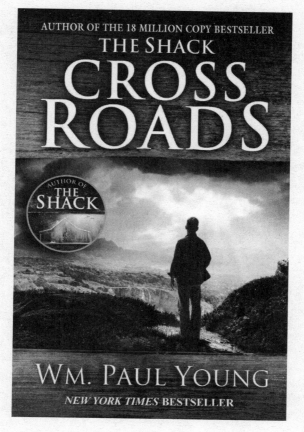

Available in Hardcover, Paperback,
Ebook, and Audio

An imprint of Hachette Book Group

CENTER
STREET

CONTINUE YOUR EXPERIENCE WITH *THE SHACK*

We invite you to continue your experience with *The Shack* at our website: WmPaulYoung.com.

- Share how you feel about *The Shack* and read what others are saying.

- Communicate with the author.

- Purchase additional copies of *The Shack*.

For information about having the authors speak to your organization or group, please contact Wes Yoder at (615) 370-4700, Ext. 230, or Wes@AmbassadorSpeakers.com.

THE SHACK STUDY GUIDE

In this study guide companion to *The Shack*, Wm. Paul Young partners with seasoned psychiatrist and family therapist Brad Robison, M.D., to offer readers an experiential guide to their own personal journey towards renewal after profound loss or pain. With excerpts from *The Shack*, questions to guide personal reflection, and some instructions along the way, this one-of-a-kind guide invites you to join Mack and Papa on a healing journey.

THE SHACK REVISITED

Continue your experience with *The Shack Revisited* by C. Baxter Kruger (foreword by Wm. Paul Young), the book that guides readers into a deeper understanding of God the Father, God the Son, and God the Holy Spirit, to help readers have a more profound connection with the core message of *The Shack*—God is love.

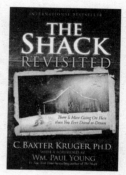

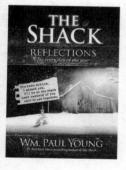

THE SHACK REFLECTIONS

This 365-day devotional selects meaningful quotes from *The Shack* and adds prayers by writer Wm. Paul Young to inspire, encourage, and uplift you every day of the year.

CROSS ROADS

Wm. Paul Young, author of the international bestseller *The Shack*, tells a story of the incremental transformation of a man caught in the torments of his own creation, somewhere between heaven and earth.

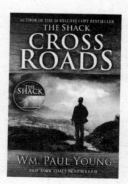

Also from Windblown Media

windblown
MEDIA
www.windblownmedia.com

HE LOVES ME: LEARNING TO LIVE IN THE FATHER'S AFFECTION
by Wayne Jacobsen

If your spiritual life feels more like an empty ritual rather than a joyful journey, let Wayne help you discover this Father who loves you more than anyone on this planet ever has or ever will, and how you can rest in his love through every circumstance you face.

SO YOU DON'T WANT TO GO TO CHURCH ANYMORE
by Wayne Jacobsen and Dave Coleman

Frustrated pastor Jake Colsen meets a man who talks about Jesus like no one he's ever met. Could this be one of Jesus' original disciples still alive in the twenty-first century, and should he believe the crazy way he talks about life, faith, and community?

MY BEAUTIFUL ONE

Seldom do songs transcend the realm of words and touch your spirit, but these songs do. This music will capture you, restore your soul, and draw you near to the very heart of God. What *The Shack* did with words, Chris DuPré does with music. That's why we are proud to release *My Beautiful One* as our debut album for Windblown Records—a definite "must hear."

BO'S CAFÉ   by John Lynch, Bill Thrall, and Bruce McNicol (September 2009)

High-powered exec Steven Kerner has no idea his tightly wound American dream is about to come crashing down. His high-profile, high-octane life has always provided everything he's wanted—until now, when a bizarre invitation from an enigmatic stranger may be the biggest opportunity to come his way in a long time. . . .

THE MISUNDERSTOOD GOD: THE LIES RELIGION
TELLS US ABOUT GOD   by Darin Hufford (November 2009)

Scripture calls him the God of love, but religion often portrays him with the vindictive personality of the devil. Which one is he and how can we be sure? If you've ever struggled to understand the nature of God, this book will help you come to see that God is truly the definition of love.

Compelling stories that unveil God's heart to the spiritually curious
www.windblownmedia.com
(805) 498-2484